Don't Stop Me Now

Holly Kerr

Three Birds Press

cover figures by simplydylandesigns

www.threebirdspress.ca

www.hollykerr.ca

For those who wanted Neely to end up with Grayson,

I hope this book will make you want to give Dawson another chance!

Don't Stop Me Now

Chapter One

Pepper

I'M NOT MUCH FOR weddings.

I used to love them; getting the pretty invitations with the swirly letters in the mail, relentless requests to my older cousins to be a flower girl, and countless hours pouring over bridal magazines planning my own special day.

And then my father left and weddings became an ordeal.

I've waited all night long for Ellie's wedding to transform into one of the nightmares of my past. It's now early Sunday morning—the darkest-before-dawn early—and I'm still waiting. We're still celebrating...and it's fun. I've had fun tonight.

Weird.

"Do you usually go to the beach in the middle of the night?" I ask as Dawson and Emmett throw handfuls of sand to extinguish the fire Shae built.

She built a fire without matches.

Who does that?

The after-wedding pancakes were one thing I could get behind, but I admit to have been hesitant about going to the beach. I like water well enough but walking through the streets of Toronto at three o'clock in the morning to sit on the shores of Lake Ontario isn't ever going to be the first thing on my list, especially wearing heels and my only little black dress. But neither Emmett nor my brother Grayson made any moves to cut the evening short, and I missed my chance to get a ride back to the hotel with Ethan and Rufus because Dawson smiled at me.

Not only smiled, but the quick, "You coming, Pepper?" sealed my fate.

I like Dawson. I like him more than any man I've met in a while. I have no idea what's going on with him and the bombshell he came to the wedding with, but she's long gone and now he's throwing hangdog eyes at the Neely girl.

I don't understand the constant movie references, but I guess it's his thing.

"We have this awesome beach here." Shae spreads her arms wide, knocking Adam in the back of the head. "And I always like to come down here when we get back. Neely's part mermaid and Dawson—" She points to Dawson's lanky frame. "Swimmer's body, obviously."

"Obviously," I murmur. "But it's the middle of the night." I point to the low-hanging crescent moon for emphasis. "Almost morning." This is a different world than what I'm used to. These people move in a different world—full of overnight flights, vacations that last longer than getting a sourdough starter up and bubbling, and applying to be on Survivor.

Who does *that*?

Actually, Grayson would be up for the reality show part, but not the surviving on an island eating rice and raw fish.

I live in a world where I should be getting up to go to work soon, not wondering if I'm even going to get to bed.

"You okay, Pep?" Grayson asks, wrenching his attention away from Neely. He's been cozied up to her all night, which is going to be a problem, one that he's not going to want to deal with.

Which means I'll be dealing with it.

"I'm fine," I assure him. "It's just...different. But fun."

Yes, fun. I've almost forgotten what it's like.

"See?" Shae smiles like she alone is responsible for my having fun. And who knows—maybe she is? "I like people to have fun, whenever or wherever the mood arises. I'm a spontaneous type of gal and—" Her slight pause is the perfect opportunity for Neely and Dawson to chime in.

"Impulsive."

"Impetuous."

"Reckless."

"Uninhibited."

"All spoken with such love," Shae says airily.

"We love you." Adam throws an arm around her shoulders. "But you do come up with some weird ideas." He swings his other arm towards the soft waves rolling onto the dark beach. "Here. Middle of night."

"You came up with the idea to go to Pain au Chocolate," she counters, folding into his arms like some origami duck. "Fire's out. Let's get moving because I'm hungry again."

I've never met anyone like Shae. She's like a long strip of sticky fly paper, attracting every bug within reach. You can't help but be drawn to her—at least I can't. I keep trying to catch her eye, get her to talk to me, rather than Emmett.

That's a tough one, because Emmett's right in there. I've never seen him move so fast.

I've actually never seen him move at all.

I want to be around Shae to soak up whatever effervescence she has in her blood. But even when I happen to be standing right beside her, I know no one sees me. It's like Shae eclipses all the light in a room.

I wonder how Neely and Dawson put up with it. They're some travel gurus slash social influencers slash reality stars without a reality show. From what I see, Shae is the Harry Styles of their One Direction, and having a semi-famous brother myself, I know it's a tough act to follow.

"Does Adam usually hang out at work after hours?" I ask after we find ourselves back on Queen Street, waiting for an Uber. Even at this early hour, the area is already alive with a few cars passing by mixed with the constant hum of the street car. There are a few all-night places open—Fred's Diner and a convenience store on the corner—but it's easy to tell it will be bustling in only a few hours.

Toronto is so different from Ashbury, where lights-out at eleven means lights-out, except for the odd streetlight. I know for a fact that I keep the earliest hours in the entire town.

"It's a good bakery," Dawson says as he slides into the backseat of a Honda Civic beside me. "Where Adam works. Good coffee."

Dawson is warm. The May night suggests spring, but I hadn't realized how the breeze from the lake had chilled until Dawson presses against my side. I fight the urge to curl into him, which surprises me—not that I have such an urge, but that I fight against it. I'm not a romantic, and I don't like to be lonely. My attraction varies—men, women, tall, small, light or dark—but when I'm interested in someone, I have a tendency to go after them.

Much like my brother, only I'm a little more discreet. Plus, I know the word subtle.

I haven't decided about Dawson yet. He smells good, but I haven't missed the looks he's thrown at Neely all night.

It would be nice to have someone look at me like that.

"It's a patisserie," Neely corrects, her voice tinged with annoyance. "Pain au Chocolate Patisserie. And it's great—good coffee, good pastries and Reuben, who works with Adam, makes the most amazing gourmet cupcakes."

"What's the difference between a bakery and a patisserie?" Grayson, who picked the legroom in the front seat over cuddling with Neely, wants to know.

"I have a bakery," I say. "I make breads and cakes and some sweets and pastries. A patisserie focuses on sweets. You can only call yourself a patisserie when you have a maître pâtissier working there."

Dawson seems impressed at my accent. "Whoa. I didn't know all that. Do you think M.K. is this mater person?"

"I've no idea, but I'm sure she knows the rules," Neely says. "Reuben might have the designation."

"Reuben is awesome," Dawson adds. "He looks a little like Hagrid—"

"Or one of the dwarves from Lord of the Rings, only taller," Neely cuts in. "But the beard—"

"His beard goes to here." Dawson slaps a hand to mid-chest. "Looks like a biker dude, but a seriously good guy."

"And a great baker."

"That means you're the mater patiserer, Pepper." Grayson mangles the French term even worse than Dawson. "She makes the best bread ever. Your cheese bread is to die for, and the rye-sourdough mix with the flecks of caramelized onion is my favourite." He grins over his shoulder at me.

"How long have you owned it?" Neely has struck me as being difficult to impress, but she does seem interested.

"I bought it two years ago. It's been tough, but I'm doing okay." I'm not doing okay, but there's no way I'll admit it. Not even Grayson knows how Pepper's Pies and Pastries is struggling.

It doesn't take long to get to where we're going. I stare hungrily at the wide windows of Pain au Chocolate shining brightly against the darkness. This is what I want for Pepper's Pies and Pastries.

As Adam unlocks the door, I quickly step in, moving away from the others to take it all in, like a welcome breath of fresh air. Even with the dim lighting, the patisserie is gorgeous. When I bought my place, I visited as many bakeries in the area as I could to get ideas on décor and what to serve. I wished I'd hit this one. Clean and crisp, with an aura of French-ness from the framed photos on the wall to the tiny tables sprinkled around the space, looking like they belong and not forced where they don't belong.

Loud music blasts from the back of the shop, but even so, even this early, there's something about the place—I would want to sit and have a coffee here. The display case is empty, the overhead light glinting on the glass and I know I'll come back here to find out what this Reuben fills it with. Plus, the smell is irresistible—sugar and cinnamon and chocolate, not to mention the wonderful scent of coffee.

If it smells this good at five thirty in the morning, then I can only imagine how amazing it will be when the display is full.

I turn in a circle, almost like I'm slow dancing, taking in the patisserie; the sights, the smells...if I could taste it, I would. This—Pain au Chocolate—*this* is what my place could be like.

I have to make it happen.

The music masks Adam's cry. "Reuben," he shouts. "Turn the music down. He usually listens to—" The sudden silence interrupts and the kitchen door swings open. I take a big step back towards the others.

He's...very tall.

Reuben stands in the doorway, his shoulders wide enough to block the space, a confused expression on his face. I don't know what Hagrid Dawson was talking about because this man is nothing like the Harry Potter character.

"It's a wee bit early for you, I'd say," he says, the Scottish accent reminding me of the sexy Highlanders of the Outlander series.

"It's a wee bit late," Shae rushes forward to give him a hug. "I can't get used to you without the big beard," she adds. "It's a whole new you. Love it."

Reuben touches his cheek. This is no Hagrid, no biker guy. This is...attractive. Handsome. Dare I say—hot? And he bakes? "It was time for it to go," he says in a deep voice. "Whereabouts are ye comin' from?"

"The wedding," Adam says with a wave of his arms. "And then we went for pancakes and then we went to the beach and now we're here. Surprise!"

"I've been up for twenty-four hours," Neely says in astonishment.

Grayson smiles easily at her. "And you still look as fresh as a daisy."

"Supposin' you need your coffee. Just so happens that I've already put it on." The accent, plus the smile, makes things start to flutter inside me, things that haven't fluttered in a long while.

"Actually, I've got someone here who wants to meet you." Adam pulls me forward and I stumble over my feet, looking up at Reuben with a foolish grin. "This is Pepper, another baker. And this is Reuben, who is a genius in the kitchen involving anything butter and pastry."

"Hi." My voice squeaks.

I never squeak.

Dawson

CAMERON SAID IT BEST in Ferris Bueller: "I'm not going to sit on my ass as the events that affect me unfold to determine the course of my life. I'm going to take a stand."

But am I taking a stand?

No. I am not.

Grayson smiles that stupid big smile at Neely, his knees close enough to touch hers under the table. I sit, the fifth person crowded around a table for two in Pain au Chocolate patisserie at five o'clock in the morning. I've been relegated to the fifth wheel. Even worse—I'm the spare tire strapped under the car, forgotten until you need it, and then it's all rusted.

Emmett and Shae make moony eyes at each other, and Neely smiles every time Grayson says something. Like a kid misbehaving when the babysitter is busy, Grayson moved in on Neely as soon as Pepper disappeared into the kitchen, which tells me his sister wouldn't approve.

I don't approve. The guy was on The Suitorette. He's going to be the next *Suitor*. What is he doing with Neely?

Why wouldn't he want to be with Neely? She's Neely.

Can anyone else see what's happening?

All night, I've waited for Neely to give him The Look, the same cold expression in her eyes that turns them tiger-yellow. Grayson Grant is the type of guy that Neely has no tolerance for—a handsome hunk without much between the ears, the kind who loves 'em and leaves 'em.

She shows a surprising amount of restraint tonight, smiling and looking happy instead of baring her teeth in a growl.

She actually growled at me once.

But not Grayson. There's been no curt responses, no snappish comebacks that leave you reeling, thinking there's no point in existing if that's what she thinks of you. Tonight, Neely actually seems to be...almost like she's...encouraging him.

Am I the only one having issues with this? Doesn't Shae see what's going on? Or even Adam? He cares about his sister enough to stop her before she makes a mistake.

Emmett laughs and Shae rests her hand on his arm, looking into his eyes like she looked at the cupcake earlier. No. Shae does not see.

I remember the hair cut of 2010; no, Adam won't stop Neely from doing something stupid.

It's only me watching this train wreck.

"Speaking of to die for, what happened to Reuben?" Neely leans forward, resting her elbows on the table. "New hair, no beard...what happened?"

"I did," Adam says from behind the counter where he's fussing with the coffee maker. "And a girl—sweet little thing, too bad it didn't work out. But she inspired him to make some changes in the Reuben outfit, and I have to say it worked out rather well." Adam glances towards the swinging door that leads to the kitchen, where Pepper had been quick to disappear with Reuben.

I thought for a half second that Pepper and I...maybe...

I shouldn't have even thought about it for that half second. Not that there's anything wrong with Pepper. There's a lot right about her, but Natasha and I ended things only a few hours ago. If I'd moved on with Pepper, that would make me no better than The Suitor's love 'em and leave 'em attitude.

"He looks amazing," Shae says, always happy at someone's happiness. "I've never seen him wear jeans before."

Adam leans forward. "His bottom is to die for," he whispers. "Never saw that coming in those baggy cargos he used to wear."

I stare into my coffee, wanting to talk about anything else but Reuben's backside, but I keep my mouth shut, afraid of what is going to fly out if I open it.

What are you doing with him, Neely?

My heart is as heavy as if I'm carrying around a fifty-pound bowling ball.

Samantha's Dad in Sixteen Candles said it best: "That's why they call them crushes. If they were easy, they'd call them something else."

I don't have a crush on Neely. I love her.

It doesn't make it easy at all.

Chapter Two

Pepper

I CAN'T BELIEVE I'M getting a tour of the kitchen of Pain au Chocolate.

Once I got over my wedding phase, I got fixated on kitchens. This happened at the same time as I started baking, so it's not as weird as it sounds. I used to keep a scrapbook of my dream kitchen. Counters, cupboards, backsplashes—I was into it all. Add in appliances, especially the stainless-steel kind and I was in heaven.

Reuben holds open the swinging door to the kitchen and I slide in under his arm. I shouldn't bother to compare it to my kitchen, but how can I not? Despite the name, my shop focuses on breads, sweet and savory, with some toothsome treats popping up in the glass display counter whenever the mood stirs me.

This is a French pastry shop with croissants and pain au chocolates glistening with butter and a gleaming egg wash. This place—

"Ooh." I poke my head into the most perfectly laid out kitchen I've seen outside House Beautiful Kitchen edition.

—is perfect.

Within a second, I'm in the room dancing around with delight; me, the non-dancer whose display of emotion is a quick clap of the hands. But this is different. This is my dream—right here in someone else's kitchen.

I run my hand along pristine counters, touching the spiral mixer in the corner like a caress. "I want one of these," I moan. "It looks brand new."

"M.K.'s prized possession." A timer dings and I jerk back to Reuben, who is staring at me with a bemused expression.

"Is it okay that I'm back here?" I don't care if it's not okay—the only way Reuben is getting me out of here is if he throws me over his shoulder and carries me out.

Which might also be okay. Very okay. His shoulders are super wide and even with an apron—

I shake my head to stop those thoughts as Reuben pulls out a tray of croissants, the scent making my mouth water. "Depends on why ye're back here."

"To check it out...I have a bakery in Ashbury, about forty-five minutes outside the city. Not that it compares to this." Reuben bends over to slide another pan into the oven and the sight of *that* is even more impressive. I've never been in a kitchen with a man other than my brother and it's...it's doing something to me.

Or maybe it's the sight of Reuben's backside that's doing something. For such a big, burly man, Reuben has a bottom that should be seen in baseball pants.

Football pants would be better.

He stands and I look away. "A fellow lover of the dough," he says with a quirk of his mouth in a half-smile.

"You can say that." I turn to the stainless-steel table lining the back wall, at the neat rows of tools laid out. A scale sits beside silicon mats rolled into tubes; different size sifters, rolling pins. I keep my spatulas and whisks in a earthenware jug, but these are laid out with the precision of a surgeon.

I can learn a lot from this M.K. person.

"You don't want to be with your chums?"

I turn back to Reuben. "They're not my chums. Friends." He blinks with surprise and I flush at the harshness of my words. "I mean, maybe someday, but it's only my brother...and Emmett...that I know. The rest...Shae and Neely. Dawson...we met at Adam's brother's wedding. But I guess you know that."

"I do."

"James, he married Ellie, who is Emmett's sister. Ellie used to be my best friend back when we were kids." I find it hard to explain my relationship with Ellie, probably because I don't understand it myself. We shared so much that it should have brought us closer together, but ended up splitting us apart. "Maybe she still is. But—her mother and my father ran off together, abandoned us, left a family without a mom and my own family without a dad." The words tumble out of my mouth, like pastry flakes when you've taken too big a bite and I do my best to stop the mess. "I don't know why I just told you that. I didn't say a word tonight. I imagine people already knew...they might be already talking about it, so why do I need to say anything? It's none of their business. It's none of your business."

I said that. All of that. Out loud.

I don't need a mirror to tell me I have two bright spots of red on my cheeks, which is never a good look for me.

"Aye, it's your business," Reuben says easily, his hands folding another chunk of dough. I stare at those hands—wide palms and long fingers, looking curiously out of place among the pastry but somehow right at home. "I find it's easier to tell strangers your business than those you're close to. Before coming here, I was on a cruise ship working as a barista. You've no idea the little gems people dropped before me." His smile goes right to his eyes and this crinkle around the corners. "Still do."

"Yeah, I can see that," I say, thinking of my verbal diarrhea. "You've got an ease about you. I definitely don't have it."

"No? How be if I say you're the first lass I've had back here?" He smiles shyly and the hard crust around my heart cracks a bit.

How's that possible? Why is this guy's smile making moves on my insides?

"How be I say that I'm honoured to be your first?" I smile at Reuben, wider than I smiled at anyone tonight and let that crust crack a bit more. "Cruise ship," I muse, leaning my hip against the counter. "You must have travelled all over the world, just like Shae."

"Aye, but not like Shae. I don't share the need to advertise my travels around the world as they do."

"No, that would be something I'm not sure I could get used to. It seems like they're having fun with it, though."

"She's a lovely wee lassie, is Neely. Dawson too."

"Dawson's a lovely lassie?" I tease. "I really love your accent."

He looks at me long enough for me to notice his eyes are about twenty shades of green behind the black-framed glasses, long enough for my stomach to give a strange little squeeze. "A *deagh dhuine*."

"A doo—what's that?"

"A good man."

"He seems to be. But like I said, I don't really know him. So how did you end up here?"

Reuben shrugs those massive shoulders. "I've no idea. I got off the boat, thought I'd go home for a spell, and ended up in Toronto instead. I've been here ever since."

"I've never been anywhere," I admit. "I mean, I've been to the States to watch Grayson play ball, but that's it, and I didn't see much other than the baseball field." I hold my breath, waiting for Reuben—like most men—to start with the Grayson baseball questions. Everyone I meet seems to be a fan, either of baseball or the reality show he was on.

"World-travelling is not for the faint of heart," Reuben says and relief makes my shoulders sag.

"My heart is not faint," I protest, with a smile so wide it's about to break my face.

"My apologies if I offended you." He looks at me with those eyes.

"You didn't. I have an older brother, so it's pretty impossible to offend me."

"I'll not attempt to prove you wrong. I only mean, it takes a certain sort to leave behind the loved ones. Or takes someone who hasn't much at home, to leave so freely."

I cock my head. "Which one are you?"

Reuben stares at the ceiling as if he's looking for answers. "I thought I was the first, but the more I've been away, the more I think the latter."

"I'm not sure I could ever leave my mother," I confess.

"I once thought so, too, but seems she had a push for me to see the world. And the timing was right."

"Why's that?"

One last fold of the dough and Reuben pushes it aside. "Who's looking after your wee bakery this morn?"

The abrupt change in subject has me taking a step back. "It's not wee."

"Who's looking after your humongous bakery this morning?"

I smile. I *laugh*. "I have a woman who helps me out, and a co-op student who I pay to work weekends. They're opening today. I should check in."

"You shouldn't. I'm sure they're right as rain without you poking in." He looks at me carefully. "Aye, you don't take much of a break from the bread, do ye?" I shake my head. "You're one day off then, and you're in someone else's *cidsin*?"

"What's that?" I ask with delight.

"Kitchen. I've lost a bit of the Gaelic, but it pops in now and again."

"I like it," I say shyly. "And I like your *cidsin*."

"Oh, it's not mine. I know well enough not to take it over from M.K. I just work here." He cocks his head at me. "You've a look that says you've a lot on your mind."

"Bread," I say without thinking.

Reuben blinks. "Bread?"

"It's what's on my mind. Do you know how difficult it is to perfect a nice gluten-free roll?"

"Can't say I do."

"I spend a lot of time on it, and I still can't make it work. Or make it sell." I rub my fist against my eye, the same move three-year-old me perfected whenever I cried. And a sudden sob hitches in my throat as the responsibilities of owning my bakery weigh me down like a month's worth of gluten-free flour. "It doesn't matter."

"It does to you." The gentleness in his tone has me blinking back a surprising wetness.

"Yeah." I heave a halting breath. "It's hard, you know. Owning your own place. All the responsibility and I've got no one watching my back. I've got my mother and Grayson but—" Where did the pity party come from? All the way from left field, to show up when I'm talking to a really nice guy, with the same interests and looking great in jeans... "It doesn't matter. I don't know why I'm telling you all this."

"Aye, it does. And I do know. But, failing means yer playin'," he says and then it's my turn to cock my head.

"Is that some Scottish saying? Because I don't know what it means."

"It tis. I'll fill ye in another day."

"I should let you get back to your work." I gesture to his hands, now working at another pat of dough, folding over and over to make the delicate layers that will be light and flaky enough to melt in my mouth. Reuben may not have the maître pâtissier designation but he certainly has the skills. "Not that I've stopped you."

"Aye." Reuben looks over at me with a shy smile. "You're a bit of a distraction, though."

"Oh..."

That sounds like a good thing.

"Reuben, I need you!" Adam's voice jams a barrier between us and I laugh nervously at the timing.

"He has trouble with the machine at times." Reuben looks at the pastry before him, and at me. "Jus' a mo...stay?"

I nod, making no move to follow him. He's...this kitchen...

I was ready to burst out in tears in front of him. I don't do that.

I lean against the counter, the day and night and everything piling up so that I feel like a cupcake that's had the oven door opened one too many times and is threatening to sink in on itself. I'm going to end up with a big gooey hole in the middle of me if I'm not careful.

I pull my phone out of my tiny wedding purse that's been loped around my shoulder all night. Five sixteen. AM. It's no wonder I'm emotional. I need a bed.

I need a kitchen laid out like this.

With Rueben gone, I take the opportunity to really study the kitchen, having felt too awkward to stare. Or touch. Or...taste. I break off a corner of one of the pains of chocolate cooling on the shelves and hum with pleasure at the taste.

I need to make these for my place. Every few weeks I like to come up with something new, something that will let the customers know I'm not a simple bakery. Baked goods, squares, tarts...every sweet I introduce helps the bottom line. Bringing something like French pastries will set me apart from the other bakeries in the area.

But is Ashbury ready for French pastries?

I need to do something. The next loan payment is due in a week and a half and it's going to drain my savings unless I can come up with an influx of cash, and quickly. But I have no time to create and perfect new recipes by then. I need—

My eyes fall on the laminated pages of the binder on the far counter.

Recipes.

With a guilty glance at the door, I flip through the pages like I've stumbled onto a treasure. As I take in the ingredients and directions, I realize it's even better than I thought.

These aren't the recipes for Pain au Chocolate's famed pain au chocolate. Instead, it's page upon page of cupcake recipes.

Before I let the stab of guilt stop me, I start taking pictures.

♥

Dawson

"**D**AWSON, WAKE UP."

It takes a moment for Neely's voice to sink into my sleep-deprived fogginess. At first, I think I'm back on the plane, that I fell asleep with her head nestled on my shoulder, her long ponytail dangling onto my chest.

Then I open my eyes.

We're at Pain au Chocolate and I fell asleep at the table with my head propped against the wall. Neely's beside me, but she's wide awake and looking at me with annoyance.

"Whoa." I blink quickly and check for drool. "Didn't know I fell asleep."

"You were snoring," Shae accuses with a grin.

"You weren't," Neely says. "You only snore when you have a cold. I called an Uber. We should call it a night."

"A morning," Emmett corrects. He hovers by Shae, and even half asleep, it's easy to tell he doesn't want to say goodbye to her.

Pushing myself away from the table, I follow the others to the door. Pepper has returned, more subdued that when she danced into the kitchen with Reuben. And Reuben—even though we interrupted his morning routine, he seems almost as reluctant as Emmett for us to go.

I must really need sleep if I think that.

Outside, the early morning chill hits me like a smack to the head after the warmth of the patisserie. The sight of Neely pulling Grayson off to the side to say goodnight is even more effective in waking me up.

"It was nice to meet you." Pepper is suddenly beside me, and I yank my attention away from Neely. "It's been a fun night."

"It was. I always give Shae credit for nights like this."

"I don't think she needs the credit if she's got that." She jerks her chin towards Shae and Emmett, both with silly smiles on their faces. Neely is also smiling at Grayson. Everyone is so happy and cheerful and paired up—

"Ah. Yeah." I look down at Pepper, the dark smudges under her eyes a mix of exhaustion and mascara, at the full lips and wide smile. "It was really good to meet you," I say truthfully. "Maybe we'll see you again?" I turn it into a question, which can be construed in different ways, which might not be the best idea. I like Pepper; she's cute and fun but...

Even with the *but*, I hug her goodnight before crawling into the Uber.

"Well, that was fun," Shae says as the car pulls away and immediately drops her head onto Neely's shoulder, eyes closed. While it should be impossible to fall asleep that quickly, anything is possible with Shae.

"I can't believe what time it is," I say in a low voice. "We haven't stayed up this late since we—"

"We graduated," Neely finishes.

"Shae wanted to watch the sun rise."

"She insisted." Neely glances down on the head propped on her shoulder as Shae gives a snort slash snore, like she knows we're talking about her. "And then you both fell asleep lying on the beach."

I remember that night. The graduation party itself was a blur of tequila shots and promises to keep in touch, some from classmates that hadn't spoken to me in four years. As the night wore on, Shae had announced that we should head to the beach to watch the sun rise.

I remember thinking that I was the luckiest guy to be lying in the sand with a girl on each side of me. I had always been aware of how attractive both of them were, as most eighteen-year-olds would be, but—in all of our four years of friendship—managed not to be an idiot about it.

It had been easy with Shae; after one disastrous kiss, we both stayed firmly in the friend zone. But it had been more difficult to stay there with Neely.

She was—still is—so beautiful that it hurts to look at her at times.

I don't know why I never made a move back in high school. Too afraid—of rejection, of Shae's reaction, of Neely herself. Plus, my mother and I had moved around so much that good friends had been hard to come by and I wasn't about to do anything to put what I shared with Shae and Neely to the test for the sake of highly charged male hormones.

Later on, however...

"I remember it being a good sleep," I say, pulling my thoughts away from the abyss of the later years. "No guy would ever complain about falling asleep between the two of you. I'm surprised she's not awake and watching now." I point at the pink-orange glow of the sky. "Do you think we should wake her?"

Neely shakes her head. "Let her sleep. She needs it."

"So do you."

"Are you telling me I look exhausted? Thank you," Neely says with an annoyed twist of her mouth. "It's what every woman wants to hear."

"I think you look beautiful." Either the exhaustion or my frustration at seeing her with Grayson makes me speak with raw sincerity. "You always do."

Neely's lips part like she's about to say something.

And the car pulls up to my building.

"Guess this is my stop." I unbuckle the seat belt and lean over to kiss the top of Shae's head. Then, because she's so close, I touch Neely's cheek with the back of my hand. "Get some sleep."

Is it my imagination, or does Neely press her cheek into my hand?

"You too," Neely whispers, holding my gaze with those big, golden eyes, like she's trying to give me a secret signal. "'Night, Dawson."

I really wish I could read whatever she's trying to say.

"'Night, Neely." I heave a deep breath and duck out of the car, still holding Neely's gaze. "See you, Adam," I add as I'm about to shut the door.

"Later, bro." Adam gives a sleepy wave.

I must really need some sleep, and head inside to crash.

This building isn't as seedy as some of the others we've lived in, but there's an unmistakable scent of cat pee and curry drifting through the hall. My mom's apartment—and mine, even though it's been years since I've been home longer than a couple months at a time—is on the first floor, but not close enough to the front door for my liking.

I unlock the door, wincing at the loud creak, only to find my mother awake and sitting at the cramped kitchen table.

"What are you doing up?" I demand in a loud whisper. "You better not have been waiting up for me."

Mom looks up from the computer parts scattered across the table, her warm smile tugging at my heart, slapping me with the usual guilt for going away so often. "I stopped waiting up for you years ago, for your sake as much as mine. What are you doing here? I didn't expect you for hours." At my blank expression, she nods expectantly. "You told me you were staying at Natasha's tonight?"

How can I have completely forgotten the break-up? We may have only been together for a few months, but telling Natasha that it was over shouldn't have been that anticlimactic.

Did I even say those words? That *it's over.*

"Me and Natasha are over." There. I said it. I drop a kiss on Mom's head before slinging my jacket onto a chair and heading for the fridge.

"What happened this time?"

"I should never have invited her to go on the trip with us," I say, neatly sidestepping Mom's use of 'this time.' Yes, there have been many 'this times' when I've come home and told Mom about breaking up with Ashley or Amy or Tyesha, but now's not the time for a reminder. I stare into the depths of the refrigerator like it has the answers as to why I waste my time with women like Natasha. They may look pretty on the outside, but there's no gooey chocolate centre when you get there. "Want me to make you breakfast?" I rouse myself enough to ask.

"I'm still perfectly capable of making my son breakfast after he comes home from a night of debauchery. Other than breaking up with Natasha, did you have fun storming the castle?" she adds with a grin as mischievous as Shae's.

I come to the habit of quoting movies naturally.

"I assume that's what you've been up to," she adds, with a pointed look at the time glowing on the microwave. "For most of the night."

"Shae wanted to do a bunch of Shae stuff." My head hovers in the fridge but I'm not hungry, not after the snack at Pain. And I'm going to Neely's later for the post-wedding breakfast, and Mama S. always makes more than enough food. I pull out the jug of milk and look for a glass.

"Such a Shae." Mom bends her dark head to get a closer look at the motherboard she's working on. "Mike stopped by a few times when you were away. I assume you asked him to again."

"It was three months. I like knowing there's someone around to look after things if there's a problem." Mike is Shae's step-grandfather and I get him to check in with Mom whenever I'm away.

"And you don't think Claudine and I can handle anything that comes up?" She looks at me over the half-moon glasses perched on her nose. My aunt Claudine has lived with us since we moved from the Philippines when I was two.

"I know you can. But why should you have to? That's what I'm here for. And when I'm not, there's always Mike. He says he doesn't mind," I remind her. "Probably gives him a break from playing Fortnite and making muffins."

"I think he's a bit busier than that."

"Yeah, with all those women he dates," I laugh. "At least that's what Shae says."

"Yes, well, how was the wedding?" Mom asks as I pour myself a glass of milk. It's the one thing I miss when we're away—cold milk. Shae always says she misses Mike's cooking the most, and for Neely, it's her bed, but to me, milk never tastes the same as it does at home.

"It was good. Nice; they seem happy. It was fun, except for Natasha." As I take a seat at the table, gently pushing away the video and Ethernet cards, I give her a recap on the night.

I also get my computer savvy slash tech skills from my mother. After my father died, Mom went to school for computer science and now works as a technician. She can fix anything, and luckily her boss lets her do most of it here, since the wheelchair makes getting around with a stack of hard drives a bit of a challenge.

"How are things here?" I tilt my head towards the hall leading to the living room where Mom parks her wheelchair. She's had the chair since I was twelve, but still prefers the cane or walker. The multiple sclerosis seems to be in remission, but there's always that chance that things will get worse, fast.

"Nothing new." She keeps her head bent, poking a tiny screwdriver inside the motherboard, so I can't see her face.

"Anything old?"

"I am the same as I was when you left all those weeks ago." She finally looks up when I finish the milk and set the glass on the table. "You should get some sleep."

"I'm going to Neely's for breakfast at nine."

"Then you have time for a three-hour nap. I didn't make the couch up for you," she apologizes.

"You don't have to." We've been in this two-bedroom apartment for three years, and for three years, I've slept on the couch pushed against the wall, my clothes in boxes in a corner of Mom's room. Having girlfriends with their own place is always a plus. "I can do it." I push away from the table, my face creasing into a huge yawn. "I think I am going to get a couple hours before I go to Neely's."

"I'll keep Claudine quiet," Mom promises.

"Good luck with that."

"How's Neely?"

There's a knowing tone in my mother's voice that brings a frown to my face and I pause on my way out of the kitchen. "She met a guy tonight."

"Dawson..."

"Mom. Don't start something you aren't willing to finish."

"Oh, I have no problem finishing anything," she says lightly. "It's you with the unwillingness and once again, I don't understand why. You've been friends for years—"

"Maybe that's the problem. We're friends. Me, Neely and Shae."

"Shae wouldn't have a problem with you and Neely."

"You don't know that. *I* don't know that. Plus—" I swallow at the sudden lump in my throat. "Neely won't let anyone come between her and Shae."

"But you won't come between them. You love Shae, too."

"Neely can't look after both of us." Sadness grips me. I must be tired to admit this to anyone, even Mom. "As long as Shae is sick, no one has a chance with Neely. *I* don't have a chance with Neely."

It's why I've never pushed it with Neely, because I don't want to compete with my best friend for Neely's love. I want a person who puts me first; a strong, enduring love. A movie love, with grand gestures and happily ever afters.

I can't have that with Neely because Shae, as long as she's dying, will always come first. I don't want to be a distant second.

"I'm going to sleep." Before I leave, Mom catches my hand.

"I'm sorry, sweetie."

"I know. Can't be helped."

"It's good to have you home."

I kiss her dark head again. "It's good to be home."

Chapter Three

Pepper

I AM NOT CUT out for a life of crime.

At the hotel, my purse sits on a chair closest to the door, mocking me. Inside, my phone nestles innocently between my wallet and my e-reader. I don't look at my phone. I don't look at the pictures. I don't even check to see if there's an emergency with the bakery. If anyone was to break in, they would take my purse and that would be the end of everything.

It's still sitting there when I wake up, only a few hours after I fell asleep. A round ball of guilt bounces around my stomach.

So why do I suggest going back to the scene of the crime?

"Ye're back."

After we check out of the hotel, Grayson and I head back to Pain au Chocolate for coffee before we make the trek home. There are a few customers sitting quietly at tables as we walk in. Reuben looms behind the counter, standing head and shoulders and a bit more over the tiny dark-haired woman beside him, whose smile is as bright as the green apron she wears.

I let my breath out in a huff when he smiles at me. There's absolutely no suspicion in his eyes. He doesn't know what I did. But the ball of guilt lingers, even after I silently vow to delete the recipes.

"Couldn't resist," Grayson says, smiling down at the woman. "We only had a taste last night. Plus, I could do with some of that coffee to get us back home."

"These are the folks who stopped by early this morning," Reuben explains to the woman. "Adam's friends."

"Ah," the woman nods. I can't read the glance she gives Reuben and I'm doing all I can not to stare at him. He looks the same as he did when we left early this morning, save the clean shirt and apron; yet, in the light of day he seems different. "I heard about that."

"I hope we didn't get Adam in trouble," Grayson says easily.

"I don't think Adam needs any help with that. Was it you who asked for a tour of the kitchen?" She turns to me. "I'm M.K., by the way."

I took your recipes.

"Pepper has her own bakery," Grayson answers, somehow realizing I can't open my mouth without a confession zipping out. He gives me a shoulder nudge that snaps me out of it.

"Ah. Competition."

"Hardly," I say, finally finding my voice. "I do bread, although it might be a good idea to branch out." I scan the glass-fronted display case, where trays of pastries glisten in the light. "Plus, I'm in Ashbury, so it's not like I'm around the corner."

"Ashbury..." M.K. frowns. "Isn't that where Pike's Farms are?"

"Emmett." Grayson beams at her. "We were at Ellie Pike's wedding. Emmett was with us last night."

"He's a nice man," M.K.'s smile suggests Shae isn't Emmett's only admirer.

"My best friend," Grayson says proudly.

As Grayson does his best to impress M.K., I sneak a glance at Reuben.

He's staring at me, and when our eyes meet, his shoulders slump like he's let out his breath, as his face creases into a smile.

"I should send Reuben out to check on your place." I whip my attention back to M.K., my own smile wide across my face. "Get some samples of your bread."

"That'd be great," I say with more enthusiasm that is necessary. "Pepper's Pies and Pastries, Main Street. Can't miss it."

"Unfortunately, Ashbury is one of those places you can easily miss. Blink-and-you-miss-it little place," Grayson says with a rueful smile. He's never loved the little village like as I do.

The bell over the door tinkles and Grayson and I turn in unison to see a blonde burst in like a storm. "I need coffee and I need it fast. Is Adam here? Because I think I might kill him for keeping Patrick out so late last night."

"Patrick—Adam's boyfriend—the wedding," I say without stopping to think that it might not be the same person. "We were there. He did go home early. Earlier." I smile sheepishly.

The woman looks at M.K. with confusion. "They were at the wedding with Adam and showed up here last night," M.K. explains.

"Without Patrick," Reuben rumbles.

"No, I know, because I had him up at the crack of dawn yesterday," the woman heaves a sigh. "I'm surprised he stayed awake through the wedding." She grimaces as she turns to us and does a double take at the sight of Grayson.

"Hey! Can I ask—?" she starts. "Are you—?"

Grayson doesn't even glance away from his study of the display counter. "Chrissa's season of The Suitorette."

"You're the baseball player."

This warrants an interested glance. "Either you know The Suitor or you know baseball."

"We watch the show," she says with a hint of patronizing in her voice.

"Flora knows baseball," M.K. cuts in. "And softball." They both look like they're waiting for Grayson to comment. "This is Flora Shaughnessy."

Thankfully, my brother picks up on the change in mood or else the male chauvinistic side of him is still asleep. "You played. One of you did. Or does."

Flora jerks a thumb at her chest. "And my fiancé plays. Did you ever come across Dean Coulson when you were playing?"

Grayson's eyes widen. I know him enough to understand the reaction. Even I've heard the name. Dean Coulson is another pitcher who got injured, but unlike Grayson, he got a second chance.

When Grayson heard, it sent him in a sullen mood that lasted more than a week.

"I never had the pleasure of playing with him, but I know of him," Grayson says. "How's the arm holding out?"

"We're cautiously optimistic," Flora says with a happy smile. "He's down in Buffalo now, but there's talk of him moving up soon. We'll see."

"I read an article on him," Grayson says. "About how he credits his girlfriend to get him back into the game. Something about her playing in the Olympics. That's you?"

"Almost in the Olympics," she corrects with a wince. "If the IOC hadn't changed the rule on women's softball, I would have been there."

"And then they changed it back and she missed her chance." M.K. rolls her eyes.

The two of them remind me of Shae and Neely from last night, and my heart gives a pang that's the complete opposite from what I felt when I saw Reuben.

I've never had a friend like that. Not even Ellie.

"How long has your wee bakery been open?" I blink with surprise at Reuben's question, like he knew I need the distraction.

"Two years, but I worked for them before I bought it." Beside me Grayson is peppering Flora with questions, so I move further down the counter to better hear Reuben. Not that hearing him is an issue, but his accent is strongly Scottish and comprehension takes a moment.

"I'd like to see it."

"Ashbury's about forty-five minutes north-east of the city, so it's not far..." I finish with a smile, trying to hide the unease after last night. The guilt.

"I'd manage that."

"What should we get, Pep?" Grayson interrupts.

"One of everything to try." I say it like a joke, but I'm serious. If I could offer pastries like these, it would do a lot for sales. Already my mind is calculating costs and any new equipment I'd need.

Grayson takes me at my word and starts pointing to things, including a cupcake with a cloud of fluffy white frosting that looks almost too beautiful to eat. "Roasted coconut," Reuben offers.

"Reuben makes the best cupcakes," Flora sighs.

"It's really helped business," M.K. agrees.

Reuben gives me a shy smile as he collects the sweets in a white box. I like him. That's what makes this so, so bad.

I can't use the recipes, no matter how it might save my business.

Dawson

NEELY'S HOUSE ALWAYS SMELLS like garlic, even when the table is covered in casserole dishes and plates of pancakes, with nary a garlic clove in sight.

Garlic and tomato, and onions, with pots of basil adding sweetness. Good food smells. It makes my stomach rumble with hunger every time I step in the door.

I was invited to the post-wedding breakfast, like I get invited to Christmas and Easter dinners, as well as Sunday lunches when we're in town. I might not have the big family like Neely does, but this one makes me feel like I belong.

Even when Neely is talking to some other guy on the phone.

Emmett dutifully heads to the dining room, but I wait, studying the framed pictures of Neely and her brothers and trying not to look like I'm listening.

Her voice is different from when she talks to me on the phone, or Shae, but it's the expression on her face that makes the shiver of dread run through me, as quick as that curry ran through me in Singapore, leaving me stuck in place.

Neely is talking to Grayson. She's smiling.

That's a laugh.

I stare unseeingly at one of the photos on the wall. One of my favourite things about Neely's place is that there's so much family around—the pictures of Neely and her brothers through the years, the huge dining table big enough for bowls of pasta and the ever-extending family.

I want this for myself someday.

And yes, part of me—more than a part—has given thought that maybe Neely...

It never goes farther than that. It can't. There's too much at stake; namely my heart because I can't handle another Neely rejection.

Silence really does speak volumes, especially when you're questioning how someone feels about you.

With a last laugh, Neely hangs up. "Was that Grayson?" I demand, sounding harsher than I meant to. Neely's smile falls from her face like melted wax. "Moves fast," I mutter.

"Is there something wrong with that?" Neely asks in a sharp voice.

I spread my hands in a gesture of peace. "There's nothing wrong with anything, Neely. Mama S. called. We better get in there."

I don't wait to see if she follows me.

The table is long and packed with food and people—both the bride's and groom's families, and me, the only outsider. I thought Shae was coming, but she needs more sleep than I do. I'm sure Mama S. will box up enough leftovers to feed her for a week.

As I take my seat at the end of the table, I do my best to push back the unsettled, uneasy thoughts of Grayson Grant. He's infringed on family time—my time with Neely and her family. All I want is to forget I saw Neely smiling at another guy.

But as a wise man once said in Pretty in Pink: "Whether or not you face the future, it happens."

Neely takes the seat beside me. Without a word, she reaches across me to snag two of the zucchini fritters and drops one on my plate. I retaliate by scooping a heap of egg casserole on her plate before serving myself.

It distracts me from the words burning in my mouth. I want to ask Neely what's she doing, what she's doing with Grayson, because if he's The Suitor, it can't end well.

But it's not my place to say anything. She's only sitting beside me. There's no holding of hands out of sight of her parents, no legs tangled under the table.

We're *friends*; only friends.

"So, you two?" Emmett waves his fork in our direction, his plate overflowing with a bit of everything on the table. When Mama S. says eat, you eat. "What's the deal?"

Neely doesn't even look at me. "Friends."

"She's my best friend," I add, struck by the way Neely's lips tighten when I say that. Does she not consider me her best friend? "Her and Shae," I correct. "We've known each other forever."

"Dawson keeps my girls safe when they travel the world," Mama S. cuts in from the other end of the table. "Why they insist on gallivanting all over the world I'll never know, but at least I trust Dawson to keep them safe. He's such a good boy." Mama S. gives me the warm smile that always makes me feel like I'm a true member of the family.

"Such a good boy," Neely murmurs in my ear. "So I shouldn't tell her about that night in Thailand when you played bartender and we had to carry Shae home?"

When she pulls back, I see the half-smile on her face and it's like watching the sun rise. Neely isn't annoyed with me, and so everything is all right in the world. "You're the one who suggested it," I say in a teasing voice, keeping my voice low even though Mama S. has moved on to eavesdropping on another conversation. "Since you were unhappy with the quality of the drinks."

"They watered down everything. Remember that one Thai bucket we got on the beach? It was all Coke and no *Sangsom*."

"And not much Red Bull, either. But you seemed to like the *lao khao*." I grin at the memory of Neely at the bar propped between two of the locals and matching them shot for shot of the fiery fermented rice spirit. I glance at Emmett who is following our conversation with a look of confusion, and his nephew Rufus beside him, eyes wide with delight. "Local alcohol. Nasty stuff."

"You need a stronger stomach," Neely chides me.

"I did better with the *khao-soi* than you!"

"That's because you like curry. Plus, they put in extra chilis. I still think you told them to."

"Why on earth would I do that?" I slap my hand across my chest. "Just because you ordered me fisheyes and octopus?"

"You deserved that." Neely's laugh is contagious, and I grin at her.

"Why did you deserve it?" Rufus demands but Neely only shakes her head, blonde hair spilling over her shoulders. She looked amazing last night for the wedding—radiantly beautiful with her hair and the dress—but I prefer this. This is the true Neely.

"I have no idea what all that stuff is, but you guys sound like you had a great time," Emmett says with an uncomfortable smile. "And Shae was there for all this?"

"We do have a great time," Neely says, leaning against me. "It's all Shae. She makes us eat all the local dishes; really anything that's out of our comfort zone."

"I have a bigger comfort zone than she does," I admit.

"And the three of you always go together?" Rufus asks.

"Since we were eighteen," I tell him. "We stuck to Canada for that trip and drove to British Columbia."

"That was such a long drive," Neely groans.

"Especially when Shae insisted on listening to her playlist."

"So much Justin Bieber. He's better in small doses."

"And Ke$ha." My smile fades as I remember Shae loudly singing the lyrics to Die Young.

"The three of you do all this travelling together?" Ellie cuts in, leaning across Rufus to join the conversation. "Just—" Her eyes shift to Emmett. "The three of you?"

"I've gone with them." Adam actually raises his hand. "And Dawson often brings a friend."

"Do you and Shae ever bring friends?" Emmett asks Neely.

Emmett's got it bad. I wonder how many times he's going to mention Shae while he's here.

"I don't have friends," Neely says quickly. "I mean, I do, but not ones I'd bring along. I mean..." I look at her in surprise. It's not often she stumbles. "It's difficult to have relationships when you're away so much. There's not much time."

"And there's a lot of Shae," Adam murmurs from the other side of me.

Ellie shakes her head. "And you do all this travelling because of your vlog? How do you—how do you afford it? Do you have jobs?"

"This is our job," Neely says. I recognize the steel under the words. I know she likes her new sister-in-law but Neely hates anyone questioning our trips. "We have sponsors, we work with different companies. ExpiryDate is one of the most influential travel vlogs out there."

"You're happy with being gone all the time?" Emmett asks. "Myself, I like being home, so I don't really understand. But Shae likes all the travelling?"

I glance at Neely out of the corner of my eye. The table has gone quiet. Neely's family all know about Shae; about the terminal illness that she was diagnosed with back when she was a teenager and they all know that Shae hates anyone knowing she's going to die.

If Emmett is asking, then it means Shae hasn't told him, and no one wants to be the one to let it slip.

"Shae loves it," I say firmly, and I see shoulders relax. "Can't get enough of it."

"Do you?" Ellie asks. "I mean—Neely, you're twenty-seven and brilliant. Don't you want a career? What you get to do is incredible, but don't you want a life? A husband?" She gives a self-conscious laugh. "I can't believe I said that, and it's only because we just got married—"

Adam lifts his glass to her. "You can say anything you want today."

His interruption is the signal for conversations to resume, but I notice Ellie is still focused on Neely.

"I'd like a career someday," Neely says in a quiet voice. "A future with someone I don't have to leave every few weeks. Someday."

My breath catches at the wistful note in her voice. For years, the two of us have been following Shae around the world, having the time of our lives, neither of us asking if that's what *we* wanted.

No one asks us.

This is for Shae; we live this life because someday soon, Shae won't be a part of it, and neither Neely nor I want her to miss out on anything.

But what about us?

What do I want?

Chapter Four

Pepper

WHEN WE FINALLY GET back to Ashbury, the interior of the car is covered with flakes of pastry and smells of coffee. I ask Grayson to drop me off at the bakery, because that's where my car is, and also, I need to check in. It's been twenty-three hours since I left the bakery, the longest I've been away.

"Are you sure about this? Why don't you come home and get some sleep?" Grayson smothers another yawn with his hand as he stops at the curb. The Sunday afternoon line is Saturday morning long, snaking through the tiny tables to the door. Part of me is proud of the business but another part is just really tired. So tired that I let the conversation with Grayson stall once we left the city limits and didn't ask him about Neely and what's going on with her.

"Look, lineup," I tell him, pulling myself out of his low-slung car with difficulty. "They need me. I won't be long."

We both know I'll close the bakery, plus set up for Tuesday. Monday is the only day of the week I'm closed and I'm looking forward to playing catch up on my sleep.

"Suit yourself." Grayson gives a toot of his horn as he pulls away from the curb, but I'm already at the door.

"Pepper! You said you wouldn't be in." Behind the counter, Mrs. April gives a mock frown, but I've worked with her long enough to recognize the relief in her blue eye shadowed eyes. Neither of us expected Sunday afternoon to be like *this*, and Mrs. April would have let Lexi go home at noon, so she's been on her own since then.

Not that Lexi would have been much help. She's a godsend with the espresso machine, but we're still working on her customer service skills.

"I can't stay away," I call over the low rumble of voices. "Looks like I got here just in time."

"How was the wedding?" Mrs. April asks as I make it to the counter.

"Ellie was beautiful," I say. At seventy-four and a former nurse, Mrs. April knows most of Ashbury, and loves to tell anyone who will listen how she was in the delivery room when I was born. It makes for a strange twist that I'm now her boss, but she's great with people, and knowing everyone means she brings in a lot of business for me. "It was a lot of fun."

"You had fun!" She claps her hands with delight. "That's so nice. But you look tired. You should go home. I'll be fine here."

"I'm sure you're as right as rain." I don't realize I've echoed Reuben's earlier words until Mrs. April gives me an amused smile. "I told Grayson I won't stay long."

Grabbing the chef's jacket that I like to wear, I take a run around the tables, scooping up the colourful plates sprinkled with crumbs of brownies and scones and empty mugs. When I bought the bakery, there was no spot for customers to linger, only a reputation for good bread. Two years later, Pepper's Pies and Pastries still makes good bread, as well as pies, but now there are tables for customers to linger with their flat whites, iced frappuccino's and sweet breads and slices of apple tart. Even without a Starbucks in sight, the sleepy little village of Ashbury has gone latte crazy for the high-tech espresso machine I put in last year.

With smiles and polite hellos, I clear the tables. Even though I'm in dire need of sleep, there's no place I'd rather be.

Not even back in Toronto enjoying the scents of Reuben's *cidsin*.

I wonder if he'll come to Ashbury.

"I love the lemon-poppy seed cake," one customer tells me, pulling my thoughts away from Reuben. Now who's the distraction?

"I'm so glad you like it." Even though the cake was a family recipe from Mrs. April, it was still my decision to include it on the menu and my chest warms with pride.

My place can compete with Pain au Chocolate any day. I don't need anyone's recipes.

"Pepper Grant." The voice slices through the bustle like the proverbial warm bread knife cutting through butter, bringing back memories of the mean girl who ruled Ashbury High four years running. "We need to talk."

I close my eyes for a split second, caught out in the open with dirty plates stacked in my hands, mugs dangling off my fingers. This is not high school; this is ten years later and I'm a grown woman with my own business.

I throw my version of a carefree smile over my shoulder and walk, not run, behind the counter to drop my load. "Hi, Jena. What can I get for you today?"

Jena Markov pushes her way to the front of the line, and it says something about her status in the tiny town that no one complains. "Something's happened."

Nothing good, from that expression. When Jena Markov purses her lips like that, it bears an unfortunate resemblance to the backside of her pug, barking at shadows outside the big window.

I pull my gaze away from her mouth and focus on the blue eyes, as cold and calculating as ever. "What can I do for you?"

"I want nothing from you other than an explanation as to *why* I found a hair in my loaf of gluten-free bread!" Jena shakes the over-sized Ziploc bag at me. "Look at this!"

It *has* to be the gluten-free bread. I give the bag a look. "I...don't see anything."

"Well, *I* did." Her chest puffs like the cocky white rooster on the Pike farm. "I found a long, curly, brown hair inside my loaf of gluten-free bread, which I bought from *you*. What do you have to say about that?" And then she sticks her hand in the Ziploc bag, pulling out what I guess is the hair and waves it in my face.

"I don't have brown hair," I say, giving my head a shake so my ponytail swings to the side. "I'd say it's blonde. And no curls."

"I found it in my loaf of bread!" Jena's voice rises and Mr. Samms, who hasn't forgiven me for raising the price of the whole wheat boules, whiplashes his head from his seat by the window to watch.

Customer service skills reluctantly click into place even though every inch of me aches to snap that Jena herself has long, curly brown hair. There's no point arguing or explaining. "I'm very sorry that happened. Can I replace the bread?" I ask, fighting to keep my face expressionless.

The first thing I learned back in school with Jena and her friends is to never show weakness. People may think small towns are full of busybodies who really *care* about each other, but the truth is that there are cliques and a hierarchy, just like in high school. And I don't belong to one, nor am I far enough up the ladder to tell Jena where to go.

Plus, I really need the business—Jena and her friends. Jena sniffs. "Well, I don't know."

"Please. A loaf of gluten-free and I have a fresh pumpernickel right here so you can make your spinach dip."

How is it possible for someone that short to look down her nose at me? "Well, I was thinking of making my dip for book club tomorrow night..."

I let out a soft hiss. This is all a game to her. "Let me get it for you."

A few of the customers watch from the tables, including those in the lineup behind Jena. With a sinking stomach, I wonder who else will come up with the same ploy for free bread. It's such a simple thing, but every one of them eats into my much-needed profits.

Even worse is how Mr. Samms gets up from his table and walks out, followed by one of the members of the baby book club group who have been meeting here for the last six months.

I don't know what's worse—let Jena see how angry I am, or how much this hurts. I pull a loaf out of the basket, glad my back is towards her so she can't see the wince of pain. It has to be the gluten-free.

As much as I try, I can't make a decent loaf of gluten-free bread. I wasn't kidding when I told Reuben that I had bread on my mind. I've tried brown rice, oat, almond and buckwheat flour and nothing works. The loaf I grab is the last in the basket, part of one of the best batches I've made in weeks, and I'm giving it away to Jena Markov as some sort of weird punishment.

I put the loaves in their simple brown bags and pass them to Jena, the smile pasted on my face with difficulty. "Thank you," she simpers.

"You're so welcome." I mimic her tone perfectly and annoyance flashes in her eyes.

"I'm sure I'll see you at the barbecue Saturday—oops, you're not going, are you. Shame you'll miss it."

"Shame you couldn't make Ellie's wedding yesterday." My smile widens at the chance to get the last word and Jena throws back her hair. "Have a great rest of the weekend."

And then my smile fades as from the back of the line, Amy Pringle follows her out, along with Mrs. Cope; both long-time customers.

Maybe I would have been better off going straight home to bed.

Dawson

"Go—shoo," Mama S. says to as I present her with a stack of dirty dishes from the table. Neely is faced with the mountain of dishes, but Mama S. still does her best to kick me out of the kitchen. "No men in here. Go sit with the boys."

"If I don't help you clean up, Mama S., my mother will never forgive me." Ignoring the order, I continue to scrape the plate into the compost bin before dropping it into the sink of soapy water. "You go sit with the boys. I can help Neely."

Neely stares open-mouthed, not even bothering to wipe away the bubbles I'd splashed on her shirt.

"No, no," Mama S. mutters as I begin to load the dishwasher. Living with two women, who both who hold full-time jobs means I'm as comfortable with dirty dishes. And I definitely wasn't taught the old-fashioned garbage about a woman's place being in the kitchen.

Although I won't go as far to say that to Mama S.

"Sorry, Mama S." I say with a grin. "But look at everything you've done for this wedding, and with Neely not around to help you? Cleaning up after you fed me the best breakfast ever is the least I can do to make up for her being away."

I've never seen Mama S. speechless.

Luckily, Adam calls to her, and she walks off with an ominous mutter, leaving me with Neely. The ghost of Grayson hovers between us, like some annoying Casper.

"Wow," Neely says, eyebrows raised in what might be admiration. "I haven't seen that before."

"I've wanted to do that for years," I admit. "My mom always asks if I help with the cleanup when I eat here, and I hate telling her Mama S. never lets me. It just took a little time to get my nerve up."

"I'm impressed."

"It must drive you crazy that your brothers get out of helping." I pick up the frying pan to dry it.

"You have no idea. There's no way I'd ever let my husband or kids sit there while I did all the work like she does. But she likes it that way," Neely finishes ruefully. "*I* don't, but she's perfectly happy with the system. While I keep living here, that's how it will be."

"James is in for a rude awakening with Ellie."

"Definitely. I think she'll teach him a thing or two."

"Two thumbs up for a sister-in-law?"

"Much better than…" I know exactly what Neely thinks of her older brother's wife. "Christmas might be bearable now."

"Or you can always hang out with Ellie's family, now that you and Emmett are so tight."

I don't know why I say that. Why would I even want Neely with Emmett's family, because that means I couldn't be with her.

Or maybe by mentioning Emmett, it's my roundabout way of finding out what she thinks of Grayson.

Is that who she was thinking about when she said that bit about wanting a future with someone? But how does she expect to have a future with a guy who's about to go on a reality show to meet the love of his life? Does Neely think Grayson is going to give up that chance?

Would I?

Neely's frown makes me regret opening my mouth, even going there in my thoughts. "Emmett and I aren't tight."

"If things work out with him and Shae you will be."

"I think I've made it clear that I don't have to be close to whoever she's dating. Or you."

Oh. We're going here, are we?

"You really never liked Natasha, did you?" I tread carefully because there are a lot of land mines in this area that can set Neely off.

"Do you blame me?" There's bitterness in her voice. Frustration. "She was only around to get her fifteen minutes."

"Yeah," I admit. "I realized it a while ago, but it's hard to break up with someone when you're half a world away from home. I felt bad dumping her in Thailand."

"So it was okay to make Shae and me miserable while you kept her around?"

"You're never miserable, Neely. It's what I love about you."

Did I really just say that?

Neely laughs. "I think you're confusing me with Shae."

"No, you." I turn to face her, but her focus is on the soapy water, trying to find the last of the cutlery. "No matter what, you deal with it, push through it. You never let anything get you down. It's admirable."

"I'm admirable. Good to know."

Neely pushes me away, sure as if she's physically giving me a shove. She doesn't want me. She doesn't want *us*. "You know what I mean," I say, hiding my own frustration.

"I really don't."

"Like the way you deal with my girlfriends," I say, a subtle reminder that if she doesn't want me, there are others who do. "It can't be easy."

"Why do you say that?" Neely asks in a strange voice.

"Well, like Natasha. It couldn't have been easy for you and Shae to deal with her."

Neely gives a choked laugh. "That's what friends are for."

Friends...

Neely pushes away from the counter and reaches for my dishtowel to dry her hands. "I'm going to see if there's anything left on the table."

"I can check—" I speak to myself because Neely is gone. "Or not."

Natasha was nothing but a mistake. Drying the last of the serving spoons from the rack, I stare unseeingly at the glass-fronted cupboard door. Almost as big of a mistake as when Mr. Scalzo decided to renovate the kitchen for Mama S., which meant she was banished from her favourite room in the world for two weeks.

Mama S. took over the kitchen at Shae's house next door. Neely and Shae can be together twenty-four seven, but it was quickly apparent that their families could not. We left for London in the middle of it, and I've never been so glad to see an airport.

Would Natasha and I have made it if we hadn't spent almost three months on the other side of the world?

Probably not. None of the girls I end up with are ones I see a future with. Maybe that's why I push them away so quickly—because that's what I do. When a girl gets too close, that's when I back away.

Which is strange, because I do want someone I can have a future with. "I want a serious girlfriend," I mutter, quoting the oft-quoted Jake Ryan. "Someone I can love, someone who's going to love me back."

There's a bing, like the universe heard me.

It's Neely's phone. Of course I look to see who is texting her; I carry her phone in the pocket of my cargo shorts most of the time when we're away.

Grayson.

In my head, I growl the name, but my expression is calm as I reach for the phone. And then I stop growling when I realize it's not Grayson.

GRAYSON: Hi Neely, it's Pepper texting for Grayson who is driving and I won't let him touch the phone. He says to tell you that we just left Pain au Chocolate and it's even better when it's open. Thanks to Adam for taking us.

NEELY: Hi Pepper, it's Dawson, on Neely's phone. Really glad you went back.
Best treats ever!

GRAYSON: You do realize I own a bakery and might just have comparable treats?

NEELY: My apologies! Reuben can't compare to your baking expertise.

GRAYSON: He really can.

NEELY: We should have a bake-off. Cupcakes. How hard can it be to bake cupcakes?

GRAYSON: you'd be surprised.

NEELY: Well, I'm going to make the drive to Ashbury to taste-test your treats either with or without a bake-off

Does that sound too much like I'm flirting? Because while I liked meeting Pepper, I didn't really see her as someone to flirt with.

Why can't I flirt with her? It's not like it would make it weird for Neely if I took out Grayson's sister.

Would it?

GRAYSON: How about tomorrow? I have the day
off

NEELY: I have plans with my grandma tomorrow.
What about Tuesday? What time do you close? I   I
can come later in the day and we can grab something
to eat after I get the tour.

So maybe I'm not flirting, but does that mean I should ask her
out? Because I think that's what I just did.

GRAYSON: Sounds great! Come around 4. I'll give
you a tour of Ashbury.
Should take about 10 mins.

I respond with a laughing emoji, hoping Pepper was joking, as
Neely comes back into the kitchen. "Why are you on my phone?"
"Pepper texted you to say thanks for introducing them to Pain.
They're heading home."
"On *my* phone?"
"Grayson is driving, so don't go distracting him." I text Pepper
that I'll see her Tuesday and give Neely her phone.
"You have a date with her?" The crack of Neely's voice is like
breaking glass as she scans the text string.
"I wouldn't call it a date."

"*I* would. The problem with you Dawson, is that you treat all these women like me and Shae and they're not. Women like Natasha want something from you."

"And you don't want anything from me?"

Neely's golden eyes widen as she catches my gaze and holds it. Her mouth opens like she's about to say something, but she only swallows twice before looking away. "I think you have to be careful not to lead Pepper on," she says.

"Because it will mess things up with you and Grayson?"

"What's your problem with him? I'm allowed to date who I want."

"So you're dating him? You're actually going on a date?"

"I can do what I want. You do—you have your line of girls that you go through—"

"I don't go after anyone who's not available," I point out. "Grayson is going to be the next Suitor, and you're not on the show. What do you expect will happen?"

"I don't know, and what do you care?"

"Of course I care."

"It's not like anyone is available to me," she mutters, thrusting her hands back into the sink.

"You can have anyone you want."

"What world are you living in?"

"Neely…" I sort through the words I want to say, trying to find the right way to bring it up. "Do you think you're missing out by sticking so close to Shae?"

She looks at me with bewildered eyes. "What do you mean? Of course I'm sticking with her. She's my best friend."

"She's mine too. You both are. What you said to Ellie...you want more than this, don't you? More than living out of suitcases and eating weird food. Looking after Shae."

Neely sucks in her breath like she's about to blow out candles on a cake before her shoulders sag. "I want Shae to live. I don't want to lose my best friend."

"Neither do I. That's not the point."

"What is? How can I plan on a future when she can't have one? How can I want to finish school and find a good job when Shae can't have one?"

"Shae doesn't even want a job."

"Of course not! How do you take a job when you don't know how long you'll be alive for?" She turns to the kitchen door. It's good that Emmett and his family have already left because Neely's voice has risen to make it easy for anyone in the living room to hear.

"I can't." Her next words are so quiet that I have to strain to hear her. "As much as I might want to, I can't think of anything—I can't plan for anything—while Shae is still with us."

And that's why I don't have a chance with Neely.

Chapter Five

Pepper

Despite the lack of sleep, my body still wakes me up at my usual four forty-five on Monday.

Not bothering to stifle the groan of frustration, I bury my face in the pillow, wishing, for once, I could sleep in. Today is the only day of the week the bakery is closed, but still, my stupid mind starts racing about what I need to do...

And what needs to be done.

I make the best bread in the area, taking my grandmother's recipes and adding my own touches over the years. Oma was from Germany, home of the best bread in the world, taught by her mother, who trained as the traditional bakester, or female baker and I like to think I might have surpassed her skills, with my tangy sourdough, the baguettes that are chewy in the middle and perfectly crusty on the outside, and my traditional pumpernickel, making it the old way which takes twenty-four hours. And my quick breads are legendary—the cornbread mini loaves are best sellers, the beer bread that flies off the shelves. and the cheese and chives scones.

I have everything I need to make Pepper's Pies and Pastries a raging success, so why hasn't it taken off like I want it to? And why am I stuck in this mess?

The mess being how to find a way to bring in more business so the loan payment due at the end of the month won't wipe out my entire savings.

It's my own fault. I didn't exactly *need* the new mixer, forgetting for a moment how sluggish the old one had been, having seen Ruth Liu through thirty-so years of bakery business. I started adding a prayer when I turned it on and when I heard about the practically new one for sale in Whitby, I jumped at it.

I had a day to play with my shiny new toy before sticker shock hit me. And then the basement of the bakery took on water thanks to an abnormally insane amount of rain and ruined six months of flour with the damp. And then, a week later, a group of town teenagers, bored and stupid drunk, broke the huge front window by falling through it during a wrestling match on the sidewalk.

Somehow that became *my* fault. I'm not sure if it was because the bakery window is seen as too big, or too tempting—idiots see the clear pane of glass and immediately have the need to push each other through it. Two of the boys fell through the window, with no injuries, save ten stitches between the two of them. Everyone was so relieved to have the town hockey phenom Marshall Platt—who was probably an instigator, as well as one of the idiots who ended up inside the bakery—emerge relatively unscathed that no one thought of forcing him to pay for the damages.

That was all on me, unless I wanted to sue for damages. Which I do, but can't because I'd look like the Wicked Witch of the

Northeast GTA, and business would dry up much quicker than the wet spot in the basement.

Along with the window, the boys had cracked the sill and broken the table under the window, along with the antique salt and pepper shakers that sat on the table, part of the collection that I inherited from my grandmother. And then they'd tracked dirt and bits of glass through the bakery into the kitchen, looking for a snack.

I'm still furious about the whole thing, and everyone in town knows it, just like everyone in town knows everything else about my life. It's one of the downfalls about living in a small town, especially one you'd been living in since you were born.

All the expenses keep adding up, and it's everything I can do to stay afloat.

I can't ask for help because of a combination of pride and the fact that my mother doesn't have the cash to bail me out. Grayson might, but there's not much of his professional baseball salary left, another reason he was so interested when the producers from The Suitor came calling.

Since sleep is out of the question, I grab my phone from the nightstand beside the bed and start scrolling, anything to keep me from checking out the photos of the recipes I took.

Because if I look, then I'm going to end up trying them out, and then what happens if those cupcakes are the way to get me out of the financial mess I'm in?

"Why aren't you doing that in your bakery?" Grayson asks when he appears in the kitchen many hours later.

Flour and eggs and other ingredients are strewn across the counter, one batch of cupcakes cooling on the rack and a second in the oven, warming the room with the scent of vanilla.

I looked. I read all of Reuben's recipes that I took pictures of.

Stole. I stole them. I'm a thief.

Once I read them, I had to try them out to see if they taste even half as good as they sound. But before I started, I sat down with my notebook and carefully copied out the recipes, so I don't have to go back and forth checking my phone. Once I double and triple checked the amounts with the pictures, I deleted them.

Evidence gone. These could be recipes I came up with myself, or ones passed down through the family, like most of my bread recipes.

No one will ever know that I took them, except me. And eventually, I'll make myself forget. It's not like I'm ever going to see Reuben again. And even if I did, how would he ever know that my cupcakes are his cupcakes?

It's not like the recipes are much different than the usual Mary Berry recipe.

Actually, they are.

If these are Reuben's recipes, it's obvious from the notes and scratch outs that he's taken the time and effort to perfect each one. There are the names of cocoa and vanilla brands scribbled in the margins, adjustments to cooking times and temperatures, substitutions of whole milk, sour cream, and apple sauce, as well as different oils to try.

I push back my guilt as I get started on the first batch—coconut carrot cupcakes. Then I move on to lemon lavender with Greek yogurt and fresh honey from one of the local farms.

I'm not worrying about frosting yet. I need to perfect the cake.

I'm well into the third batch—simple vanilla—when Grayson strolls in, looking rested after fourteen hours sleep.

Unlike me, with the dark circles under my eyes.

I ignore his question with a flip of the mixer switch.

"Do we know what she's making?" Grayson asks Mom loudly, pulling open the fridge to find the orange juice.

"Cupcakes." Mom flips the pages of an old cookbook, looking for inspiration for me. She came down midway through the second batch, smiling but sleepy eyed. Both she and Grayson are used to my early hours and even though I do my best to keep the noise to a minimum, when the muse strikes, I can be pretty loud in the kitchen, what with the mixer and the timers and my music.

I need background noise. Mom once told me I use it to drown out the voices inside my head, and that sometimes it's okay to listen to them. I disagree, because they whisper things I don't want to think about. I ignore them more than my brother's voice.

"Ah. A little friendly competition, is it?" Grayson asks over the noise of the mixer.

"I can make cupcakes as good as he can," I tell him.

"I'm sure you can," Mom soothes, turning another page. "Who's he?"

"No one," I say quietly.

"He sure looked like someone when you dragged me back there yesterday. She met a guy," Grayson informs Mom.

I make slashing motions, glare at him with dagger eyes.

My brother smiles. "Actually, she met *two* guys," he continues.

"Did Grayson tell you that *he* met a woman, which is totally stupid because he still hasn't signed the contract for The Suitor," I burst out, almost shouting over the mixer.

"Wouldn't it be more stupid to have met Neely *after* I sign the contract?"

"Are you going to?"

"Not that it should be any business of yours, but yes, I plan to." Grayson has that smile on his face, the one that is guaranteed to infuriate me.

Not that I need any help today.

"Is this before or after you lead Neely on and break her heart?"

Grayson slaps a hand across his chest. "You wound me. Plus, I think you give me too much credit. Neely's a nice girl, but I'm not planning on marrying her."

"No? So it's not bad to make her care about you and then up and run off and do the show? That's no better than—" I snap my lips closed as Grayson's eyes widen.

"Grayson is nothing like your father," Mom says, still calmly turning the pages of the cookbook. "Nor are you, so stop being afraid of being vulnerable."

"I'm not afraid," I burst out.

"Of course you're not," she says in a voice that is the epitome of cool and composed. "But it wouldn't kill you to give these two very nice men a chance."

"Why don't you want to talk about the mess Grayson's about to make of his love life?" I demand.

"Because I've been sitting here for hours waiting for you to tell me something interesting about this weekend and I'm very excited to hear it." She closes the book and folds her hands on top of it with an expectant smile.

"Oh, I want to hear this," Grayson says, settling back at the table with a grin.

"There's nothing to tell," I mutter. If I say one word about Reuben, then I'll tell my mother everything about stealing the recipes and why I need them for the shop, and then it'll all come out about the money and loan payments, and everything will spin out of control, just like if I lift the arm of the mixer before the paddle slows, which sprays batter everywhere.

"I need to make these cupcakes," I finish with a scowl.

"I'm here whenever you need me to listen," Mom says in that super-calm voice that makes my skin crawl with frustration, because I can never be that calm.

Also, because when she uses that voice, it's impossible to get mad at her.

"And I'm here to taste-test anything that looks good," Grayson says.

I fight the urge to throw a handful of batter at him.

Dawson

ONCE I LEAVE NEELY'S with a full belly and aching heart, I head home and sleep the rest of the day away. Mom and Aunt Claudine keep their voices down just enough, but luckily, I can sleep through anything.

I wake up Monday morning feeling more rested, at least enough to attack the jet lag that will have me dragging by the end of the day. It's the worst thing about the constant travel. It takes a while to get the body clock on a regular schedule; harder still when we're usually off again pretty soon after I've shaken it off.

There's been no talk about planning the next adventure. Sure, Shae has her heart set on Antarctica, but there's no way I can afford the expense without a full ride from a generous sponsor.

Ellie's comment at breakfast yesterday got me thinking, more than I usually do about the future. I'm with Neely in that I want Shae to have what she can out of life. It's only fair, in a very unfair situation. I never put much thought into what I'm getting.

Or what I'm losing.

Twenty-seven years old, and I live with my mother and aunt in a two-bedroom apartment, which means, I have no room of my own. I wake up, my legs tangled in blankets, my nose shoved into the cushions of the couch.

This is my bed when I'm home.

I never look at the option of moving out because there's no point paying rent on a place that I might be in for four months of the year. Nor can I afford it. Neely was right about the sponsors—they pay for the majority of the travel expenses, but if we stopped going places, the money would soon dry up. Without a job, I've got no way to pay for an apartment, or even buy myself a decent futon to sleep on.

Being poor is never fun, especially when you know my father's family, his other children, want for nothing.

I throw off my blankets. While I have no love for my father's first wife nor their children—my half-siblings—my grandmother is the coolest Grammy ever. Every time I come home, I make a point to go see her as quick as I can, because since she's pretty old, I have no idea how long I'll have her around for.

That's my plan today—some Grammy time. And then maybe sleep some more.

Along with not having my own place, I also don't own a car, so it's public transit for me. Toronto doesn't have a bad system—not as good as some, better than others, but at least the bus drives a lot smoother than the *tuk tuks* we used to get around in Thailand. And it gives me a chance to respond to the countless comments on the vlog.

The three of us share the vlog and the Insta page, and it's not unheard of for all of us to respond to the same comment. We each have our own fans; @redheadswinga being one of my most vocal admirers. But there's been a few guys that I've followed back, a couple that I game with, and talk online. I've made more than a few friends with the vlog, and I would miss it if we stopped.

I'm not sure where that thought came from. No one is talking about stopping. How can we? How could I do that to Shae?

I'm distracted by a comment on the zip lining post from @k_gretchen. "Looks like fun. Love to catch up when you're back."

It's the last part that grabs me. *Love to catch up* isn't unheard of from people who want to believe they know me. The use of *you're* rather than *u r* suggests it's from a non-Gen Z. The name...

It's from my brother. Half-brother.

I look up in time to see the bus approaching my stop and pull the cord. My phone is still in my hand as I hit the sidewalk, my backpack slung over my shoulder and I stare at the comment again with disbelief before stuffing the phone in my pocket.

Is Keith suggesting we catch up for all the twenty-seven years, or just the ones since his mother contested my father's will, which left Mom and me with nothing?

It might be an interesting question to ask.

When I get close to Grammy's, I hear the dogs before I see them, a cacophony of barking that can mean anything from *I'm so excited to see you that I think I might pee*, or *I'm so hungry that I might chew off your ankle in a moment.*

I don't understand dog, but Rachel does. "Hey, Dawson." Rachel flashes a smile before slowly opening the back door of her SUV parked in the driveway she shares with my grandmother. Instantly the barking becomes louder and a tiny, fluffy thing leaps out of the car. "Grab her!"

I step on the leash as the dog dances around my feet yapping with excitement. "How many do you have in there?" I ask warily. I like dogs, but they don't like me. Or more importantly, they play havoc with my sinus system. Already I feel a sneeze coming on.

"Six. Plus one of mine." A wave of slobbering, smiling canines bursts out of the car, Rachel scooping their leashes into her hands. I hand over the pink leather strap under my shoe.

"Rusty." It's easy to pick out the black-and-white dog in the pack of golden labradoodles, plus the tiny Pomeranian.

"You remember." Rachel has shared a drive with Grandma for years, and I've had to endure Grandma's attempts at matchmaking for almost as long. Rachel and I almost got together about three years ago—two really good dates—but then Shae booked us for Brazil at the last minute, and when I got back, Rachel had moved on.

"You named your dog after the kid in National Lampoon's Vacation," I say. "How can I forget?"

"Ah, yes, the John Hughes aficionado."

"Could be worse." I stuck my hands in my pockets as I glance over my shoulder at Grammy's front door. "How's everything around here?"

"Mrs. Gretchen is as awesome as ever," Rachel says with a grin. "Do you know she brings over bottles of schnapps to drink with me?"

I wince at the memory of my grandmother pouring me shots the day after I turned nineteen. "You should stay away from that stuff."

"Don't I know it. Has she said anything about the new neighbour?" The grimace on Rachel's face mirrors my own.

"Just that a young guy moved in."

"*Boen*," Rachel says with disgust. "He doesn't like dogs."

"The horror." As much as I like Rachel's company, that many dogs would send me into sneezing fits for the rest of the day.

"Did Mrs. Gretchen say if he complained about me?" Rachel asks, a little too eager to find out someone is bad-mouthing her.

"Ah—no. I haven't been around much, but I haven't heard anything."

"Astonishing." She rolls her eyes. "That he didn't say anything. I saw the video of your last trip," she adds, jumping topics like one of the excited dogs. "Who's the new girl? I've never heard anyone scream so loud."

"Natasha." I say ruefully. "She won't be in any more of the videos."

"Break another heart?"

"I didn't," I begin, then stop myself from apologizing. "Honestly, I don't think she has a heart. Maybe an emoji one."

"Another one who likes the spotlight?"

I cock my head to the side at Rachel's question. "What do you mean?"

"You're a good guy, Dawson, but really—find a woman who isn't that concerned with how many likes they get."

I nod slowly, thinking of what Neely said about Natasha. "I'm beginning to realize that."

"But, I liked you for you," she adds quickly. "I still think you're pretty cute, but I think the timing is wrong."

"Found someone else."

Rachel's eyes flick to the semi attached to Grammy's house. "No. Maybe."

I raise my eyebrows at her indecision. Ah—the new neighbour. "Good luck with that. I'd better get in. You know my grandmother's watching us out the window."

Waving goodbye, I smile at the sight of tiny Rachel trying to shepherd the dogs down the street. Knocking twice, I let myself into the house. "Grammy?" I call out.

"Is that my very favourite grandson?" she calls back, popping her snowy white head out of the kitchen down the hall. The whole house smells like lemon Pledge. Grammy is meticulous about dust.

And also wearing shoes in the house. "Do you say that to the others?" I kick off my Vans and meet her halfway down the hall, my arms open for a hug.

"I would if I ever spoke to them." Her arms tighten around my waist, surprisingly strong for a woman her age. "You forget that I've had practice lying under duress. But not to you." She pulls back and pats my cheek.

"It's good to know I don't cause you duress."

Grammy snorts, a most un-grandmotherly noise. "You, my grandson, cause me no end of worrying about your love life. Come and sit down and tell me what happened to the last girl." Taking my hand, she pulls me down the narrow hall into the living room where shelves are filled with books and bottles and other knickknacks, many of them that I brought back from our trips. "I noticed she vanished in the pictures at the wedding."

"I don't want to talk about her," I complain. "Wouldn't you rather have your present?" I dig through my backpack and pull out the plastic bag full of trinkets.

"Of course, if it's making a clinking noise." She settles onto the couch and pats the seat beside her before resuming the television show that was paused. "It's always a good time for a drink."

"You're watching Bridgerton?" I recognize the show, having been forced to sit through the series with Neely and Shae.

"I quite like that Duke," Grammy says in a sly voice. "You're safe to watch it with me. This is early on; none of the sexy business of episode six."

"Great. I brought you a bottle of Chalong Bay rum," I say, rummaging in the bag. "But I'm not drinking it with you." The memory of a night spent with a group of backpackers from Australia is still fresh in my mind, and even the smell of the liquor suggests being near it might not end well. "But you can try this." I hold up a bottle of *lao khao*.

"Go get some glasses," Grammy instructs, turning up the volume.

"Don't you want to know what it is?"

"Surprise me."

No grandmother I've ever met would drink fermented rice wine in the middle of the day, but my Grammy is not like any other. "Just because I'm old doesn't mean I still can't enjoy new experiences," she would say. "I'm not dead yet."

She refuses to tell me her age, but if she's telling the truth about her work with the resistance in World War two—I have no reason not to believe her—she's got to be in her mid-to-late nineties.

"Neely took a liking to this stuff." I pour a stiff shot into the jelly glasses I retrieved from the kitchen.

"Neely did, did she? How are my girls?" Grammy gives a cautious sniff before throwing it back. I laugh at the grimace on her face as it hits her stomach. "That's nasty." But yet, she refills her glass.

"Shae met a guy at the wedding this weekend," I report, taking a cautious sip. "He seems nice."

"Which means she'll scare him off by the end of the week."

"Probably." I sigh, remembering Emmett's face from yesterday's breakfast when we talked about the next trip. He's already falling, which means Shae will start running soon.

"Shae's a good girl but makes stupid moves." Grammy tips back another mouthful of *lao khao* and even I wince as it goes down. "And you indulge her too much."

"She's sick." Grammy is one of few people outside our immediate families who know the truth.

"I understand the living your best life—after what I've been through—but what about this nice man? Will he indulge her like the two of you? He'll want a life with her."

"They just met."

"Stranger things have happened. I knew my first husband for all of six days before I knew he was the one."

"Wasn't that during the war? And you know a life with Shae isn't in the cards for Shae."

"You can have part of a life. No one knows when their time is up." She sips delicately at her glass before tossing the rest back with a smack of her lips. "Look at me, I should have been snuffed out years ago and here I am, still kicking along having a drink with my grandson. You made a good move getting rid of the loud girl."

And back to Natasha. "Thanks," I say drily.

"She wasn't with you for the right reasons. What do you say about impressing people? From that movie you made me watch?"

"Spend a little more time trying to make something of yourself and a little less time trying to impress people," I recite the line from Breakfast Club. "That one? Have you been talking to neighbour Rachel?"

"Now that's a nice girl. You should meet a nice girl like that, not the poser." Grammy purses her lips in an impression of duck lips. "Every picture was like this. You can't see her soul, and pictures are for seeing into the soul." She holds out her hand for my phone and quickly opens my Instagram app, scrolling through the posts. "Every picture. I want to see *eyes* in a picture. That's how you get to know a person—look into their eyes. With this girl, all you saw was the lips."

Natasha did have beautiful lips but what came out of them wasn't nearly as nice. I'm not about to give Grammy more ammunition though.

"With Shae, you know what person she is when you look at her. She's almost too open for her own good." Grammy holds up my phone, frozen at a picture of Neely smiling at one of the baby elephants knocks off her hat. "Neely has a secret."

"What secret?"

"How would I know? You say you're her best friend."

"What can you tell about me?" I ask, filing away Neely's potential secret for later.

"You're a good man," she says in a proud voice. "And you're a romantic."

"Like my father?" While I love hearing Grammy's stories about her time in the war and her travels, I grasp every nugget she drops about my father like a mouse clearing crumbs. Five years with him wasn't enough. There's still so much I don't know.

Two days after my dad died, my mother sick with shock, Grammy showed up at our door.

"Caroline Gretchen," she said in a brisk voice, steel-blue eyes taking in our dumpy apartment in an instant. "I'm your grandmother."

She's like no other grandmother—tinier than even my mother, with a shock of white hair and those blue eyes that don't miss a thing. That day, Grammy waved off my mother's feeble insistence that we were *fine* and proceeded to take charge, her tiny body as sturdy as a tree my mother could lean against until she got her life back on track.

Grammy shakes her head. "Your father became a romantic only after he met your mother. Before that, he was cold. There wasn't a lot of love in his life, because of *that woman*."

There aren't many people in this world that I dislike, but my father's first wife, is tops on that list. It's nice to know she's not a favourite of Grammy's either.

"So, tell me what happened with the last one. Natasha," she adds, her voice full of contempt.

"Have you ever liked one of my girlfriends?" I wonder.

"I like Neely."

"Neely's not my girlfriend."

"Maybe she should be."

I close my eyes. "Why not Shae?"

"You're too good of a man for that girl," Grammy says after a pause. "I know there's not much hope for her, but it wouldn't be a fair fight. You'd give all of yourself to her, and she's not ready to do the same. She needs a man with his own heartache."

To change the subject, I lift the bag of gifts I brought back from Thailand, showing her the slippers and trinkets I brought back, soon to have their own spot on the shelves for her to dust.

But Grammy likes them, and I like Grammy, so I always fill my suitcase with things for her.

"Keith called a few days ago," Grammy says later as she walks me to the door.

I stiffen and pull my arm from around her shoulder. "The one who isn't your favourite grandson?"

Grammy sighs. "He's better than his brother. He wants to talk to you."

"Why?" Even I don't recognize my voice. Cold and unyielding, not like me at all.

"Does he need a reason?"

"Considering he's part of the family who contested my mother's claim to my father's estate, then yeah. I think he needs a pretty good reason for that."

"I think he might want to make amends," Grammy says carefully, not looking me in the eyes, which is never a good sign.

"And how does he expect to do that? Give back half the money? Because Mom wasn't asking for all of it. Just enough to give her a break."

"How is your mother?"

"Do you really want to know?"

Grammy frowns at the sharpness of my voice. "Of course I do."

My shoulders slump. Almost three months away from family drama had been a nice change. Too bad it's over now. "What does he want?"

"I think he wants to offer you a job."

Chapter Six

Pepper

A DOZEN CUPCAKES SIT in the display case, the lights glinting off the silver sparkles. I hate myself every time I look at them.

And then I think of the six dozen I started with this morning—two dozen each of chocolate caramel with dark chocolate frosting, lavender with honey, and a simple vanilla that I think is beautiful in its simplicity.

They sold out before noon.

Out of the over hundred cupcakes I made yesterday, I brought in only those I deemed worthy. And now there are only twelve left.

Eleven. Mrs. April must have sold one when I was in the back.

Just looking at them makes me feel queasy with guilt.

But then I think of the *cha-ching* of the cash register, and the hungry look in the customers' eyes at their first look at the perfect little cakes sitting there and the queasiness settles a bit.

They look good. Even I—my own harshest critic—have to admit that.

"Pepper, you need to always have cupcakes now," Tina Freeman exclaims. She's one of Jena Markov's group, one of the nicer ones, and I had breathed a sigh of relief when she walked in this morning with her yummy mummy yoga group.

If they came back, it would mean Jena hasn't labeled me a pariah or worse—a bad baker.

Between the four of the yummy mummies, they cleaned out a full dozen cupcakes, prompting me to send my co-op student, Lexi out to the office supply store to find some sort of take-out boxes.

Which prompted me to consider an online ordering system. Customers could order cupcakes for birthdays or special occasions, which would be an added profit on top of what I can make for the store—

"Pepper!" Mrs. April calls, waving the receiver of the old-fashioned landline that hangs by the door to the kitchen.

I've been so caught up in my thoughts that I missed the ringing. Taking the receiver from her with a wan smile, I pause to clear my head. "Pepper's Pies and Pastries. How can I help you?"

"Aye, this is Pepper?"

The voice doesn't register—only the accent. And the accent brings a smile to my face, so wide that I turn away from the counter to face the wall. No one needs to see this. "Yes, hello, is this—?"

"Reuben, from the wee bakery in the city. Hullo."

"Hi." I slip into the kitchen, the phone cord pulled tight around the doorframe. I don't need an audience for this. I have no idea for what but maybe—

"Hullo." Reuben clears his throat, sounding like cars driving along an old dirt road. "I was calling to see—"

"Yes?" The word trips out of my mouth before I can catch it.

"You see, aye...I have here an extra Madagascar vanilla, and I thought, well, I wondered, seeing as you're a baker as well, I thought you might have a need for it."

"Oh." That is not what I expected to hear. "Um, sure. In fact, I have—" I look wildly around the kitchen for something to trade. "I have some sourdough starter I can trade if you like," I say, pointing to the mason jar on the counter, full with the smelly flour-and-water concoction. "If you're interested in making bread. And like sourdough. I like it. I like it better than regular bread and I use rye flour to give it extra flavour and—"

"I'd love some of your starter."

I stifle the giggle that threatens, happy that he stopped me yattering on. Reuben says love like *luuve* and it sounds so *lovely*. So sweet and—"Well, that's great." A long pause and I wave my hand in the air, trying to think of something to say. "I don't know if I'll be in the city anytime soon—"

"I'd like to see your place. Your bakery."

"That would be great."

"I've a day off on Thursday."

"Thursday. Thursday is...great." I really need another word. "Great. What time...?" My mind jumps to what needs to be done before he comes—a good cleaning of the mixer, tidy the shelves in the back, organize the spatulas like M.K....

"We could have a meal," he says carefully, like he's extending a hand into the lion cage. "Later in the day, when you're through with things. If there's a place or pub nearby."

Do I sound like that when I talk to him? And who would dare to hurt him enough to make him that cautious? I already hate her.

"That would be...really nice." My smile widens. This is...this sounds...I think I have a date.

With Reuben.

"I'd like that," I add, wondering if he can tell I'm smiling from my voice.

"Aye, well, 'til Thursday."

"Aye—yes. Ashbury's not too far, just follow...I guess look at a map? I'm not good at giving directions."

"Aye—no. The GPS tells me it's not too far."

He already looked it up. Another giggle threatens. "Great."

"Great." Another pause, this one stretching awkwardly. "Until then. Pepper."

"Bye, Reuben," I whisper. When the phone disconnects, I stand there with it in my hand, silly smile on my face. "Thanks for calling."

I have a date. On Thursday. He's coming here, for a meal, which means taking him to Bollocks, which has the best menu, unless he likes fish n' chips, but would that remind him of home? Do they eat fish n' chips in Scotland, or is it only England? What do they eat in Scotland?

"What does it matter?" I say aloud. "He wants to see me."

I let the giggle escape, become a full laugh of delight, and give myself a hug.

I have a *date* with Reuben.

And then my ecstatic gaze falls on the box I used to carry the cupcakes in this morning and everything falls flat.

Dawson

I DON'T DO ANYTHING about my brother. Half-brother. No text, no response to his comment—nothing.

It's better that way, at least until I decide what I want to say to him.

Of course it's an automatic *no* to any job offer. Like Neely said, maybe someday, but not now. Not when Shae... But working with my brother? Keith is a tech guy, with at least two start-ups under his belt. It's why it makes seeing my mother's struggles to establish herself so hard. Mom knows computers; Keith works with computers. It wouldn't be too difficult for him to give his stepmother a helping hand.

But then there's the whole problem of Keith, his brother Kevin, and younger sister Kylie acknowledging Mom as anything but the former housekeeper that seduced their father and wound up pregnant.

That's not how it happened, but that's what their mother told them.

And Mom wouldn't accept help from Keith even if he offered. "If somebody doesn't believe in me, I can't believe in them," Mom always says, using the Pretty in Pink quote.

So I shouldn't either.

I push any thoughts of Keith firmly to the back burner and head over to Shae's for a much-needed round of Call of Duty with Mike.

I miss milk the most when we're away, but video games are a close second. At seventy-five, Mike is one of the best gamers that I've had the pleasure playing with, and a morning destroying things with him will help make up for the weeks without a controller in my hand.

And then I'm off to Ashbury to see Pepper.

I'm still not sure of the reasoning behind that, but I borrowed Aunt Claudine's car to make the drive. It should be fun. Pepper is fun.

She's not Neely, but maybe that's best. Besides, there's hope that I can come away with some insight on Grayson and what I need to do to make Neely forget about him.

If I was the type of person to do that.

I'm still debating that as I knock on Shae's door.

Mike yanks it open. "Do you know where Shae is?"

I take a step back at Mike's tone, as accusatory as a pointy finger. "Ah, no. Have you talked to Neely?"

"Not yet." The word ends in a hiss, his normally easy-going expression clouded with worry. "She didn't come home."

"Neely didn't come home?" My heart stutters.

"*Shae* didn't come home."

"She didn't text?" I follow him into the living room, taking my customary spot on the couch, Call of Duty already queued up on the screen.

"I wouldn't be this worked up if she had." Mike scrubs his hand through his short silver hair. "I know she's an adult and I have no idea what the three of you get up to when you're halfway around the world, but when she's home..." He trails off as he sinks onto the couch beside me.

"I'll check Insta." Keeping tabs on Shae is a full-time job as I well know, but it's not only because Shae has a tendency to jump at any idea or plan, regardless of potential consequences.

It's because when you don't know where Shae is, you don't know if she's alive.

But thanks to Shae's Instagram account, it's usually fairly easy to track her down. "Here." I show Mike my phone where a photo of the night sky has already reached thousands of likes. "She went to Emmett's yesterday, right? Looks like she stayed the night. Cool pic."

"She could have called," Mike mutters, picking up the controller.

"She should have called," I correct.

"She missed a doctor's appointment."

"I didn't know she had a doctor's appointment. Did Neely know?"

"Neely should not have to be Shae's keeper. Neither one of you should. She's a grown woman who should know how to keep appointments and check in."

Mike's frustration with Shae ups his game, and for the first fifteen minutes, I have trouble keeping up with him. I think it helps because when he finally defeats me and tosses down his controller, his face has lost some of the tension. "What's this Emmett guy like anyway?" he asks, heading to the kitchen. "Want a Pepsi?"

"Please. He's a good guy," I say loudly. "What I know of him."

Mike returns with a can. "Did you check him out online like you do?"

"I did that once, and only because Neely told me to."

"Do you do everything Neely tells you to?" Mike asks with a teasing smile.

"No." Even though now that I think of it, I kind of do. "She scares me." I stare at the wall behind the TV. Outside that is the shared drive between Neely's and Shae's houses. Neely is probably home, doing Neely things.

Planning for her date.

"She scares everyone. What about this guy she met at the wedding? Shae didn't say much."

"Grayson Grant. Former baseball player, soon to be the next Suitor."

"Tell me how you really feel."

I guess I didn't do as good a job as I thought keeping my own frustration out of my voice. "He's a nice guy," I say flatly.

"The Suitor? Isn't that the dating reality show?"

"Exactly. How is that going to work if he takes off to meet twenty other women and leaving Neely with a broken heart."

"He's going to break her heart?"

"How am I supposed to know? Do you think he'll break her heart?"

"I think maybe you're jumping the gun. It was just one night."

"She's never had her heart broken."

Mike takes up the controller again. "I think she's had her heart broken."

"Who?" Mike gives me the raised eyebrow. "*Who*?"

"If you don't know, I'm not going to be the one to tell you."

"What are you talking about?"

Mike heaves a sigh and completely destroys a building onscreen, while I get two shots in. "Seems to me our Neely was pretty upset back when you started going out with that girl."

"Which girl?"

"*All* the girls."

My surprise means my avatar is distracted and takes a round of machine gun bullets to the chest. "What are you talking about?"

"Dawson, buddy, for such a smart guy, you've been pretty stupid when it comes to that girl. Neely's always had a thing for you. Always."

"No, she hasn't." I'm adamant in my protest. "Not at all. She thinks of me as a *friend*."

"I think you should take a closer look at that friendship," Mike suggests, attention still on the screen.

"No," I say, my voice as flat as the floor. "I told her I was in love with her and I got nothing from that."

"What?" Mike allows himself to be killed onscreen. "When was this?"

"Years ago." Dropping the controller on the cushions, I lean back against the couch, rubbing at my face. "We were in Italy. It was my Lloyd Dobler moment—we finally hooked up—"

"You hooked up with Neely? Why didn't I know about this?" Mike demands, sounding nothing like a seventy-five-year old grandfather but rather my gamer buddy.

"Because you're Shae's grandfather," I remind both of us. "And if you heard about us hooking up, then you might start thinking that Shae is hooking up..."

"She spent the night at the home of a strange guy. I'm not stupid."

"Emmett's a good guy. I met his dad, too. He lives with him. You'd like Peter."

"I'd like to know what happened with you and Neely over in Italy all those years ago. We'll get back to Emmett later."

I turn away, not trusting my expression. I like thinking of the night I spent with Neely—what guy wouldn't—but I also hate it, because it hurts so much.

"Look, I know it's none of my business," Mike begins, and I shake my head in response.

"It's not that." Talking about Neely like this is something I would have done with a father, if mine hadn't been in New York during 9/11. Mike's the closest thing I have to a father and I think we both know that. "I've never told anyone. I think Shae knows...what Neely told her."

"What would Neely have told her?" Mike asks gently.

"We were working for the vineyard in Tuscany with a bunch of Australians and every Friday we'd meet up for pasta and wine. One Friday Neely and I ended up being the last ones up and..."

I can't drink red wine without remembering the taste of it on her lips. The eagerness of how she kissed me, the softness of her skin. How her tanned arms and shoulders made her pale breasts seem almost ghostly in the moonlight.

But they had been real and they fit perfectly into my hands.

"And we..." I trail off with a shrug.

"Got it. I'm sure Neely would have given Shae a few more details," he says with a rueful smile. "Girls, you know?"

"Maybe." I hate the thought of them talking about me like that. Did Neely tell her details? How I held her after? My face grows hot at the thought. "So...it happened...and we...we just stayed there outside looking at the stars. And I told her I loved her."

"You told her that? Those very words? Not some quote from Sixteen Candles?"

"I think I can figure that out on my own. *I love you, Neely.* That's what I said. Those very words. And a bunch of other stuff. And she...she didn't say anything."

"Nothing? Not even a thank you?"

"Nothing." I heave a sigh, taken back to staring at the night sky, with Neely in my arms, her golden hair spilling onto my chest. Of how the words leapt out of my mouth before I could stop them, brought about by the utter perfectness of the moment.

It was my Samantha and Jake moment from Sixteen Candles.

"I said what I needed to say." My voice is quiet, like back then when I didn't want to disturb the quiet of the night. "Neely just lay there. I didn't know what to do because I kind of poured my heart out to her. It was... Eventually, I fell asleep. In the morning, I went and got her coffee and it was...awkward. I haven't said a word about it since." I turn to him. "Do women actually say thank you? I thought that was a movie thing."

"Wow." Mike sips from his can, his eyes wide and thoughtful over the edge. "She said nothing. What you told her...it was nice?"

"What—do you think I'd be a jerk to her?"

"Of course not, but it was a few years ago, and you know, buddy, you are a guy."

"What's that supposed to mean?" Maybe I did it wrong? "What would you say to a woman if you were telling her how you felt?"

"What do you mean?" Mike pulls his arm off the back of the couch. His expression switches from interested to wary.

"I mean, how would you tell someone you loved them? That's a thing you've done, right? Shae says you're always out on dates. Who was the last woman you said I love you to?"

"Dawson..." Mike doesn't meet my gaze. "We shouldn't be talking about this."

"Why not? What's the matter with her?"

"There's nothing wrong with her. She's wonderful."

"That's present tense. Are you dating someone?" Mike shifts uneasily. "You have a girlfriend? That's great, really great. Who is she?"

This is when Mike looks me full in the face. "Your mother."

Chapter Seven

Pepper

I HAVE RUINED EVERY relationship I've been in so it's almost a relief to know that I won't have to wait to mess up this one.

Not that there's a relationship with Reuben. I'm really jumping the gun if I think that. Right now it's just a man calling a woman to have a meal.

But even such a little thing fires up the butterflies in my stomach, which are then caught and squashed by the fact that I stole his recipes.

I can't really get past that.

Lexi arrives for her shift at noon, and she and Mrs. April excitedly scroll through Pinterest for more cupcake suggestions. Lexi is a junior at the local high school, with an interest in anything culinary. She's doing her co-op with me; I'm sure I wasn't her first choice, but I was the only food-related business in town who agreed to take her on. It's worked out well—she works every other afternoon, and once I got her trained to my liking, I started giving her other shifts on the weekends, which means I haven't had to hire anyone else.

I'm not sure what's going to happen in June when she's got her credit, but I'll deal with that when she tells me she's found another job for the summer.

"Something with peanut butter!" After eating three of my non-perfect cupcakes, Lexi is clearly on a sugar high, hopping up and down as she shouts suggestions down the counter. I make a mental note to keep her from the second latte.

"What about all the allergies?" Mrs. April points out.

"We can put a little sign," Lexi says. "Everyone knows this isn't a peanut-free place."

"Do you think I should try a gluten-free one?" I ask, Lexi's enthusiasm rubbing off on me.

"No!" she cries, and even Mrs. April shakes her head. They've watched the trials and tribulations of me trying to make the perfect gluten-free bread.

"I don't think it's necessary," Mrs. April adds.

Lexi brings a freshness to the shop on the days she works, even though the blue hair and multiple piercings still get a few concerned glances from the older customers. The afternoon regulars have gotten used to her, and I've gotten used to using the hours she's here to plan and prep for the next day so I don't have to stay so late.

Alone in the kitchen, I pop a CD in the stereo and let autopilot take over. I've been making bread since I was seven and started developing my own recipes a few years later. Everything I know is in my head; no recipes left out in a binder, with laminated pages catching in the light.

Why can't Reuben be forgettable?

Knowing I'll see Reuben Thursday has me swinging a pendulum between excitement and dread with a healthy dose of terror in the middle. It would have been easy to justify taking the recipes if he'd only been someone other than Reuben with his sweet, shy smile. If he hadn't been as big as one of the maple trees I used to climb with Ellie, or hadn't had the best Scottish accent.

I fell asleep watching Outlander on Netflix last night.

Why can't he be like anyone else I've ever met? If he was, I wouldn't think twice about this.

Lexi pushes open the kitchen door with an empty tray in her hand. "More cupcakes needed," she sings. "There's a gaggle of mean girls from school out there. I've half a mind to stick something nasty in Rylee's but I couldn't do that to you." She grins, flicking the stud in her tongue against her tooth.

"I appreciate that, especially since I know how strong the urge would be," I say. Lexi is more of a rebel than I ever was, but I pegged her as a kindred spirit the first time we met. She hasn't found her place in Ashbury, or in the world—something I can relate to since that's how I felt all through high school.

To be completely honest, I still don't feel like I belong.

But that's not anything I need to reflect on. I take advantage of Lexi being there to hide out in the kitchen for most of the afternoon to whip up both a milk chocolate batter with the last of my Valrhona cocoa, and one with dark chocolate. The kitchen soon fills with the scent of baking chocolate, which is as much a great selling technique for the cupcakes as baking bread.

There are only two cupcakes left in the case by the end of the day. I tell myself it's a good sign that there will be no chance of Reuben ever finding out I used his recipes.

"The cupcakes were a great idea." Mrs. April takes off her apron and hangs it neatly on the hook in the kitchen. The wall clock by the door, with the rooster in the centre and colourful chicken numbers, tells me it's only a few minutes before four o'clock. Lexi has already left for the day.

Today, the hours I've spent here don't weigh on me as heavily as they usually do. Most days, I'm itching to get away from the customers, the smell of bread, and get home. Today, all I want is to get back into the kitchen and try my hand at more cupcakes. "Why didn't you tell me you were thinking of something so different?" Mrs. April asks, watching me stack the clean plates and mugs behind the counter.

"It just came to me."

She cocks her head. "You just came up with the idea to sell cupcakes in a bakery that specializes in bread?"

"Why can't I do both?" But she's still watching me, eyes narrowed like she knows the real reason. "We went to this place in Toronto on the weekend," I relent. "It was a patisserie, real upscale French place, but they sell cupcakes and I thought—why not?" I don't meet her eyes. Maybe it's my guilt because I really have to remind myself that, even though Mrs. April has known me since the moment I was born, she can't actually read my mind.

"Why not, indeed? I think it's a great idea and will only help business. Have you figured out the sales totals today?"

"I know what I started with." The décor of Pies and Pastries is vintage, with the salt and pepper shakers on every available surface, the mismatched chairs, and even the clock. The cash register fits right in; made in the 1940s, it's big and bulky and as heavy as sin. It's always been a great conversation piece for tourists in the area, but seriously limits me with sales totals. Luckily, both Mrs. April and I know the ins and outs of the thing, as well as how to keep track of inventory and sales throughout the day.

"Well, I know those cupcakes are going to bring in the hungry masses." Mrs. April bustles behind the counter to find the scraps of paper I use to keep track of what I sell during the day.

"Thank God," I mutter, pulling a mug with a tooth-sized chip out of the pile. Not for the first time, I wish I'd gone for plain white instead of the bright yellow and red plates.

"What was that?" Mrs. April has the hearing of a much younger woman.

"Nothing," I say quickly.

"Pepper...you haven't asked me to check the books for you lately." Mrs. April looks at me with a mix of curiosity and concern and all I want to do is throw myself in her arms and tell her everything, confess about the expenses from the window and the water damage, and how I'm running out of money.

But I don't.

"I'm good with the books," I lie. Back when I first bought the place, Mrs. April looked after the bookkeeping for me while I did my best to figure out the business end of the bakery. I'm very good with the baking aspect, but numbers have never been my thing.

I was diagnosed with dyslexia when I was ten. My father used to sit at the kitchen table with me for hours, patiently helping me with my homework. After he left, it was six months before anyone noticed how much I was floundering, and I've never really recovered from it.

I'm good at hiding when I need help.

"Which is your favourite?" I ask Mrs. April, pointing to the leftover cupcakes.

Mrs. April's eyes gleam, forgetting all about my books, just like I knew she would. "I really liked the lavender and honey. I'm surprised they're not all gone."

"Take what's left," I say quickly with another glance at the door. "I don't want to sell day-olds. I'm making chocolate for tomorrow. Dark chocolate with salted caramel and chocolate with peanut butter frosting."

"Where are you coming up with these?"

I tap the side of my head. "I came up with a bunch of ideas last night." And technically I did.

"Sounds like good ones. Keep it up." She drops a hand on my shoulder as I pass. "I'm very proud of you, Pepper. You've done a really good thing with this place. Ashbury appreciates you, and so do I."

I reach up and squeeze the hand on my shoulder. "Thanks, Mrs. A. I—"

The bell over the door interrupts what I was going to say. And then I forget about everything when I see who walks in.

Dawson

"DAWSON, TALK TO ME," Mike calls after me as I stumble away from him, tripping over Doris, the ancient yellow Labrador who jumps up to race me to the door.

Are you dating someone?

Your mother.

He's in love with my mother. I think. Sure sounds like it.

My mother. My mother, who is still grieving over my father.

"I'm not talking to you." I don't know where I'm going, but it needs to be away from Mike—my so-called friend who took advantage of my mother being alone, her vulnerable condition. She has MS, for God's sake. I needed someone I can trust to take care of fixing things in the apartment, not someone I have to worry about making a move on her.

Oh, God, did Mike make a move on my mother?

"Dawson, wait." He gets a hand on the front door just as I'm about to yank it open and escape.

"I—I don't...I don't have any idea what to say to you," I stammer, my hand still on the doorknob.

"Tell me what you're feeling," Mike urges.

"What I'm—you sound like some therapist, not the guy I was playing CoD with!" I snort. "What am I supposed to feel? Give you a high five? Threaten to break your face?"

That surprises me as much as Mike as I've never been a violent person.

"I'd rather you not break my face," Mike says with a hint of a smile, the sight of which might possibly produce violent tendencies in me.

"You tell me this." I step back away from him and I gesture with my hands. "This—about you and my mother. What am I supposed to think? What am I supposed to say to that?"

Mike gives a resigned sigh. "This is why we didn't tell you."

It's the *we* that gets me. "You talked about me?"

"Of course, we talked about you." Mike reaches for my arm. His fingers slide across the sleeve of my flannel before dropping to his side. Doris wags her tail in anticipation of a walk. "We didn't know how you'd react. This isn't a usual situation."

"No, this is a situation where I asked you to look after my mother when I'm away, not fall for her."

"I spent a lot of time with your mother," Mike says. "She's a very special woman."

"Yeah, my father thought so too."

"Dawson, your father is dead."

I step back another foot and run my hand through my hair. "I can't believe you said that."

"Because it's true, as sad as that fact is. Your mom has spent most of your life grieving for him, trying to keep his memory alive for you. Don't you think it's time she had some happiness for herself?"

It's like he hit me. Punched me right in the stomach. "With you?" I manage.

"Yes. With me."

I stare at Mike, not seeing the eyes that show how much he cares for Mom, for me, but the silver hair. The lines around his eyes. Not how fit and strong he is, but the slight paunch visible under his T-shirt.

Mike is a good guy, but he's seventy-five. Seventy-five, and my mother is not even fifty. They could have what? Ten years together? Fifteen? And then Mike will die, and my mother will be alone again.

Doris's wet nose touches my hand. "We can't have dogs in the apartment," I say. Then I push past Mike, step outside and carefully close the door behind me.

Instinct has me crossing the driveway to Neely's front door.

She answers at my first knock. I take a step back at the sight of her, remembering Mike's *other* words.

Neely's always had a thing for you. Always.

"What are you doing here?" Neely's wearing the jeans that I've always liked, the faded ones with the rip in the knee. A real rip, not one of the manufactured ones.

I was with her when she ripped them.

"I—" *Do you love me?* I almost ask. I almost say the words that will ruin things. Because if I ask, and she says no, that's it. No more Neely-Dawson-Shae.

I need Neely-Dawson right now. Does Shae know about Mike and my mother? I think not, because Shae can't keep a secret other than about herself. She would be yelling about a love match to everyone who'd listen, which is quite a few people.

I'm not ready to yell anything. I want Neely to tell me what I should be feeling, because she's so good at that.

"I thought you were going to see Pepper." Her voice is cool, which it usually is when she's talking to me. Eventually she warms up, like a non-morning person who needs a hit of caffeine before she's ready to talk to people.

"Pepper?" Pepper is not part of this conversation.

"Pepper Grant?" Neely holds up her phone and I see the ... bubble on the screen. And then the name at the top.

Grayson.

"You were going to see her today. Says so right here." She waves it in my face, and I take a step back, vaguely remembering something about texting Pepper at the post-wedding breakfast.

"Uh, yeah."

"So? Why aren't you there? She's probably waiting for you."

It's like she's accusing me. I'm a bad guy for going to see Pepper, and I'd be a bad guy if I cancelled. How can I cancel when I don't even have her phone number?

How can I go anywhere? All I want to do is talk to Neely about Mike and Mom, but it's becoming clear that Neely doesn't want to talk to me about anything.

That...stings.

Actually, it hurts enough to double me over.

"Uh, yeah. I wanted to ask if I can borrow Adam's car. Your car." Neely and her brother share a beat-up Jetta that they let me borrow. Driving to wherever Pepper lives is the last thing I want to do, but Neely isn't the good idea I thought she was.

"Cutting it a bit close, aren't you?" Neely asks with a sneer on her face.

I nod, something akin to betrayal making my insides feel like they're shifting into something new. My heart is my stomach, my stomach is my spleen...

"What's the matter?" Neely's voice sharpens with concern. There. That's the Neely-Dawson that I need. I open my mouth to let it all spill out—

She looks down at her phone and smiles as she reads what Grayson wrote.

"Nothing," I say in a hollow voice. "I'm late. To see Pepper."

"You better go," Neely says, the smile fading from her face. "Ashbury's not too far, but it will take you long enough, and you said you'd be there before she closed her bakery." She backs away, phone still clutched in her hand, and grabs the car keys hanging by the door.

She read my texts to Pepper. I wish I could reread them, remember what I said.

"Take pictures for the vlog," she instructs, handing me the keys. "We can do a nice little small-town thing. I'll go visit Grayson soon—"

"Thanks for the car," I interrupt, backing up down the steps. The last thing I want is to have to listen to Grayson, or anyone else who made a love connection. "I'll fill it up when I bring it back."

And then I leave.

Chapter Eight

♥

Pepper

"Dawson?" My surprise brings out the snarky tone in my voice and Dawson blinks with surprise. For a moment I wonder if he's about to turn and leave.

"Hey, Pepper." Dawson waves, looking like one of the hipsters that have invaded Ashbury with his dark framed glasses and beat-up Vans. "Cute place you got here."

"What are—?" I clamp my lips shut as I remember texting him on Sunday. It was on Grayson's phone, so I haven't looked back at the text string. I totally forgot about it, about how Dawson offered to make the drive to Ashbury to see my shop.

Why would he do that?

"Thanks," I say instead. "Good to see you. You found it okay?"

"You forgot I was coming," he says, a grin spreading across his face.

"I did not."

"I think you did."

"I...why—yes," I confess with an embarrassed puff of breath. "I'm sorry, I completely forgot about it. It was on Grayson's phone and that he should have reminded me, but of course he forgot." I know it's not Grayson's fault; I should have remembered. I should have written it down or copied the texts into my own phone, or *something*.

There's a guy—a very cute guy—standing in my bakery, after driving to Ashbury to see me, and I forgot all about it.

Definitely not a good start.

What exactly am I supposed to start?

"No worries." Dawson picks up one of the saltshakers lining the counter, and suddenly I see my shop through his eyes—full of bright colours and kitschy *stuff* like the salt and pepper shakers, and the retro chicken clock, and how the black-and-white framed photos of old Ashbury look out of place on the walls. "Is this a bad time?"

"No." I glance behind me. Mrs. April's expression is a mix of delight and confusion as she looks between us. I hope I don't look the same.

"We're just about to close, so it's perfect." It's not perfect. I want to start baking for tomorrow, but Dawson did drive all this way so the least I can do is be polite.

"I told Pepper that I'd stay in case we had a rush, but a nice, tall stranger like yourself walking in is just as nice. Now, Pepper..." Mrs. April draws out my name like my third grade teacher when I got caught passing notes to Ellie. "Don't be rude. Wouldn't you like to introduce me?"

I am never going to hear the end of this. "Mrs. April, this is my friend, Dawson. Dawson, Mrs. A."

"*A friend*," Mrs. April breathes, hands clasped under her chin. "Where did you meet this *friend*?"

"Dawson's just a guy I met at the wedding—"

"You didn't tell me you met a *man*!"

I sigh. "And you wonder why I never tell you nice things," I mutter.

"Of course you have to tell me nice things!" To my horror, my seventy-five-year-old employee bumps around the counter to sashay over to Dawson. She holds out her hand like she expects him to kiss it. "Helene April," she simpers with a flutter of mascara-ed eyelashes.

To his credit, Dawson never blinks. "Dawson Jacinto," he says with a boyish grin. "Great to meet you. You work here with Pepper?"

"For as long as Pepper has. I've known her since the day she was born—literally. The stories I could tell you about this girl—"

"Please don't," I say in a flat voice.

"But I could keep you amused for hours."

"Dawson doesn't have hours," I say, quickly boxing the remainder of the cupcakes for her.

"Some other time," he says politely. "I'm sure they're great stories." He glances at me. "This is fun," he says, waving an arm to encompass the brightness of my shop. "I don't frequent a lot of bakeries, but this is amazing, so different than Pain au Chocolate. I hardly believe you sell the same stuff."

I slide the box across the counter. "You might as well head out, Mrs. A. I'll close up early since it's pretty quiet."

"Are you sure? I really don't mind staying longer if you're otherwise occupied." She gives me a dramatic wink. The producers of The Suitor have nothing on the matchmaking skills of Mrs. April.

"It's not like that," I say, laughing despite myself.

Actually, I really don't know what it is. Dawson stands there with a bemused expression on his face, so he's no help. Frantically, I try to think back to what I texted him. It had been when Grayson was driving home; he wanted to tell Neely something, and I wouldn't let him touch his phone, and then Dawson had replied...

Purely friendly. There's no way I would have flirted with him, because I'm really bad at flirting, especially over text.

"You should show Dawson the kitchen," Mrs. April suggests, making no move to leave.

"I will, after I lock the door after you." I pull her coat from the little cupboard under the counter, along with her purse.

"Ah." She gives me a knowing nod. "I'll be off, then."

"See you tomorrow." We wait in awkward silence as she puts on her coat with exaggerated slowness, slings her purse over her arm and takes the white box of cupcakes with a resigned sniff. I give her a wave after I shut the door, flipping the sign to closed.

"Sorry about that," I say to Dawson. "She finds the need to try to fix me up with just about every person who comes through that door, as long as they're within her age group."

"Like an age group as old as her?"

"Thankfully, no, but she once had it in her head that Mr. Mc-Dougall would be a good match for me, and he's pushing sixty."

"I think I'm in the wrong place if you're into men that much older."

I glance at him quickly and Dawson gives me a slow smile. And then I really look at him. Cute and cheerful, but there's something different about his eyes today, like he witnessed an accident or walked in on his mother naked. "Are you okay?" I ask. "You look like you got hit in the face with a shovel."

Dawson blinks with surprise. "A shovel?"

"You look like you've seen a ten-car pileup, or your mother naked. Both are things you can't unsee."

"Are you speaking from experience?"

"I saw a tractor overturned in the field once, killed Larry Redman. Or it might have been the heart attack that killed him, then the tractor flipped over, which is very hard to do, and therefore a bit of a shock to see. But the whole seeing mothers naked—" I gesture to my chest area quickly with a flush rising to my cheeks. "Woman. It wouldn't bother me, but Grayson had the misfortune of walking in on our mother once when he was fourteen and apparently it was quite traumatic. I'm babbling," I add, trying to stop myself. "I tend to do that a lot. I also say things before I really think about the consequences."

If I was trying to impress him, I'd have already failed miserably. But I'm not, and the realization calms me as much as my weighted blanket does.

"That's cool. I'm a good listener of babble."

"So what got you looking like that? The shovel-to-the-face look."

"Funnily enough it has to do with my mother. Apparently, Shae's step-grandfather is in love with her." Dawson runs his hand through his dark hair. "With my mother. I think. Maybe."

Even with my lack of people skills, I know there's more to it than that.

"Huh."

"Yeah. Huh."

"Mother in love with friend's grandfather…that sounds complicated." I know about father and friend's mother, but this is Dawson's issue and doesn't need my sad story to muddy the waters.

"Yeah…complicated. The thing is, though, I don't think it should be," Dawson says slowly. "But it seems to be."

"Everything about parents is complicated, especially when kids get older. I think they make a point of it, just to mess us up. Look, I thought maybe we could go to Bollocks—"

Dawson gives a surprised guffaw. "What's a bollocks? I mean, I think I know what it is, but why would we go there?"

"Local pub." A noticeable rumble interrupts and our attention flies to my stomach area. "Obviously I have food on my mind. Are you hungry? I think we said something about eating…a meal." Reuben's shy smile flashes through my mind at the word. Is it bad that I'd rather Reuben be here instead of Dawson?

"I can always eat."

"Why don't I grab something from the back, and then you can tell me all about mothers and grandfathers and how Shae is involved with all of it," I say, pulling my thoughts away from sounds of Scotland. "If you want to, that is. You don't have to."

Dawson gives me a rueful shrug. "I came all this way, so I better talk about something. Let's check out your kitchen."

Dawson

SOMETHING ABOUT PEPPER TELLS me I can talk to her about this. Maybe because she's not Shae or Neely with their opinions on things. And I know there's no way I can drive back to the city without dumping all this on someone.

Mike is in love with my mother.

The rejection of Pepper forgetting I was coming would sting more if I hadn't forgotten myself. Plus, I'm spiraling with thoughts of Mom and Mike; Mike and Mom, and it makes it difficult to focus on anything else.

What does it mean? Is he in love with her? Does she love him? Are they—?

With a quick wave of her hand, Pepper beckons me to follow her behind the counter. I catch my breath as she pushes open the kitchen door. Her Mrs. April was eclectic enough, but this is something else.

It smells amazing.

The back space is almost as large as the front of the store, and just as bright, with each wall painted a different colour. A square island cuts the room in half, with a long swath of countertop flanking one side of the wall, with bowls and baking tools stacked neatly. There's a huge appliance off the side that looks like a giant-size mixer. The back of the kitchen is a wall of ovens and shelves and in the corner, away from the potential mess, is a tiny desk with what looks like a pre-2000 PC and old-fashioned stereo.

"This is..." I trail off, at a loss for words.

"I know," Pepper says with a frustrated hiss. "The whole place needs an update but I haven't had the time or money since I bought it. I don't think anything has changed since 1990."

"The computer certainly hasn't." I head over to the desk, marveling at the box-like monitor sitting on the hard-drive. "This might be an antique. How do you function with this?"

"I don't know much about computers," she admits.

"I've got to get a picture of this to show my mom. She's a computer tech and..." My thought stutters to a halt with thoughts of Mom.

"I'll make us some sandwiches," Pepper offers, opening the door to the monstrous refrigerator. I glance over in time to see it stocked with milk and butter and plastic tubs of other things important to baking. "Ham okay?"

"Sure." Pepper takes out packages wrapped in brown butcher paper and tied with string. They seem old-fashioned amid the stainless steel of the fridge, but then the whole place is old-fashioned. A hodge-podge of so many things—the colours, the salt and pepper shakers, the computer...

"You've got CDs." Beside the desk is a red milk crate jam-packed with plastic cases and I kneel down to get a better look. "A pretty good collection here."

"I listen after hours," she says, slicing open a scone. "They were my father's. One or two?" She gestures to the sandwich fixings before her.

"Maybe two?" My own stomach starts to rumble at the fresh bread and chocolate smell of the kitchen. "I didn't think I was hungry until I got here."

"I think I must have Italian ancestors," Pepper says as she stacks ham and cheese inside the biscuits, adding a squirt of mustard. "I feel the need to feed people. Which is good since I own this place."

"Like Neely's mama," I say, stepping away from the desk. "Mama S. She's always pushing food at me. Neely says it's how she shows that she cares."

"Neely," Pepper muses. "You and her and Shae—I've never seen a friendship like that. At the wedding, I thought that you and Shae and then—nope."

"Nope," I agree. "We kissed one time. She laughed."

Pepper cringes. "That can't be good."

"I laughed too. She said it was like kissing her brother, if she had a brother, which she didn't, so she said it was like kissing Neely's younger brother Adam."

"Oh, boy!"

"We didn't even know each other." I laugh. "I told her it was like when Ginny kissed Harry Potter. They had no chemistry. And then we started arguing about how she thought Harry and Draco should just make out and get it over with. We've been best friends ever since. People ask me about it all the time and I don't get it," I admit. "We're just friends."

"I've never had friends like that," Pepper says, her eyes wide and solemn and something pricks inside of me. I can't imagine what my life would be without Neely and Shae. "I haven't even had a real male friend," she continues. "I'm sure people ask you about it because they're jealous."

Her tone is matter-of-fact, and I study her closely, wondering about the layers of Pepper that people don't see. "You must have friends. Look at you."

"What does that have to do with it?" She laughs. "If I'm cute, I should have friends? It doesn't make me a good friend, and that's my problem. I don't make them a priority. I have Grayson, and you met Mrs. April. That's about it." She waves her hand around the kitchen. "I spend too much time in here."

I sidestep the lack of friend detail, somehow sensing Pepper won't want to go into it, but filing it away for later. I already know that I want to be Pepper's friend. "Mrs. April is something else. I'd say let's set her up with Shae's grandfather Mike, because he's the same age, but he just told me he's in love with my mother, so that won't really work."

"Yes, the big reveal." She cuts each sandwich in half and sets them on plates. "I can make coffee or I have..." She opens the fridge and I see the familiar red cans. "Coke?"

"One of those will be great."

"Let's go sit at one of the tables out front and you can tell me everything." I follow her to the front of the shop to the table at the window, where the late-afternoon sun streams through. If I were a cat, I would nap here.

"Start from the beginning," Pepper says. She picks up the sandwich with both hands and takes a bite, her gaze never leaving mine.

I flip open the can and take a long swig. "I don't think I need to go that far back."

"Of course you do. How can I be suitably sympathetic that your mother has a suitor?" She winces as soon as the word escapes. "Admirer. I hate that word. *Suitor.* I can't believe they named the show that."

"Well, *The Bachelor* was taken."

"*The Suitorette* is worse."

"Yeah, that's pretty bad. I take it you're not in favour of your brother being the Suitor." I keep my voice even as I tiptoe into enemy territory.

I'm not sure how I feel about Grayson and his reality show career. On one hand, I think it's great for him to go on the show, but he needs to leave Neely out of it. I don't want her to be hurt. It's a slippery slope, one that sends my thoughts speeding back into Mike's comments. *Neely's always had a thing for you. Always.*

"Grayson can do what he wants," Pepper says, pulling me back to the present. "I'm his sister, not his keeper."

"I don't have a brother," I offer. "Well, I guess I do. Two half-brothers, and a half-sister, but I never talk to them."

"This is why you have to start at the beginning."

I smile ruefully. "I guess. I don't talk about it much."

"Sometimes it's easier to talk to strangers."

"I think so. My father was married before," I say in a rush, wanting to skip past the backstory to get to the good stuff. Neely and Shae already know that. I wouldn't have to explain.

Neely didn't want to hear about it. She wasn't interested in what I had to say.

"They lived in a big house, in a *bougie* neighbourhood with their kids." I pause before I get to the part that always makes me uneasy. "My mother was the housekeeper."

"Ah." Pepper does her best to keep her expression blank, her tone judgment-free, but surprise sneaks out. It doesn't bother me; not anymore. I know how much my father loved Mom.

"Don't worry, she wasn't the nanny," I hasten to add. "That's too much like some Hollywood scandal. She came over from the Philippines when she was seventeen and got a job working for my father's family. My father was older—quite a bit older—and his kids were only a couple years younger than Mom. She worked for them for a few years."

"And fell in love with your father?"

I hear the skepticism in Pepper's voice. "They did fall in love. I know what it seems like—did he take advantage of her? Did she set out to seduce the rich, older man? I know what it looks like."

Pepper shrugs, her bottle of water in her hand. "I have no idea what it looks like. I don't have much experience with love. My father ran off with another woman when I was twelve. Emmett's mother, actually."

"Whoa." I lean back in the chair to give myself room to take it in. It's not unlike Mike and Mom—Shae and I will have to deal with the new relationship and what it does to our existing one, but Mike and my mother aren't married to other people.

Your father is dead. Your mom has spent most of your life grieving for him, trying to keep his memory alive for you. Don't you think it's time she had some happiness for herself?

I try to shut off Mike's voice to focus on what Pepper is saying. "It was kind of whoa. So forgive me if I'm a little skeptical about the process of true love."

"Well, they did fall in love," I say. "But they didn't act on it. Mom said she had no idea that he felt the same way until...I guess they figured it out. Mom didn't want to do anything that would hurt his marriage, but according to him, there wasn't much of a marriage left. And the kids were older...all it takes is one time." I point to myself.

"She got pregnant."

"She didn't even know she was pregnant. She thought she had the flu, but the wife—I can't really call her anything else," I say apologetically. "She heard my mother in the washroom and accused her of seducing her husband and how getting pregnant was her way of stealing him. She fired my mother, threw her out of the house. Apparently, my father was away when all this happened, so he came home and Mom was gone. Really gone, like back to the Philippines. She had nowhere else to go; no family in the city, not really any friends. Plus, pregnant."

"And young. How old was she?"

"Twenty. She took all her money and spent it on a plane ticket back home."

"And your father?"

"Had no idea where she went or what happened. He didn't know about the baby, just that she left without a word. It took him two years to find her. I have no idea how he found us either. We lived in this pretty awful neighbourhood in Davao City, and one day he was just there. He took us back to Canada, along with my aunt Claudine, who looked after me. He divorced his wife and we all lived happily ever after, at least until he happened to be in New York when the plane hit the World Trade Center."

"I'm so sorry. But that does sound like a real fairy tale," Pepper says, a wistful note in her voice.

"It was. They were meant to be together." I take a deep breath, always moved by the story. "They had one of those epic love stories that they make movies from. He was so romantic, did all these things for her. He went around the world for her, saved her really. But she saved him too, from his marriage."

"They saved each other," Pepper says.

"Like in Pretty Woman." Pepper's eyes narrow with confusion. "When Richard Gere tracks her down in the limo with the flowers and climbs the fire escape? Julia Roberts has that line that she saved him right back."

Pepper raises an eyebrow. "You must watch a lot of movies."

"Me and my mom—it's our thing."

"It's nice to have a thing."

I nod and finish my sandwich. "Now Mike tells me—Shae's step-grandfather," I explain. "My mom has MS now, and I always ask him to check up on her when we're away. They're friends. I thought. Now..." I bite my lip, thoughts in a confused tangle. "What am I supposed to think about her moving on? All my life I've heard nothing but her love story with my father. Is it over?"

"But I thought he died?" she asks gently.

"He did. He's gone, but she still loves him. I know she does."

"And she always will, but that doesn't mean she can't love someone else. This might be the beginning of her epic love story with this Mike."

"I want that," I admit. "I want the epic love story. My mother always reminds me that I'm meant to be with someone too. I want the soul mate and the grand gestures and the love that never ends." Hunching my shoulders, I look at Pepper. Usually when I tell a woman the story, they get all soft-eyed and I get the sense that they think they're meant to be with me. I'm not saying that I'm so irresistible, but there's something about a good love story that can win over even the most hard-hearted person.

She nods, pulling my empty plate from in front of me to stack on hers. "You want the movie version. I'm not there yet."

"I didn't mean that you—"

"Not with you," Pepper says scornfully. "I only just met you. I definitely don't believe in love at first sight."

"Why not? It could happen."

"You sound like Grayson. He thinks he's going to walk onto the set of that show and meet his one true love like that." She snaps her fingers. "I don't believe in true love. I don't believe in soul mates, " Pepper says flatly. "Because that would be admitting that my mother wasn't my father's soul mate; that Emmett's mother was. So at this point of my life, I don't really believe in love. Or maybe I..." She trails off, her dark eyes cast with a vulnerable shine and I wonder what's made her look that way. Or who, because I don't think it's me. "I don't know. What happened with you and the girl at the wedding?"

I blink with surprise. I thought we'd stick with the dad thing, or keep debating the idea of true love. "Natasha broke up with me. Or I broke up with her. I'm not quite sure."

"Were you together long? Sorry, rude. You don't have to tell me. I ask a lot of questions and never stop to think people might not want to answer."

I shake my head. "It's all good. I met her about three weeks before we left for Asia. It was a spur of the moment decision to invite her, and I really wished I didn't."

"Not a good travel companion?"

"I knew we weren't meant to be together about ten minutes after takeoff, but it seemed rude to break up with her in another country."

"I imagine she wouldn't take that well. Look how she reacted with you dancing with me. She threw a glass at you!"

"Neely was not happy about that outburst. She didn't want me to invite her to begin with. They never got along." I glance down at the empty plates. "This has been a real True Confessions," I say with a smile. "I don't usually get this on a first date."

"Is that what this is?"

"Do you think it is?" I counter.

"A first date? I'm not sure."

"Ouch." But I smile, happy that Pepper is on the same wavelength. She's great, and definitely got me talking, but there's no spark, no certain something drawing us together.

Thinking of Natasha, I wonder about the spark that pulled me to her, because whatever it was died out pretty fast.

Like Denise before her, and Amber before that...

I keep looking for that certain something that will show me she's the one, but no one has it.

She's out there somewhere, but Pepper isn't it. At least I'm pretty sure she isn't.

"I think you're a really good guy." There's a twinkle in Pepper's eyes that replaces the sadness from a moment ago, and her gaze shifts noticeably to my mouth. But still it takes me by surprise when she leans across the table and cups my face in her hands. My heart beats frantically, from Pepper's cool hands on my face, and from the fact this is as close to the reenactment of the Jake and

Samantha's iconic table kiss in Sixteen Candles that I'm ever going to get.

And then she kisses me.

I'm stunned enough to take a moment to react to the feel of soft lips pressed against my own. And then I tuck a hand at the nape of her neck, drawing her closer. There's the heady excitement of a first kiss; the promise. The potential. The power that a good kiss has over me, like I'd be willing to follow Pepper anywhere just to keep kissing her.

And then Pepper pulls back, running her tongue over her lips like she's savouring the touch. "Nope," she says, her mouth widening to a grin. "But I had to check."

"What?"

"Did you feel anything?" she demands.

"No," I say reluctantly. It was a good kiss, but not the kiss of true love. It was nothing like Spider-Man and Mary Jane in the rain, or Claire and Bender after a day spent in detention. "Didn't exactly measure up to when Jake Ryan kisses Samantha over her birthday cake." I see Pepper's frown and my heart sinks this time. "Sixteen Candles?"

"I don't remember much of that movie," she admits.

"It's a classic."

"I'll give it a rewatch. But this—nice." I wince at the description, and she smiles sympathetically. "But not a classic. Or at least not for me."

I study the woman sitting across from me. She reminds me of Neely in so many ways, yet Neely would never be that cavalier about someone's feelings. "I'd be heartbroken if I didn't feel the same," I tell her dryly. "Besides, you need to watch more movies."

Chapter Nine

♥

Pepper

I CAN'T SAY I feel too bad about there not being that special something between Dawson and me. I like him. He's easy to talk to, and easy on the eyes, but there's nothing else. No special spark.

I can't believe I kissed him.

I knew there was nothing there, but I had to check. Dawson's a good guy, but he doesn't make me want to giggle like I do when I think of Reuben. But talking to him, seeing his expression change when he talked about love, and the softness when he mentioned his mother, I found myself wondering...what if?

So I checked to make sure, like some people stab the skewer into a cake when you think it's finished baking, and found no gooey mess.

After our snack, I take Dawson around Ashbury and this time I talk; about growing up in Ashbury, about Grayson, about buying the bakery. But it's not until later that I realize I didn't say much about *me*.

But I give him nice content for their vlog, plus I get advice about setting up a website for the shop.

After he leaves, I spend an hour finishing in the kitchen, setting dough to rise and make the frosting for the cupcakes. Everything else can wait until the morning.

I love this time of day; alone in the kitchen while the scent of bread fills the shop.

When I get home, instead of crashing into my bed like I usually do, or leafing through old cookbooks trying to find inspiration, I turn on Netflix.

When I search *1980s movies*, Sixteen Candles is the first that pops up.

The house is quiet tonight, with Mom at her book club and Grayson off doing Grayson things, and it looms, seemingly too big for just me.

What kind of house would I want for myself?

I never think about moving out.

Twenty-six years old, owner of my own business, and nothing else in this world. No car, no property...I don't even own the love of someone special.

I scoff at how sappy I sound. It's almost as bad as watching a movie that came out almost forty years ago.

But maybe Dawson is right. Maybe I do need to watch more movies. And so, I find myself curled up on the couch in my pajamas with a bowl of leftover pasta, getting sucked into the world of John Hughes.

I make it as far as watching Farmer Ted holding up Samantha's panties before I lose the fight to keep my eyes open, only to be woken by the not-so-dulcet tones of my brother.

"Pepper. Pepper, *Pepper*!"

Groggily, I open one eye since the other is smushed into the pillow to see my brother standing before me with a gleeful expression that would be better suited on the face of a ten-year-old who managed to convince his little sister to make him cookies in the middle of the night. "What?"

"You're asleep," Grayson says.

"I *was*." Pulling myself up to a sitting position, I blink at the screen partially covered by Grayson's legs.

"What're you watching?"

I point to the screen. "I was trying to watch that, but someone is in the way."

"I think your eyelids were in the way. You were snoring up a storm in here." He flops onto the couch beside me and removes my discarded bowl from under his hip.

"Was not."

"Was too. I really should record you some day to prove it to you."

"No need." It seems I've missed a good part of the movie since onscreen, Samantha stands in the doorway of the church as her family drives off.

"Why are you watching this?" Grayson scoffs, but his eyes haven't left the screen.

"Dawson," I mutter.

"Dawson—Neely's Dawson?"

This pulls my attention away from the sight of Jake Ryan. "Is he Neely's Dawson?"

"I have no idea."

"I thought *you* wanted to be Neely's Grayson."

My brother only shrugs and together we watch the iconic scene where Jake and Samantha share their first kiss leaning over her birthday cake. "It's a good kiss."

"Since when do you comment on kissing?"

"Why wouldn't I comment on a kiss? It's classic."

"Maybe so, but you've always been extra close-mouthed on your relationships."

"As compared to you, who wants the world to watch?"

He looks at me carefully, like he's weighing what he wants to say like he's deciding if I'm worthy. The thought fills me with shame. There's never been anything that Grayson hasn't been able to say to me. I've spent years debating pitches and players and everything baseball with him, his insecurities about his ability to make it to the major leagues, and what would happen if Emmett got there and he didn't.

He also shares the good stuff which makes it all worthwhile.

"Do you think I should do it?" Grayson asks like his two hundred pounds are weighing down each word.

I've been expecting this conversation since the wedding. "Gray, we talked about this. Whatever you want, I'm behind you. But if you're going to pull out, you should do it soon."

"You've never even asked why I want to do the show."

"You have your reasons." I shrug. "Plus, they asked. It was a dare the first time, and now the fans want you. You're in demand."

Just like his whole life. Grayson has always been wanted by everyone—first picked for teams, for playdates, for parties; most popular with women and men both. It doesn't surprise me that he has this chance to show the world how great he is. The Suitor will be one more thing that Grayson excels at.

"I don't think I can do it myself," Grayson admits, and I turn to him with bewilderment. "That—" He grabs the remote, rewinds to the spot in the movie where Jake and Samantha are leaning towards each other and pauses it just before they're going to kiss. "Do you think you're capable of that?"

"Kissing a guy over a cake? I'd worry a bit from the candles and not wanting to spoil the cake, but sure."

"I don't know if I am." Grayson seems oddly vulnerable for my big brother. "I've messed up every single one of my relationships. Usually because of stupid reasons, or maybe because I'm bored or realize she's not the one, but every single one. I'm thirty-two years old and I haven't ever had a relationship that lasted longer than three months."

"I didn't know the stats."

"Emmett has been married. Lots of my friends have, and what do I have?" He spreads his hands wide. "I'm living with my mother and watching Netflix with my sister."

"There's nothing wrong with that," I huff, not wanting to admit I shared similar thoughts just a few hours earlier.

"I know that. I love hanging with you. But when you look at the big picture, I'm missing out. And, honestly, I don't think I can do it on my own. Find my person that I'm meant to be with forever. But with The Suitor...maybe. It worked when I was on before. Chrissa...I felt something for her. She broke my heart but it was something. I felt *something*. I've never had that before."

"It might not work again," I warn. "You're putting your future in the hands of a few producers who don't even know you."

"But it might." Excitement lights up his eyes. "Do you ever think of why I make a mess of every relationship? Why you can't be bothered to make an effort when a great guy comes to see you?"

"How did you know Dawson was here?"

"Pep, the whole town knows you had a guy in the bakery tonight, and the whole town knows you walked home alone. It's Ashbury. You can't hide a thing."

"That's lovely to know," I mutter.

"It's how it is. So what happened with Dawson?"

"None of your business," I say with just enough ice in my tone. "This isn't about me."

"Oh, it is, Pep. It's about both of us. And our parents."

The credits fill the screen and for a moment I want to flip to another movie, another show, something that will distract Grayson from the conversation he seems determined to have. "Are we really going there?" I sigh. "We never go there."

"I think maybe we should go there. I've been told I'm going to have to be *vulnerable* on the show, so I need some practice."

"But I'm fine. There's no need for me to be vulnerable."

"Oh, yes there is, little sis. Maybe more than me. Our father leaving messed us both up, Pep; you know that as well as I do."

I don't say anything, which means Grayson keeps talking.

"He did the worst things a man can do. He cheated on Mom, broke her heart. Broke our hearts when he left. He *broke* us, and neither one of us has done a very good job in putting ourselves back together."

"I don't like to give him credit for that."

"It's not credit, it's blame."

"Same thing. I don't want him responsible for anything about my life."

"But he is. Your obsession about this bakery—"

"It's not an obsession!"

"It is, and I know this because I felt the same way with baseball. I wanted to be the best so it would give him a reason to come back."

My ears ring with the shock of his confession. Because that's how I have always felt. "He called," I whisper, almost overwhelmed with shame at keeping the information from Grayson. "The year you made it into the majors, he called the night before the first game. Called me," I add. "Said he didn't want to bother you, but he wanted to know how you were doing. How you felt getting your big break. And there was something in his voice—pride, but more than that. He almost sounded arrogant, like he was smug that you were doing so well. It made me angry to hear him talk like that, like he was still part of our lives, but part of me wanted him to feel like that about me. You know?" I shrug, feeling the flush of embarrassment on my cheek. "Stupid, really."

"No." It takes a moment for Grayson to meet my gaze. "It's not stupid because the same thing happened to me. When you bought the bakery and were dancing around the house all the time. I was still doing rehab for my arm and pretty miserable. That's when I talked to him. He wanted to know how you were. I felt like he was bragging about you, at a time of my life that I didn't want to hear it."

"He called," I whisper.

"He wanted to share the best of us but didn't want to stick around for the bad stuff." Grayson's words are tight with tension and resentment. "That's not fair. It's not what a father is."

"No."

"I'll never forgive him," he adds in a matter-of-fact voice.

"He made me stop believing in love," I admit. "I don't think I'll ever forgive him for that."

Grayson's hand is warm as he entwines my fingers with his. "Eventually we should forgive him. But we've got more important things to deal with. You have a business to run, and I have to become famous."

With my free hand, I punch Grayson in the shoulder, hard enough to make him wince.

"And once you've conquered the bread world, you can find a guy who looks at you like that Jake Ryan looks at Molly Ringwald," he finishes with a smirk.

"I might have already found him," I murmur.

"Excuse me?" Grayson rears back to take a good look at me. "Dawson?"

I shake my head. "I'll tell you when there's something to tell. But I kissed him."

"Dawson?"

"It was no Jake and Samantha kiss," I report with a hint of a smile.

"Samantha! That's her name," Grayson cries. "Couldn't remember. You better spill the beans about Dawson. For someone we just met, he's got a lot of influence in our lives right now."

I don't ask him what he means by that.

Dawson

I DIDN'T SEE THAT kiss coming.

I like Pepper. She reminds me of Neely; so closed-off with her no-nonsense manner. I like her laugh. I didn't hear much of it, so when she releases even a little bit, it's something to savour.

I hope she finds someone to make her happy, and I'm glad that, after the kiss, I know it's not going to be me. I'd be proud to be her first guy friend, but that's all it's going to be.

The kilometers from Ashbury fly by and the sun is beginning to set as I let myself into the apartment quietly. I had time to think things through but I'm still not sure what I want to say to Mom.

Time to figure it out, because I find her at the kitchen table again, with computer components scattered and a tiny screwdriver in her hand.

"Dawson," she calls.

There's a pleading tone in her voice that I've never heard before and I pause before I answer, turning to shut the door behind me.

"Come talk to me."

Toeing off my Vans, I pad down the hall. "I thought you might have talked to me," I say, keeping my own tone milder than it would have been had I come right home after leaving Mike.

Mom's eyes are dark and liquid as she looks up at me. "I didn't know what to tell you."

"So it's true?" I lean against the counter across the room, not wanting to get too close just yet.

"About Mike?" A hint of a smile curls the corners of her mouth. "I don't know when, or how, but yes."

I heave a sigh. "You love him?"

"I do." The smile widens, her dark eyes crinkling at the corners, and instantly she looks ten years younger. My mother is a very pretty woman—beautiful even, with her sheet of dark hair and eyes that look like a piece of the best dark chocolate, but there's been a lot of grief and hardship in her life. She rarely looks rested, or even happy.

She deserves all the happiness in the world now to make up for all the sadness.

"How?" I cross the tiny kitchen in a step and take the chair opposite her at the table. Her face brightens even more. "What happened?"

"You know Mike. He's a friend—and then he was more than a friend. I used to think he might be a nice father figure for you."

"He is," I admit.

"He's a good man," she says, her words coming quicker. "Sweet, caring, considerate. He wants to take care of me."

"I know, and that's fine. Good. I want you to be happy. But what I don't understand is how you can love him after my father." I stare at my mother, wanting nothing more than to understand how she could forget my father like that. "The two of you...that was forever. That was the epic kind of love that you can't forget."

"Is that what you think it was?" she asks in a low voice.

"That's what you told me. Dad—" My voice hitches on the word. "He used to tell me stories at night about how he went to find you. He used to compare the two of you to movie couples...Jack and Rose, Han and Leia—"

"He was nothing like Han Solo." Mom shakes her head with a rueful smile. "I can't believe he'd put himself in that category."

"He loved you." For a moment it sounds like I'm trying to convince myself. "He did, didn't he?"

"Of course. I was very happy with your father, Dawson, and no one can take that away from me. He did so much for us. But you know, it didn't start out like some great love affair."

"I know he was married."

"He was, and unfortunately it wasn't a happy one. But I never should have let myself care for him. I was young and unsure, but it was wrong. It was no fairy tale."

"But..."

"I loved your father, loved him dearly. But he wasn't perfect. Yes, he came looking for us and got us out of a not-very-nice situation, but he did that because he was a good man, not because he was hopelessly in love with me. You were his son, and he didn't want you growing up on the other side of the world. He wanted the best for you. He did everything he could to provide for you."

I glance around the apartment; at the worn linoleum, the water-marked paint on the wall, the chipped dishes and tired furniture. "He thought he had years," she says quietly, seeing my eyes ask the question I can't put into words. "He had no idea his wife would contest the will and take everything away from you. But it wasn't because of love." Mom takes my hand. "He was a good man, and he took responsibility for both of us. I know you think...I know what you want for yourself."

"What do I want?" I ask roughly.

"Love," she says simply. "It's what you've always wanted. To find your own happily ever after, just like in the movies."

"I want more than that."

"Of course you do. But you want to find your person. It's why you flip through girls like a deck of cards. You're very good about it," she adds, when I start to frown. "You're a nice guy, not some of those cocky players who want the notch on the buckle."

"Belt," I correct automatically.

"But you're a romantic at heart. You have the opinion that if you kiss enough frogs, you'll find your princess."

"If I said that, I'd end up offending a whole bunch of people," I say with a rueful smile.

"It's okay if your mother says it."

"I'm not sure about that, but okay."

"What happened with Mike was totally different than with your father. We were friends first—good friends. We looked out for each other. I know you sent him here to look after me, but he could do with some looking after too."

"Knowing Shae's mother, I'd say he could do with a lot."

"It happened naturally, and slowly, and it's...nice."

"Nice." I can think of no movie where the romance can be called nice. Nice is boring.

I don't even like it when women call me nice.

"Is it enough?" I ask, studying her face to make sure she's being honest with me. Because even though I once thought Mom would never lie to me, now I'm not so sure. She didn't exactly lie about my father, but I think both of them fudged the truth a bit.

I tuck that bit away to think about later.

"It's enough for me," she says, her gaze firm and direct, like she knows I'm in a questioning mood. "Right now, it's everything for me."

"But what's next? What does this mean? You and Mike..." I trail off, without the faintest idea what to call them. Dating? Exclusive? Hooking up. My insides shiver at the thought of my mother in that way, a completely natural reaction from a son.

"We're in a relationship," Mom says. And it's not my imagination but she sounds happy about this. Satisfied.

I do not want to think of my mother satisfied.

"We're in a relationship and we'd like to be in one when you're home as well as when you're away. Mike hasn't told Shae and her mother yet, but he will, now that you know."

"Why didn't you tell me?" Even the question makes me feel like a ten-year-old, left out of something fun.

"Would you have wanted to know? Dawson, you've hero-worshipped your father for years, and I never wanted to do anything to take that away from you. It's the reason I pushed you away from getting to know his first family."

"I never wanted to."

"You did. You were always curious about Keith and Kevin and Kylie. Whenever Duncan would visit them, you'd beg him to tell you everything about them."

"I don't remember that."

"I think I might have been wrong in not suggesting you get to know them." I know the years of painful memories and bad blood between Dad's first wife and Mom. It wasn't just being fired and told to leave the first home she found in this country; Mom had been named in the divorce, her reputation sullied as the court case went on too long. And worse than that was the reaction of the family when Dad died, both of us treated like we were invisible.

To admit she made a mistake about that must have taken a lot.

"Along with your grandmother, they're your family," she adds, like she wants to be saying anything but.

"You're my family. And Claudine."

"Yes, but they could do a lot for you. If you let them."

I look at her through narrowed eyes. "Do you know something? Keith has been trying to get in touch with me. Grammy says he wants to offer me a job."

"A job," she muses.

"Yeah."

"Is that a bad thing?"

"It is if he's trying to make himself feel better after stealing your money."

"Keith didn't steal anything, his mother did. He was always the nicest of them all."

"What's that supposed to mean?"

Mom heaves a sigh. "I think you should give him a chance," she says slowly, sounding like Duckie when he tells Andie about Blane. "He's very successful. Your father would have been proud of him. He'd be even prouder if you were the better man who learned to forget the past."

"And what do you want me to do about Mike?"

Mom looks at me hesitantly. "Does that mean you accept this?"

Do I? I have no choice, but really, the only reason I had not to accept it, was because I had been kept in the dark. And the ghost of my father looming over Mom.

Mike's a good man. He can stand up to a ghost.

"I'd like to know more about it before I give it the stamp of approval," I say finally. There's no letting them totally off the hook.

"I think that's a good start." The happy glow is back on Mom's face and it warms me to know I was the one who put it there. "He'll come for dinner on the weekend."

And that's it.

.

Chapter Ten

♥

Pepper

THE FAINT PINK OF the morning sky and bird songs greet me as I walk to the bakery Wednesday morning. I take the same route as I do every day—down Third Street, across Upton and turn onto Main—and notice the same things; the houses still dark at this early hour, the barking of the Robinses' dog watching from the window as I walk by, the way the motion-sensor light shines when I get close to Mabel Fry's place.

But something feels different about today, and it's not just the skunk I interrupt digging for grubs on the Merrystones' front lawn.

My steps are lighter, and everything is a little brighter, even in the dark.

I would say it's a combination of Dawson and Grayson, with a bit of Reuben thrown in. Men have put me in a good mood for once, I decide as I unlock the door.

It's nice, seeing how many times men have ticked me off.

As I flip the lights on, the brightness pours out the window onto the street, looking like a missing tooth in the dark buildings of

Main Street. I do my quick look around, which has become a daily event since the broken window and the flood.

Nothing out of place today other than the chairs Dawson and I sat in yesterday that I forgot to set on the table.

It's going to be a good day.

The kitchen smells like yeast and chocolate, and this time the sight of the little cakes, naked except their plain wrappers, waiting for me to frost them—doesn't bring on the guilt.

It makes me wonder what Reuben is doing.

Is he in the kitchen—the *cidsin*—in Pain au Chocolate, preparing for the day? Is he preheating the oven? Does he have a printed list of what needs to be done or is it all in his head?

Is he thinking of me doing the same?

Thanks to the talk with my brother last night, I welcome the way my thoughts drift to Reuben as I pick today's music. The Tragically Hip had been playing in Pain that morning and I remember Adam shouting to turn it down. What was the song?

Bobcaygeon. I even have the Hip CD in my collection, but that would be a little too weird to play it.

Instead, I pick Queen's Greatest Hits and soon the voice of Freddie Mercury is making it an even better day.

"Don't stop me now," I say aloud, skimming across the floor like an ice skater. I was good on skates, with strong strides taking me across the ice. But it was the dance moves that tripped me up more than the toe picks.

I was never a very good dancer. I'm still not, as anyone at the wedding could tell you. But I love to dance, letting the music fill me. Most of the time I save it for mornings when I'm alone in here.

"Don't stop me now," I sing, which is about as bad as my dancing.

Maybe instead of *don't stop me* being my new motto, it should be *get started*.

After the ovens are full of baking bread, I get started on finishing the cupcakes. Two chocolate, as per Mrs. April's suggestion. But I came up with a lemon ricotta with blueberry glaze. It's my recipe—not Reuben's—and as I finish decorating the batch, satisfaction swells inside me. I might have gotten the cupcake idea from him, but I can do this on my own.

And it's that little bit of pride and confidence that has me Googling the phone number for Pain au Chocolate before I open the shop.

"Hullo?" My heart leaps when Reuben answers the phone even though he doesn't sound all that friendly. I don't know why the urge to talk to him came over me so strongly. It might have been that I was in the kitchen, and I knew—or at least suspected—he might be too. Maybe he was finishing his own batch of cupcakes.

"Reuben? It's Pepper, Pepper Grant from—"

"Pepper, hullo." His tone switches instantly, from gruff to almost gleeful.

"Hi. Hello." I catch sight of my reflection in the glass of the door and realize I look like a grinning idiot as I stand with the phone cord twisted around my hand. "Sorry to bother you this early."

"No bother, no bother a'tall. How're ye?"

"I'm good. Really good. You?"

"Can't complain, or if I could, it wouldn't do me much good." He sounds like he's smiling. Or maybe that's just because I'm smiling. "How can I help ye?"

"You can't, that's not why I'm calling. I would have texted, but I don't know your number."

"I like talkin' on the phone," Reuben admits. "I never know if the other person really gets me when we're texting. Plus, I don't unnerstand half those emoji-things."

"Me neither. The whole peach is a bum thing, and the eggplant."

"Eggplant?" Reuben's chuckles make my smile widen. "Using food is too much for me. I don't get the smiley face that's crying. When do I use that?"

I laugh out loud. "Now might be a good time to use that. At least the big smile with maybe one tear."

"Happy to have made your emoji laugh," Reuben says in a gruff voice.

"That's why I'm calling." The words hitch in my throat. "About tomorrow."

"Aye." Even over the phone lines, Reuben's tone turns cold and distant. "You aren't wanting to see me now, is that it?"

"No. No! No, it's the opposite." I take a deep breath, wondering why I started this. "I know you must be busy, so I won't keep you, but I wanted to tell you—I wanted to say...I'm really happy that you called yesterday. That's what I wanted to say."

"That's what you called for?" he says slowly, almost like he can't believe it.

"I know, it sounds silly—"

"It—no. No, it's not silly a'tall."

"I was making my bread—" Do *not* mention cupcakes! "And I thought you might be doing the same. Not bread, but other pastry things, and I thought...I thought I'd let you know how much I'm looking forward to seeing you."

"Well, now." Reuben clears his throat. "I have to say, Pepper, you've made my day with that."

"Me too." Is it possible for my cheeks to ache from smiling? "I'll see you tomorrow, Reuben."

"You have yourself a fine day. Sell lots of bread."

I don't stop smiling for hours. I don't think I'm going to need to kiss Reuben to find out if there's something between us, but that doesn't mean I don't want to.

Dawson

On Wednesday afternoon, I planned to go to Shae's to deal with vlog stuff with her and Neely. I don't need my mother's quiet suggestions to know that I have to go over early to talk to Mike.

I didn't handle that well. Mom says it was a shock and I did what I could with it, but I still don't like the thought of me running out on Mike.

He means more to me than that.

Thankfully, he's the one who opens the door to my knock. "Dawson," he says, the expression of surprise on his face quickly dropping to wariness. "Shae's still in bed."

"I know. I came to see you. If you've got time to talk."

He holds the door open. "For you? Always."

Once we're seated on the couch, in our usual gaming positions, I'm surprised at Mike's fidgetiness. He keeps shifting, hands twitching almost like he's—

"Are you nervous?" I demand.

"*Yes.*" He exhales in a loud huff. "This is worse than when I asked my first wife's father permission to marry her."

"How many wives did you have?"

"Only one at a time. But...two," he says, his voice resigned. "I never married Shae's grandmother."

"I didn't know that. So, technically, you're not her mother's step-father."

"No. But I like to think I helped raise Cybil enough to call her my daughter."

Seeing as how Shae's mother is one of my least favourite people in the world, I don't say anything to that. "What are your intentions towards my mother?" I ask brusquely.

Mike gives a dramatic shiver. "This is worse than asking for a hand in marriage."

"So you don't intend to marry her?"

"This is pretty new for the both of us," Mike admits. "We're taking some time to figure things out."

"How long has this been going on?"

"Did you talk to your mother?"

I nod. "But I didn't ask...We mostly talked about my father. I didn't feel right asking for details."

"Good. That's good that you talked about your dad. As for the timeline, I can only give you what I know. Thanks to you, Delia and I have had years to become friends. But it's only been this last trip when things switched." Mike has a knowing smile on his face and I'm not sure I appreciate that. "It was your mother who took the next step. Made the first move, so to speak."

"My mother." I did not see that coming. "She doesn't have an issue with the age difference?"

"*She* doesn't," Mike says. "It was a hard no for me for a long time before she wore me down. Delia's an amazing woman, and still a young woman. I, as we both know, am not. I don't want her to be saddled with an old guy."

I catch my breath. "So you are looking at a future with her?"

"Dawson, I love your mother." Mike's words are careful and concise. "And she loves me. We're in this together, so whatever she wants, I'm game. With your blessing, of course."

I nod slowly, fingers pulling at the leather bracelet Shae gave me years ago. "I wouldn't stand in her way."

"That's not the same as giving your blessing."

I roll my shoulders. "That sounds so formal," I protest.

"That's what we're talking about. I don't know what the future holds for me and Delia, but I need to know you're cool with it."

I offer my fist to bump. "I'm cool with it."

There's no question about it. I want my mother to be happy, and if she's lucky enough to find a man like Mike to love her, I can't be anything but happy for her.

Mike bumps my fist, a relieved smile on his face. "Good to know. Now, what did Neely say when you told her? I haven't said anything to Shae yet."

"I didn't tell Neely."

"But you ran over there."

"Yeah." Now that the Mike thing has been straightened out, I can't help but wonder about Neely. "She's always been my go-to," I confess. "More than Shae. It's Neely that fixes things."

"Neely's a fixer, that's for sure."

"But yesterday when I went there, she was texting the other guy. Grayson. Didn't look that happy to see me. She rarely seems happy to see me, now that I think of it."

"Dawson, don't—"

"I know you said that she's always had a thing for me, but I just don't see it," I say, frustration heavy in my voice. "Maybe one time, but not now. She's always annoyed with me. And even if there's something there..." I swallow twice, trying to force the words past the catch in my throat. "I took my shot years ago and nothing happened. This thing she's got with Grayson is new for her. I've never seen her look like this. I think...I think he might make her happy. She's not annoyed with him like she gets with me."

"Has she said anything about him?" Mike asks gently.

"No, but I haven't really been listening. I have eyes, though, and she looks happy. She looked happy with him at the wedding. With me—not so happy. So whatever this thing with him is, I only want her to be happy. And I don't think that's with me."

Mike drops a hand on my shoulder that suddenly feels like it's carrying the weight of the world. "I don't know what to tell you," he admits. "But I know what might help?" He hands me the controller with a sad smile. "A little Fortnite to take your mind off it?"

Chapter Eleven

Pepper

"**Y**OU LOOK NICE THIS morning," Mrs. April says as I unlock the door for her Thursday morning. Her eyes widen as she takes in the dress.

A dress.

It's almost unheard of for me.

My work uniform is a pair of black pants or nice pair of jeans and whatever I throw on top, since the white chef's coat covers me from shoulders to hips. I've never been interested in fashion, rarely have an opportunity to wear nice clothes, nor do I feel comfortable with the hair and the makeup and the fancy stuff. I have three dresses hanging in my closet; the little black one I wore to the wedding, my prom dress still locked up in the plastic sheath, and this one—a springy sundress Mom bought for me two years ago when we thought I might have to appear on The Suitorette for family day with Grayson.

"So pretty." Mrs. April catches my hand and holds it up so she can fully appreciate the blue and white midi dress held up by the thick straps. "And your hair."

I had pulled my dark blonde hair back into my usual ponytail, but I took a few extra minutes to curl it, so I have two thick ringlets bouncing over my shoulder.

"What's going—is he coming back?" she asks, finally releasing my hand.

"Who?" I hurry behind the counter, feeling safer without the scrutiny.

"That cutie-patootie. Dawson." Mrs. April follows me behind the counter to stow her coat and purse.

I let out a bark of laughter. "Did you just call him cutie-pa-tootie?"

"Yes, because that's what he is. I thought him very nice, and those cheekbones were very impressive. You rarely see a man these days with such fine bone structure." Mrs. April is completely serious, which makes me smile even more.

"I'll be sure to tell him." Dawson and I exchanged numbers before he left on Tuesday so we wouldn't have to rely on Neely's and Grayson's phones to stay in touch. We've already texted a few times, and he gave me an update on what happened with his mother and Mike.

"So when will he be here?" Mrs. April ties the apron around her waist as I duck into the kitchen to grab the trays to finish loading the display case with scones, thick slices of banana bread, and two trays of cupcakes; coconut and lime, strawberry jam, and simple vanilla.

I ran out of the good chocolate, so it's chocolate-free until the delivery comes in.

Yesterday afternoon, Lexi came in for an hour after school and took advantage of the spring weather to walk along Main Street with a tray of mini-cupcakes. The response was amazing, and we stayed open an extra half-hour and sold out of cupcakes, scones, and cheese and garlic baguettes.

I'm hopeful for today, and stayed last night until after eight o'clock preparing.

I'm not sure what I'm more nervous about—how sales will be today or that Reuben is coming to see me.

I hope the cupcakes are gone before he gets here.

"When will who be here?" I ask, carefully sliding the tray into the display case.

"Dawson!" Mrs. April cries with exasperation. "When will he be here? I need time to fix my face. You really caught me off guard the other day. Meeting a new man should be an experience for all, and I don't think I gave him enough *me*."

My mouth drops open as I stare at Mrs. April's round figure and over-made-up face, her way of concealing the lines etched around her eyes and lips. I may love her to death, but at times I don't understand her. "You know Dawson came to see me, right?" I ask gently.

"Well, of course, Pepper!"

"All right then." I arrange the tray of scones; cranberry, apple, and cheddar chive, all thick and golden brown and sprinkled with cane sugar. "But I have no idea when he's coming back."

"But *why*?" she wails. "You look like this and he was nice and…it makes sense. Perfect sense."

"Maybe so. Dawson is a great guy, but not for me."

She fists her hands on her ample hips. I'd much rather she get to work, but Mrs. April is like a dog with a bone when she wants information. There's no stopping her until she gets her fill. "You can tell that after one meal?"

"I can tell from one kiss." I try for nonchalance but steal a grin at her expression of surprise.

"A kiss!" Mrs. April actually bounces on the balls of her feet.

I hold up my hand. "Don't get excited. There is absolutely nothing to be excited about. I mean, as far as kisses go it was perfectly adequate—"

"Adequate! That's a little harsh."

The tray of banana bread slices slides in beside the scones, along with tiny tongs to pick them out. "He agreed it was perfectly adequate. There was no...spark."

"Oh, no." Mrs. April seems to deflate right before my eyes.

"It's okay," I assure her. "I'm fine with it. There was no...no movie magic."

"Magic," she says wistfully, somehow totally understanding what I'm trying to say, even when I don't. "Magic is nice."

"Magic would be nice," I agree. "But no magic. It's okay," I hasten to add as her face falls. "We're going to be friends. I've never had a guy friend, so I'm excited about that."

"Emmett is your friend."

"Emmett is different." I survey the display case. I wonder if it would be worth having a plate of cupcakes set up by the cash register to inspire impulse purchases. They do look good today. I candied a bit of lime rind to sprinkle over the coconut ones.

"I suppose you being in love with him for all those years put a damper on whatever friendship might have developed between the two of you," Mrs. April muses.

This pulls me right out of cupcakes and back into the conversation. "How did you know about Emmett?"

"Pepper, dear. I helped pull you out of your mama's belly, all red in the face and screaming blue murder. There's not a lot about you that I don't know."

"Did everybody know?" My stomach tightens with embarrassment at the thought of all of Ashbury laughing at my unrequited crush.

"Of course not," she assures me. "You've been very discreet in your affections. Maybe too much. Maybe that was your problem with Emmett." She raises an eyebrow. "Although, considering your families, it might have been best if the two of you didn't pair up."

"Ellie and Grayson 'paired up'", I burst out. "Bet you didn't know that."

"Of course I did," she says with infuriating calm. "That girl doesn't know the word discreet when it comes to her affections."

I shake my head with a bemused laugh. "What else do you know?"

"Oh, everything...except why you made such an effort this morning. I know you plan on a big day, but this seems a bit much."

I look down at my skirt. "Is it too much?"

"Of course not! You look lovely. But not like you."

The bell over the door tinkles as Mr. Patel and Carl Duggan come in with their sun-faded baseball caps and ready smiles. Mrs. April sashays to the cash greeting them with her own smile. "This isn't over," she hisses over her shoulder. "I'll find out exactly what's going on."

I have no doubt she will.

The day passes in a haze of anticipation for me, as well as an increasing giddiness of how much I *sell*. Loaves of bread fly across the counter, the scones are sold out by mid-morning and as soon as Lexi arrives, I disappear in the back to make more. The frother works nonstop as Mrs. April mans the coffee maker, providing drinks for those who camp out at the tables to savour their cupcakes.

Every sales transaction involves a cupcake.

And at two dollars profit for every one sold, the sound of the cash register is music to my ears.

"This is the busiest we've ever been," Mrs. April cries late in the afternoon. "It's amazing. My feet are ready to walk off my legs, but I've never been prouder of you, Pepper. I'm so happy for you."

Even I can't find fault with today, other than my cheeks hurting from smiling. I'm so relieved that I think I might cry.

Not in public. No one needs to see that.

"I couldn't do it without you," I say to her. Lexi has already left but I was very vocal in my appreciation of her, topped off with cupcakes for her family.

Even Jena Markov showing up doesn't put much of a damper on my good mood.

"Look at the lineup," Jena complains as she reaches the cash. "Your little store is quite busy today." Once again she somehow manages to look down her nose at me even though I'm taller.

"It's a bakery and yes, it is." There's no Ziploc bag in her hand today, but knowing Jena, who knows what she's got in her bag of tricks. "Thanks for being so patient with the line."

"Like I had a choice." Her mouth purses like the backside of her pug, but this time it makes me want to laugh. Jena snaps off her order of two whole wheat, two white boules and one of sourdough, as well as another loaf of pumpernickel.

"Got plans for the weekend?" I ask as I bag the bread.

"Always do," she simpers. "My social life is *so* busy in the spring. Really, any time of the year." The laugh is fake and grates just enough.

"Must be nice for you."

"Oh, my goodness," Mrs. April cries over the noise of the frother. "Grayson Grant!"

I look up to see my brother saunter in, wearing gym shorts and an old T-shirt and shiny with sweat. It doesn't bother my customers; a wave of whispers cuts through the lineup and tables as the folks of Ashbury practically bow to him.

He's always been very popular.

"How was the date?" I call to him.

"Date was good." Every head turns to hear his answer. Most of the men in bakery want to live vicariously through Grayson, and most of the women would give their first born to have a life with him. He's always been the Golden Son of Ashbury, both he and Emmett, but Grayson's career-ending injury won points over Emmett's very public meltdown after Alex's death.

They're going to love seeing Grayson as The Suitor.

"New girlfriend, Grayson?" Patty Benjamin asks from the line, her voice suggesting that she rather hopes not.

"New friend," Grayson corrects, and I silently thank him. I'd never hear the end of the questions in here if he admitted to a new girlfriend.

"She's from the city," Jena sneers.

"She is from Toronto." Grayson bypasses the line to hover at the counter, but I notice he keeps a healthy distance away from Jena. "She's Ellie's new sister-in-law. I met her at the wedding."

"Neely is great." I'm more enthusiastic about Grayson's subtle dig at Jena than any excitement about Neely. She's nice, but a complication Grayson doesn't need at this time. I know he still hasn't signed the contract for the show, and I'm tired of reminding him.

"Nice wedding?" A woman in line asks.

"Beautiful," he enthuses, surprising me with his animation. "I'm sure they'll be very happy together."

"What was Ellie's dress like?" Patty asks Grayson. I can't hide my smile at the expression of confusion on Grayson's face. White. Puffy. Pretty. That's all he knows about the dress. Patty might get a better response if she asked me, but that's how it is in Ashbury. Grayson always comes before me.

"I think that's it for the day for me," Jena says, turning her back on Grayson and surveying the paper bag waiting on the counter with a sniff. "Well, I guess I should try one of those cupcakes I keep hearing about."

I have to ask. "Who keeps talking about them?"

"Oh, you know. Lots of people in this town have nothing better to do than to hang out in here. I'll have a chocolate," she adds without even a glance at the display case.

"No chocolate today," I say. "We've got some coconut-lime, strawberry jam, and I used the berries from Pike's farm, so you know they're good. And there's a few vanilla left."

"No chocolate?" She seems horrified, like I told her her dog was just run over.

"Check back tomorrow."

"Fine," she huffs, never meeting my gaze. "I guess I'll take a coconut."

"Coconut is great."

I slide the cupcake out of the case and into one of the wax paper baggies I've been using. It's not perfect, and I'm sure icing gets stuck on the top, but it's the best I've got right now. "Have a great rest of the day," I say, insincerity dripping with every word.

"Always do."

Once Jena takes her leave, I quickly get Patty's order ready to free Grayson from the constant questions. "I can't stand her," I mutter to my brother after Patty leaves. "She gets worse every year."

"Jena, or Colin's mother?" he asks, studying the glass display case. "Cupcakes look good. You've been practicing."

"And they taste great. I think I nailed Reuben's recipe." With all the success today, I've managed to push away the queasiness of taking his recipes but that admission brings it roaring back.

"Good for you."

I take a deep breath and focus on my brother. "What's up? You're running. You only do that if you're bored or thinking about something."

"Both, I guess."

I wait impatiently. With only an hour before we close, the lineup has finally died down, but there are still a million things I need to do before I close. And before Reuben gets here.

"*The Suitor*," Grayson says finally. "I should do it, right?"

"We've been through this enough," I say, unable to keep the irritated tone out of my voice. "Both when you went on the first time, and when they asked you to come back. You are the perfect person because you believe in romance more than anyone I know, and you're in the perfect position in life to do it now. So, yes. Go sign the contract."

"I don't know..." he hedges.

"Neely will be there after the show is over," I say bluntly. "If that's what you're worried about."

"But will she?"

"From what Dawson says, she's not going anywhere."

"What's that supposed to mean?"

What does he think of this girl? And does he really think enough of her to put the kibosh on the show? "It means that he doesn't think she's looking for a relationship."

"How would he know what she's looking for when he doesn't even notice her?" Grayson snaps. "If he had half a brain in his head, he would have grabbed her years ago."

"I knew it!" I do an arm pump, prompting Mrs. April to look over with bewilderment. "I knew she was in love with him. It's so obvious. Why did you go out with her if she's in love with another guy?"

"I didn't say anyone was in love with anyone." The way Grayson backs away from the counter tells me there's more I don't know.

"Grayson."

"Pepper," Grayson mimics. "She's a nice girl. I'm allowed to date who I want."

"There will be enough drama when you get on the show," I warn. "Don't go looking for it now. And don't get your heart broken before you even meet any of the women. Neely's great, but it's not a good idea."

"I think I know when something's a bad idea, and this isn't it."
Grayson reaches the door, almost falling out as a customer opens it behind him. "See you at home," he calls, leaving me shaking my head.

"What's the latest drama with him?" Mrs. April asks.

"Women problems." I can't say too much to her because Grayson as The Suitor hasn't been officially announced yet, and if I let one peep out, it will be over town in minutes. "Like always."

Mrs. April smiles like she knows what is going through my mind. "You'll find someone for yourself," she says with such assurance in her voice that I look at her with surprise. Is that what she thinks the problem is? "Someone who is worthy of you. You're still young. Lots of time."

"I know."

"I know you know. But I wonder if you believe it."

Dawson

FOR THE FIRST TIME since we got on the plane for Asia all those weeks ago, I spend the day playing video games.

All day, from when Claudine leaves for work and Mom shuffles out with her cane. The wheelchair is the last resort, and I always feel hopeful when she doesn't need to use it.

I take my big bowl of the sugary cereal that Claudine buys for me, hiding it in the top cupboards, far from Mom's reach, and eat it on my bed/couch. I don't get dressed. I don't even have a shower and have the bedhead to prove it.

I play games all day.

First Fortnite, checking in with fellow gamers and fans who are online. Mike is there, and it's back to normal, interacting via games with him. Might take a little longer in real life, but there's hope.

I still haven't talked to Neely about Mom and Mike and because of that, there's an ache deep inside me, like I ate too much cereal. I haven't talked to her about anything since her 'date' with Grayson, and when I saw her Wednesday, I annoyed her with my comments.

I can't seem to keep my thoughts about him, and them, to myself.

It doesn't help when I keep replaying what Mike said about her like a favourite record.

When I was twelve, one of my buddies told me Pasha Patel liked me. Before that, I'd never looked twice at the girl, and only knew her as quiet and smart with long black hair. That news was followed up by one of Pasha's friends telling me Pasha thought I was the cutest boy in grade six. And then a random girl in the class told me Pasha was staring at me all through math.

Of course, by the next morning, I was madly in love with Pasha Patel.

Ever since Mike told me Neely had a thing for me, I haven't been able to stop thinking about her.

Of course that doesn't mean when I'm destroying a world.

I take a break for more food around one o'clock, sitting cross-legged on the couch with a sandwich in one hand and the controller in the other as I battle an army of zombies, happy beyond belief. There's nothing on my mind other than my avatar fighting for his life—not Neely, not Shae, not my mom and Mike—and I like it that way.

Of course, it doesn't last.

The knock comes a few hours after I last ate, just when I'm feeling the need for something else, and wondering when Mom and Claudine will be back. I get killed before I manage to pause the game, so whoever is at the door already has a strike against them.

Strike two if they're selling something, although it's not common that we have salespeople wandering inside the apartment building.

In fact, the intercom usually buzzes to announce a visitor.

I open the door with a scowl, only to have it quickly wiped from my face. "Natasha," I say with surprise. "What are you doing here?"

"It's nice to see you too." She pushes past me with a box in her arms, marching into the living room. "I'm getting rid of your stuff." She drops the box on the floor for emphasis.

"I didn't know I had stuff." The box looks like it's on its last legs and it's easy to open. T-shirts, my favourite sweatshirt that I thought I left in Thailand, a pair of flip flops and two books that I had jammed in Natasha's suitcase. "I had no idea you had all this."

"I was going to burn it but didn't want to deal with the smell."

Burn it...Hell really has nothing on a scorned woman.

But what exactly did I do to her? "Look, Natasha, I know it wasn't cool getting thrown out of the wedding," I begin.

"Is that why you think I'm mad?" She laughs disdainfully. "That *was* really cool and got me tons of likes. It also made your precious Neely look pretty bad."

"She's not my precious and—"

"No? What are you calling her these days?"

"My *friend*, same as always. I thought you were mad that I danced with Pepper." I am thoroughly confused now, which isn't uncommon when it comes to me and women. They say things they don't mean, they mean things they don't say, and trying to read body language is near impossible.

"Pepper," she sneers. "Although I should thank you. Because of your little scene with her, Grayson will definitely remember me, a plus when it comes to picking the next contestants for The Suitor."

Were we at the same wedding? Because I remember things a lot differently than Natasha seems to.

"That's great," I say. If I don't try and argue, maybe she'll leave quicker.

"I've applied for the next show. I think Grayson will be great. I can't wait to get to know him better."

She's fishing. I know she's fishing. Pepper explicitly told us Grayson's role in the next season wasn't official and shouldn't be discussed. This is an easy sidestep. "I'm happy for you. Guess you've had no trouble moving on."

"Moving on? It's not like I had anything to move on from."

Even though I suspect Natasha is slightly crazy, it still stings. I shared a room with her, a bed, for the last four months. To be pushed aside that easily is more than a slap to the ego. "I wouldn't say that."

"Oh, no? Maybe if you weren't in love with someone else, we might have had a chance. I still can't figure out which it is—Shae? Or Neely? Or both?"

I scrub at the back of my neck, frustration rising. I've heard it all before, from Natasha and others. Can't people believe that the three of us are only *friends*?

Maybe if I believed it myself.

"I'm not getting into this with you."

"Of course not. The only ones you make an effort for is them. Always at their beck and call, like a little lapdog eating their crumbs." She rolls her eyes, and the gesture contorts her face into something not very pretty. I wonder what she'd think if I took a picture of her like that and posted it online.

"Thanks for bringing my things back," I say in a tight voice.

"You do know you'd be twice as popular on Insta if you dropped them, right?" she asks, suddenly serious. "They're holding you back."

"Ask me if I care."

Natasha shakes her head, long braids flying around like Medusa's snakes. She's pretty enough to turn men to stone, but she's also as mean as a viper, so it's a good comparison. "That's what I've never understood. What are you getting out of this, Dawson? The trips, the fun little trio—what's the point?"

"You wouldn't understand."

"That's where I think you're wrong." Natasha turns from slightly crazy snake lady to cool and calculating quick enough to make me shiver. "Something that I heard you and Neely say one night, something about Shae...and time left. I don't remember the exact words—"

I do. I remember it well. We'd been in a local pub in a town in Vietnam and Shae had climbed onstage, singing her heart out alongside the guitar player. Neely had wanted to pull her down, but I convinced her to leave Shae for a few more minutes.

"I guess you're right," Neely had said with an affectionate smile. "It's not like she's got a lot of time to goof off like this."

My heart stills at the memory, at the realization of what this means. Shae hates people knowing she's sick, that she's dying. I've spent the last twelve years protecting her secret. To have Natasha, of all people, ferret it out is maddening.

"I thought for a while she meant there wasn't much time left on the trip, but it was only a few weeks into it," Natasha muses. "Then I watched as you and Neely treated Shae like you were babysitting a really spoiled kid and afraid of the parents finding out that they were a brat. The whole trip—she did whatever she wanted, and you let her. The thing with Denzel Duke—Neely was going crazy that she just took off but neither of you said a word to her. If I pulled that—"

"I like to think you wouldn't have, since you were on the trip with me," I say flatly, trying to disguise my mounting fear. If Natasha knows about Shae, what's she going to do about it? Because one thing I've learned about my ex-girlfriend, is that Natasha always has a plan. A motive.

An agenda.

"If I was with my friends," Natasha corrects. "There'd be hell to pay if I took off with a strange guy, even if he was as famous as Denzel. It got me thinking—why? Why no consequence for Shae? No talking-to like I know Neely was aching to do."

"You don't know anything about Neely," I snap. "And Shae's a grown woman."

"Yeah. We both know she's really not. She's like a little kid and the world is her candy store. Again, why do you let her have so much slack?"

"I don't know what you're talking about."

Natasha laughs. "That's what they always say when you're onto something. And I already know I'm onto something. You can find out a lot on social media, if you know where to look. And I do."

The only sound in the apartment is the groan of the hot water pipes upstairs. I lick my lips, waiting for the threat. The demand.

Shae will not want the knowledge that she's dying out there, and I will protect it, and her, as best as I can.

Please tell me Natasha doesn't want to get back together with me.

Maybe if I tell her the truth about how I feel about Neely…that I do care. That maybe I do love her. Will that be enough?

One look at Natasha's cool eyes, narrowed in thought, says otherwise.

"I wonder if I should just post how she has some unpronounceable disease," Natasha says slowly and my heart does that seizing thing, like an engine without oil. "Or if I should hide it in a comment and let someone else pick it up. Deniability, and all that. I admit, I don't much like the two of them, especially after spending all those weeks plodding after you, but I have to say Neely is a force to be reckoned with."

"You should remember that." That isn't exactly hiding behind Neely—

It is hiding behind Neely, like a kid hanging onto the skirts of their mother. What can I do to stop this? Because it is my fault. I'm the one who brought Natasha into this.

Or let her push her way in.

"Look, Natasha, we had a good time together, and it's too bad that it ended like that."

"But you're not sorry. You've never once said you're sorry that she *threw me out* of a wedding. Who does that? A power-hungry witch like Neely. That tells me that there's something going on with Shae, because why would Neely just stand aside and let her have the spotlight? That's what drove me crazy when I was with you. Shae is not the star of the world."

"You're right. But they're both the stars of my world, and I won't let you hurt them."

"What are you going to do about it?" Natasha moves closer so that her chest brushes against my chest. "Dawson."

Yes, I think about kissing her, but only to shut her up. We had something good between us, good enough to make Natasha's other, less pleasing qualities, bearable. And if that's what I thought she wanted, I would have planted a big, fat kiss on her.

"What do you want?" I ask stiffly, not backing down one inch, even though Natasha clearly has me on the ropes. I wish Neely was here. She's much better at confrontations and conflict and crazy women.

"Oh, you know what I want. Any little tidbit about the next Suitor you want to share?"

"No." It's not me, but it's the only information that I have, other than Shae, that is of any use to her.

But if I say something, I'll betray Pepper.

"You sure about that? Because I think your new best friend Grayson Grant is about to be sworn in as the next Suitor. Do you think you'll be better or worse friends if he's dating Neely? And how can he be dating her if he's about to find true love on TV? Poor Neely." Natasha's expression is almost gleeful. "Things aren't going to work out for her, are they?"

A long moment passes as I battle my conscience like it's one of my video games. What can Natasha actually do to Shae? Start a rumour that she *might* be sick? It might pick up speed for a few days, but if no one confirms, it will go away.

If I confirm Grayson is The Suitor, *that* could do serious damage. Plus, Pepper would never forgive me.

Neither would Neely.

"Anything you want to tell me about everyone's favourite reality show?" Natasha urges. "Anything? Anything?"

I can't open my mouth because I'm afraid of what will come out.

"All right then." Natasha brings her hands up to my chest and pushes off with her fingers. "Nice knowing you. Tell Shae to check Insta in a couple of days, and I'll be sure to tell her where I got the juicy tidbit." She smiles, looking as ugly as I've ever seen a woman.

What did I ever see in her?

Chapter Twelve

Pepper

"Pepper," Mrs. April calls later as I finish tidying the kitchen. "Can you come out here?"

My heart literally skips a beat. It has to be Reuben. A quick glance at the clock suggests he might be early; might be if I'd thought to ask what time he had planned to make the drive.

It doesn't matter. He's here now.

I arrange the smile on my face as to be not quite as giddy as I feel and push open the kitchen door.

Only to find my mother at the counter, laughing with Mrs. April.

"Mom?"

"Hi, sweetheart," she sings, looking impossibly put together for a sixth grade teacher. My lack of dressy clothes thankfully coincides with Mom's excellent fashion sense and the fact we're the same size. "I thought I'd stop by to see if you needed any help, maybe check if we can get you out here early enough for dinner with us tonight."

"Tonight?" I stammer. "I..."

"She has plans tonight," Mrs. April oh-so-helpfully informs my mother. "Only she's driving me crazy by not telling me who he is. Or she?" Twin eyebrows jut into her hairline.

Ever since I told Mrs. April my taste has run to both men and women, she likes to say things like this to prove she's tolerant and accepting. It's very cute until it's not.

"I wouldn't feel too bad, Mrs. A.," Mom says. "She hasn't told me anything at all about this."

"There's nothing to tell," I huff. "Yet. I met Reuben on the weekend, he works for Pain au Chocolate patisserie, we got to talking, and he's coming to check out the place."

Mom shares a skeptical glance with Mrs. April. "That's it? You sure?"

I shrug. I *think* there's more of a reason than that, but I'm not about to give either of them false hope.

"Where did you meet him?" Mrs. April gets the jump on Mom.

"I told you. Pain au Chocolate."

"You picked up a baker?"

"I didn't *pick him up*," I protest. "And he's a *maître pâtissier*."

"Oh, how nice! A fellow after your own heart." Mrs. April claps her hands.

"Sounds impressive," Mom adds.

"More importantly, is he French?" Mrs. April wants to know. Like I said, she's a dog with a bone.

"Scottish," I admit.

"What else can you tell us?"

"Nothing. There is nothing *to* tell. If there was, you both can be sure I'll let you know." I lock gazes with both of them until they shift uncomfortably. "Now, go."

Mrs. April swells like a bullfrog. "You can't think we'll be leaving you here with a strange man."

"You were quick enough to leave me the other day when Dawson came by."

"Well, he wasn't Scottish."

"What does that have to do with it?"

"Who's Dawson?" Mom asks, and Mrs. April turns to her with the happiness of having more gossip to share.

"Oh, he's lovely. Very cute with those sneakers all the nice boys wear—"

I interrupt her with a snort. "I've got to finish in the back. Mom, thanks for stopping by, but I don't think I'll make it home for dinner."

"You can be so lucky." And then Mrs. April actually elbows my mother. "Get it? Lucky?"

"If you're finished..." I make little shooing motions with my hands. But as I'm standing there in the middle of the room, the bell over the door tinkles as Reuben steps in.

Instead of everything in the bakery grabbing his attention, his gaze goes straight to me and that shy smile curves the corners of his mouth.

"You're here!" My face heats up as I realize how loud that was.

"Hullo." Reuben looks from me to my mother and Mrs. April, both standing there with amazed expressions, heads tilting up as they take in his height.

I don't remember the last time my mother met anyone I dated. Is this dating? Is this a date? This is Reuben standing in my bakery, come to spend time with me.

What am I supposed to do with him?

Nerves and uncertainty hip-check any excitement I might have felt only moments ago. I can't deny I liked Reuben when I first met him. I'm attracted to him. But again—what am I supposed to do with him?

Any interaction with the opposite—or same sex—I've had in the past five years involved drinking and then going for the quick lip-lock. I even kissed Dawson a couple of days ago.

The thought of kissing Reuben...I don't know what I feel about that. What I should feel about it.

"Well, aren't you a big boy," Mrs. April says under her breath.

Thankfully Mom clicks her tongue as a warning to her and steps forward. "Hello, there. I'm Carly Grant, Pepper's mother."

"Reuben Stuart. Friend of the lass."

"The lass," Mrs. April mouths at me. I roll my eyes at her.

"So nice to meet you, Reuben. I'm about to leave, and so is Mrs. April—"

"Helene April," she interrupts, flipping up the end of the counter with a loud bang in her hurry to offer Reuben her hand. "A pleasure."

"'Tis mine," Reuben's voice, so deep and growly, elicits a titter of giggles from her.

"Oh, well." She clutches at her chest. "I'll be going, Pepper, unless you need me for something?" Her smile is nothing but hopeful.

"I'm going to give Reuben a tour of the kitchen and then I thought we'd take a walk around town." In my head it sounds like the most boring suggestion but Reuben nods like it's the best idea ever.

"That sounds like a *lovely* idea," Mrs. April gushes with more enthusiasm than necessary and sends me rolling my eyes again. "The kitchen I mean. You show me yours and I'll show you mine," she sings under her breath.

"Yeah, well, *no*," I say in a curt voice. "I mean..." There's a hint of a bemused smile peeking from under Reuben's beard. "Not like that."

"I'll see you at home, Pepper," Mom says. "Mrs. April, I'll walk out with you. So nice to meet you, Reuben."

"Ta verra much."

I wait until they're both gone, door locked behind them, before I take a deep breath. Reuben is so big and brawny...and big. He dwarfs everything in the place.

Or maybe it's because I'm so conscious of him here.

"Sorry about that," I say, more flustered now we're alone.

Hide the cupcakes. Protect the bakery.

Where did that come from? Reuben's recipes are hidden inside my brain rather than lying out in the open, and the cupcakes are safely packed away in the refrigerator waiting for me to frost them in the morning. Unless Reuben goes snooping, which I doubt he'd do, he'll never know I make cupcakes as well as bread.

Why wouldn't he snoop? I did, when I was in his kitchen.

"Why?" I pull myself back in time for Reuben's question. "It's nice to meet your mam. You look like her."

"I don't think so. My mother's beautiful." As I make an about-face and lead him into the kitchen, I realize I'm about to mess this up. Painfully, awkwardly, like every other relationship I've been in.

I push open the door. "This is it."

As Reuben looks around, I see the kitchen through his eyes. It's not as pristine and carefully organized as the kitchen of the patisserie, but everything has a place, even though there's not quite a place for everything.

In other words, it's tiny compared to Pain au Chocolate.

And even though I leave with bowls clean and tidy at the end of the day, I still have a good many hours before my end of the day, so the counters are a bit of a mess.

Just like me.

As I watch Reuben looking around the kitchen, any confidence remaining starts to crumble. Why is he here? Maybe it's a reconnaissance mission that M.K. sent him on. Maybe they want to get into bread making and want to check out the competition. Maybe he's a secret baseball fan—or worse yet, Suitor fan—and wants to ask about Grayson. Maybe he's here to pick up gossip about the rumours about Grayson—

"Nice place," Reuben says in his low rumble.

I'm not taken in by the admiration in his voice. In fact it only makes me more nervous.

What's wrong with me? Dawson was here, standing right where Reuben is not two days ago and I wasn't a tittering wreck with him.

I *like* Reuben, that's what's wrong. I like his smile, and how tall he is, and how things tingle when he looks at me. And this is only after I met him once.

"How was your day?" Reuben asks. My heart skips a beat, not from the question, but because he stops his tour beside the fridge where I have six dozen cupcakes neatly packed in plastic tubs between sheets of wax paper.

"My day?"

"Aye, your day. Was it well?"

"It was." A nervous laugh escapes.

"I make you nervous."

"What?" Another laugh. "No, of course not."

"I think so. If not, what's got you so skittish?"

"Skittish? I'm not a horse?"

His shy smile changes into a full-fledged smile and my heart literally skips a beat. The glasses and his beard hide a variety of emotions, but when he smiles like that everything is out in the open.

My shoulders relax a fraction.

"Aye, you're not a horse." His eyes rove around the kitchen, searching for— "Is that the bread?" he asks, his eyes falling on the covered bowls on the counter.

"My boules."

He lifts the corner of the towel. "First rising?"

"That one is almost ready to be punched down."

"Aye, don't let me keep you from the bread." I raise an eyebrow and Reuben nods with another of the smiles. "I dinnae ken that I've had such a lesson."

"Are you serious?"

"Aye. It's important to you."

No one has ever... "If you want." Giving my hands a wash, I move over to the long counter where Reuben is standing and pull the large bowl towards me. "You mix everything together and let it rise. Now I'll punch it." For emphasis, I punch the dough with my fist and it deflates with a hiss. "And I separate it into smaller balls and let them rise." I drop the dough onto the counter and slice through the mass with a pastry cutter. As I shape the dough into boules, Reuben places his hand on mine.

"Like this?" He molds his hand over mine.

My breath hitches noticeably and my cheeks redden. Yes, he makes me nervous. Yes, he makes me blush. Yes, he makes me...

...feel something.

Everything.

I glance up at him hovering at my shoulder and meet his smile. Looking back, I'll be able to say that the move was perfectly flirtatious without even meaning to. "Yes...but it's harder to do just like that."

"Aye, mebbe so." His hand dwarfs mine, warm as a blanket, and then it's gone.

"You've got really big hands."

Instead of answering, Reuben holds up his palm so I can press mine against it. It looks like a child's hand. "My da was six eight," he says. "Tallest in the village. Mam was six foot, and I'm horrible at sports. I played rugby, but I had no choice about that."

"Why didn't you have a choice?"

"When you look like me, and the team is a losing one, there's a certain expectation that you'll help out the lads. Now, give me a chance here."

I push a hunk of dough in front of him, and together we shape the boules. And then we start on the French loaf and the whole wheat, with Reuben asking questions about flour and technique and when I first began baking, so by the time the dough is ready, I've relaxed enough to answer his questions without the breathless nerves.

"There, that's better."

I look up into his smiling eyes. "I don't know why..." I trail off as Reuben touches my chin, rubbing his thumb along my jaw.

"It dinnae matter."

"No..."

"Aye." The corners of my mouth curl up. "What's funny?"

"I like your accent."

"And I yours."

"I don't have an accent," I whisper.

"To me, you do."

I let my eyes drift closed and lean in. But instead of the soft touch of his lips, Reuben clears his throat and his hand drops from my face.

Dawson

I KICK THE BOX of my stuff across the room. It hits the corner of Claudine's chair and splits down the side, my things spilling out.

At least I didn't spill it about Grayson.

When I refused to say anything, Natasha gave a shake of her snake braids, flounced to the door and let herself out without another word. She could always guilt me into doing anything, just with a pouty lip and a sweet, "Please. Please, Dawson?", so I feel pretty good about not giving in to her.

At least I would feel good if I knew what she was planning about Shae, so I could stop it.

I picked Pepper over Shae, and I kind of hate myself right now.

Technically, I picked Neely over Shae, but that doesn't help, only makes it more complicated.

Grabbing my phone, I open the Instagram app. There's no way that Natasha can have posted that quickly, but she might have had something ready to go—

Or maybe she'll wait, knowing it will drive me crazy. I'm always the most impatient when it comes to posting things. Plus, she knows—she must know—how bad I feel about this.

What did I ever see in her? There's nothing sweet about her, nothing good. Nothing at all. Why—?

"What the—?" I mutter.

I have a DM on my Instagram page.

Hi Dawson. This is Keith (your brother). This is the only way I have to get a hold

of you so I hope you see it. I'd really like to get together at your convenience to

talk about a few things. I can be reached—

He left his number and his office address. I don't have to check to know that it's within walking distance.

I've lived here three years and I've had family within walking distance the whole time.

Keith is not family.

I'm not sure what he is, but right now, in the mood I'm in, he's an annoyance. An irritant. He's commented on my posts, and now he sends me a DM?

It's like he's stalking me. That's not something family does.

"Let's get rid of this right now," I mutter aloud. Then I go and put on a pair of pants.

It's a quick walk to Keith's office, made all the faster by my anger-induced pace. I'm furious with Natasha, Keith, his mother, my father for dying—really, the whole world. And right on top of the pile is me, for throwing Shae under the bus.

I should have told Natasha something...anything...that would have kept her off the scent.

I walk right into the office; there's no reception area or smiling secretary to greet me. Groups of people cluster around tables, hovering over screens, wearing jeans and shorts and graphic Ts. The latest Cardi B plays loudly. The amount of Funko figurines and LEGO creations makes it more like a pre-school than an office.

This isn't a workplace; it's a party room.

Not that I'm complaining. Whenever I get a job, I'd want it to be in a place just like this.

No one pays any attention as I stand by the door, awkwardness replacing some of my anger. Maybe this wasn't a good idea. Maybe I should just go.

A guy wearing a beanie and attempting a beard looks up and sees me. "Hey," he says in greeting. Then he does a double take. "*Hey*! Are you that travel vlog guy?" He elbows the woman beside him.

Recognition floods her face at the sight of me. "You're Dawson Jacinto." It's not a question. "We were literally just watching your video." She holds up her phone.

"Literally watching it," the guy echoes. "What are you doing here, dude?"

"Ah...Keith? Is Keith Gretchen here? Is this where he works?"

"Here to see the Keefer," he cries, swinging his arm towards the back of the room where glass walls divide the space into office. There's a man in the corner office, seated at a desk and laughing on the phone. "Go on back."

"Ah...thanks."

More of my anger dies away as I wend my way through the bodies towards his office, replaced by something like awe because looking at my half-brother is almost like looking in a mirror.

He looks like my father, and therefore looks like me. I share my mother's colouring but inherited my father's etched cheekbones and divot in the chin rather than her soft, curved cheeks. Keith has the same cheekbones as us, the same mess of dark hair, similar black-framed glasses. His eyes are round rather than almond, and my mouth is bigger, but the only other difference is that he's tanned from the outdoors and I'm half-Filipino.

"Dawson?" Keith's jaw drops as I appear in his doorway. Holding up a finger, he makes a quick excuse to whomever he's talking to and hangs up. "What are you doing here?" he demands, scrambling to his feet. "I mean, I'm glad you stopped by but, wow! You're here!"

It's not often that someone seems *that* glad to see me and that brings back the annoyance. "What do you want from me?"

Keith halts about two feet away from me. He may look like my—our—father, but there's no perfectly fitted suit, no immaculate tie and pocket square. He's wearing, of all things, cargo pants and a Blue Jays T-shirt.

His face is a bit softer, his eyes lacking the intense green, but it's enough of a match for me to stand staring for an awkward moment in the doorway before I can bring myself to move.

"I mean, hasn't your family done enough?" I stalk past him, past his proffered hand, to stand at the corner of his desk. "What more do you want from me?"

"I didn't get in touch with you about that." Keith returns to his desk to stand stiffly across from me.

"Good, because I don't have anything left. I really don't." Despair tinges my voice and suddenly, everything hits me at once. Losing my father, my mother's illness...Neely...

"I want to offer you a job."

That stops the wave of sadness like a breakwater. Grammy might have warned me about this, but it's the last thing I really expected Keith to say. "Why?"

"Why would I offer you a job, or why would you work for me?" He hikes a hip on the edge of the desk.

I cross my arms over my chest and wish I looked more imposing. "Both."

"I hated your mother for a long time," Keith begins as casually as if we're talking about the weather. "I might as well be honest with you. I was seventeen when Dad left to find you. Even then I knew they didn't have the best marriage, but we were still a family until your mother ruined things."

Even though every ounce of being tells me to defend my mother, I stand and listen, maybe realizing for the first time what my parents' love story did to Keith's life.

My being born took his father away from him.

"Maybe it wasn't right of my mother to contest the will, but she was angry," Keith continues. "And I can't blame her."

And now, after hearing Pepper's side of her parents' fallout, I shouldn't either.

"So why am I here?" I ask.

"Because I can't hate *you*. And I'd really like to get to know my brother. Besides—" He circles his desk and settles into the chair, fingers tapping on the keyboard of the laptop. "Do you even know what I do? Because I know what you do."

"I don't do anything."

"You should. I know about the trips. And those two girls." He wiggles his eyebrows at me. "Got to be nice seeing the world with the two of them."

"Yeah, well..."

"That Shae's a spitfire, but I have to say Neely would be the one for me."

"Yeah..."

There must have been something in my voice, or some half-brother telepathy going on. "So that's how it is, is it?" Keith laughs, and my chest squeezes because it's the same laugh that my father had. "Anyway, it'd be tough, but I thought if you ever give that up..." He turns the laptop so I can see the screen. "My company designs computer games. And you, Dawson, are a pretty big gamer. I think we could do some interesting things together."

Chapter Thirteen

♥

Pepper

"YOU'VE ALWAYS LIVED HERE?"

After the non-kiss, I need to get out of the kitchen and get some distance between Reuben and me. Bread finished, I give the kitchen a quick clean up and we head outside.

Ashbury looks pretty in the late afternoon sun, but there's still not much to it. The wide strip of Main Street, shops struggling to stay afloat, just like me.

I know this because of the rant session at the last town council meeting. Mrs. April really does know everything that goes on.

"Born here and never left," I say. Like my bakery, I see the town the way Reuben would see it—tired and small. Any attempt at quaint and cozy and other adjectives to describe a town of that size only brings out the old-fashioned-ness of the place.

Ashbury has a real-life General Store, where you can buy anything from maple syrup to maxi pads, the Royal Bank hasn't been renovated since the 1950s and the vault with the lock like a ship's helm is still front and centre, and there's a Stedmans department store in the middle of the street. They went out of fashion in the 1980s, and most went out of business then too.

Pepper's Pies and Pastries is at the end of the street so we have a good walk to Bollocks at the far end.

"It reminds me of home." To my surprise, Reuben has a look of delight on his face.

"Where's home?" This, of course, reminds me that I know nothing about him, other than he's great at making cupcakes and looks darn good in those jeans.

"Linlithgow."

"Scotland, right?" I'm not sure what to do with my hands. My bag is slung over my shoulder, so there's nothing to hold. My right arm keeps swinging free and brushing against Reuben's and then I lurch away like he gave me a shock.

"Aye, on the Sterling-Edinburgh road. Reminds me of this." He sweeps his arm out. "Streets wide enough for carriages, stores that have been around for ages. Except for the castle, of course."

"You have a castle?"

"Aye, Linlithgow Palace, birthplace of Mary, Queen of Scots."

"You *own* a castle?"

"Not personally. I expect the National Trust holds the papers on it now. Bit rundown now, can't imagine it being the birthplace of anyone else."

"I thought you meant..." I trail off with a nervous laugh. "You're not some secret lord ruling Scotland from afar, are you?"

"Not secret," he says with a shrug. "A few of my kin reckon we're descendants, but no one's thought to prove them wrong."

"Or right," I say eagerly.

"Another shrug. "I've things on my mind other than being descendant of the king."

"Like what?" I take advantage of Reuben's pause to barrel through with more questions. "How long have you been away from Scotland? What did you do there? How did you get into baking?" I flush slightly and hope he thinks it's only the sun on my cheeks. "I ask a lot of questions. It's easier than talking about myself."

"That's my way."

"You answer mine first."

"As the lady requests—"

"Lass," I interrupt. "You said lass earlier. I like that."

He smiles down at me, his hand brushing the back of mine, only he doesn't jerk away like an off-balance drunkard. "Just a lass and a laddie out for a stroll?" He exaggerates the accent which then exaggerates my smile. "Well, now, for answers. I've been gone near four years, back for a Christmas visit with Mam. As for what I did—"

Something tells me to brace myself.

"My family owns a fair bit of land. Enough to have some golf courses. And a distillery," he adds with more than a note of embarrassment.

Because of the hesitation, I don't make a big deal about it, even though I make a mental note to Google him as soon as I get home.

"That sounds like a good family business. Businesses. But how did you end up being a pastry chef? It's not a normal jump from—what do you distill?"

"Whisky. Scotch."

Wow. Even I know Scotland is famous for whisky. And isn't golf the national sport? "From whisky to cupcakes. Bet your family didn't see that coming?"

"Aye. It's mostly my cousin who runs things, especially since I took my leave."

"Why did you take your leave?" I ask.

"That is a tale for a much less nice day. But through all that is that I helped my mate Kane open his first shop with the promise that I could do some baking. It's something I've enjoyed, but never had the time, what with the companies and businesses and all. Kane's done well; got five or six shops now. Baba's Bakehouse."

"And you...own them too?" I ask faintly.

"With Kane. He does most of the work and I...advise him of things."

"Huh." There's so much more to Reuben than I expected. I take a deep breath and tell myself he's still the same guy as the one who wanted a lesson on how to make bread.

"I dinnae unnerstand if that's a good *huh* or not."

"It's a surprised huh. Kind of amazed. I thought you were one thing and you're really not."

"I'm the same me. And if you'd seen me a few weeks ago, you'd think me a different person entirely."

"The Hagrid look? Dawson said something about that the night we met."

"Aye. Hair down to here." He chops a hand halfway down his arm. "Beard just as long."

"What made you cut it?"

"A few things. It was time, plus Adam—" He pauses to make sure I follow.

"Neely's brother?"

"Aye. He's a wee bit persuasive. Plus, there was a lassie."

"I'm not the only lassie then?" I don't know why I say that; I don't even know why I think it. But I do know that a wave of jealousy like nothing I've ever felt washes over me at the thought of Reuben with someone else.

That's not a good thing.

This time Reuben doesn't just brush my hand with his—he takes it, entwining our fingers, and the jolt of surprise turns into a warm glow that travels through my arm. "You're the only lassie I'll be wanting to take a stroll with."

His hand is warm and it feels right to walk with him like this.

It feels really right.

"That was a stupid thing to say," I admit. "Of course you've had other lassies. Look at you." We're outside the wide windows of Bab's Cut and Curl and I gesture to the window. I'm tall for a woman but Reuben is still head and shoulders above me.

He pauses and smiles at our reflection.

Even with the blurriness and haze from the late afternoon sun, even I have to admit we look good.

"Sweet." He gives a gentle squeeze of my hand. "I left Scotland because of a broken heart."

The jealousy is replaced with a wave of anger that someone could hurt this man. This baker-businessman-king.

"Who did that?"

"Glinda. Glinda the gold-digger, as Adam calls her."

"Ah." How dare she!

"Aye. She was after what was in my sporran. That's the pouch you wear with a kilt," he adds in response to my blank expression.

"Aye." The accent is contagious as my head fills with images of Reuben in a kilt and I do my best to hide my smile. "Is she the one who got you to cut your hair?"

"No, that was an age ago. It was wee Susie, from the shop who prompted the change. Nothing to tell about her, good or no. But she helped me see I'm a worthy man again."

"You've always been worthy. I don't even know you, and I can see that."

"Aye, well, there's times when it's easier to see you're not."

"I get that," I say slowly. "At least you've been in love. I don't...I haven't let myself. Maybe when I was younger, but I don't think that counts." The confession surprises me; me who has always been close-mouthed with relationships, even with my family. I don't talk about love with anyone, and now this is the second time in a week.

"It all counts."

"I wish he didn't count. I wish all of them didn't count."

Even now, I know Reuben will count. There's something about him, something that soothes and comforts and lets me be me. I don't have to pretend to be someone I'm not.

I've never felt that way before.

The last time I'd been alone with a man wasn't even a relationship but more of a one-night stand. I'd let Grayson and Emmett drag me out to Bollocks about six months ago. When Emmett had gone home earlier, and Grayson had become enamoured with newly divorced Robin Tetley, I'd let Wade Watley buy me one too many drinks. This led to a frantic make-out session leaning against the corner of the pub, where three of my customers walked by.

As embarrassing as that had been, it was better than being cornered in the back hall of the community centre during Amy Flatter's engagement dance by none other than Jena Markov.

It was like she was trying to use her lips to apologize for the years of taunts and teasing, and I had bought it, until she suddenly pushed me away and stormed off like I had been the one who initiated the kiss.

The time before that had been the loan manager of the local bank. After I signed the paperwork, he insisted on taking me out to lunch, and then back to his house to see his newly renovated kitchen, where I discovered photos of his wife. The time before that had been a six-week stint with one of the producers of The Suitorette that I had met when Grayson was on it. I should have realized that Radha's refusal to be seen in public with me had more to do with me being Grayson's sister.

And that leads back to Luke Ellis, high school sweetheart and general bad guy. At least he was bad to me for the two years we spent together.

None of them counted. But Reuben is different.

And now all I need to figure out is how not to mess it up.

"Aye. But your past matters only when you let it," Reuben says.

"How do you stop? When it defines you?" Growing up with Grayson as the Golden Son, with the memory of a father who wanted someone more than his family, with a stream of failed attempts at love. How can that not define me?

"When it makes you into the beautiful baker you are, you listen. But when you think bad thoughts about yourself, and doubt the decisions you still must make, then you dinnae."

"You make it sound so easy."

"Trust me, it's not. It takes a bit a time, and a stint on big boat making coffees to figure it out, but you can."

His words hang in the air as we reach the corner of Main and First, home of Bollocks Bar and Grill. Reuben takes one look at it and laughs, a loud rumble that sounds like his very chest is vibrating.

"Now then," he says with a wide smile. "You need to take me there."

"Our town treasure," I say as I lead him across the side street.

He gives my hand a squeeze. "Not the only one."

Dawson

I DIDN'T EXPECT THAT. A job offer. And not only a job offer, but one that, on first glance, has me seriously considering it.

But how can I even think about it? I have Shae to think about, and my commitment to her and Neely. The three of us started the vlog, and we vowed that we would finish it.

No one mentioned how we'd be finished when Shae lost her fight with the disease that will ultimately kill her.

Stopping because of an awesome job opportunity seems wrong.

That's what stops me from accepting on the spot, not the fact that his mother hates mine.

But Keith pushes aside the subject of both of our mothers and we start talking games. He shows me the rest of the office space, I meet the rest of his team and get to try out their new game—a MMORPG—that is so much fun I don't want to stop.

But I want to find out more about Keith, so I finally hand the controller back and find my way back to Keith's office.

"Hey." This time all my rage is gone as I stand awkwardly in the doorway.

"Did you like it?" Keith asks, eagerness written all over his face.

"So cool."

He motions me inside his glass box. "I think we've got some really unique avatars, stuff that's never been seen before. Release is a year away and we'll need it, because there's some serious bugs to fix—"

"The way the mage flashes in and out," I interrupt.

"And if you pick the female warrior, there's a serious lack of clothing options, which I still think is intentional rather than an oversight. Miguel was in charge of that, and he's got the maturity of a twelve-year-old." He grins, looking younger than his forty-two years. "Guess we all do to work here."

"I'd fit right in."

Keith leans his elbows on the desk. "You're thinking about it?"

"I'd be an idiot not to. Your setup is amazing. I can't believe I had no idea you were here. I live ten minutes away."

"That would make it handy." He pauses for a moment. "Look, do you have someplace to be? I thought if you wanted, we could order a pizza...I've got beer in the fridge..." His expression is so hopeful that even if I didn't like the idea, I'd still say yes.

"Sounds good," I say, surprised that I mean it.

"Do you have somewhere to be?" I ask Keith later. Two of the designers share the pizza and the first two rounds of beer before they leave for the day, leaving Keith and me alone in the echoing office. "Are you married or anything? It seems so strange not to know anything about you."

"I asked Grandmother about you," Keith admits with a sheepish smile.

"You call her *Grandmother*?"

"What do you call her?"

"Grammy. I don't know if she likes it, but that's what she's always been."

"My mother insisted on us calling her Grandmother. I always thought it was her choice. She's something else, isn't she?"

"Does she make you drink with her? I always bring her back local booze from the places we go, and she makes me do shots."

"She tried that once, when I was nineteen. I came home drunk and Mom banned me from seeing her for a year. They don't get along," he adds after a pause. "Mom's never forgiven her for going to see you guys after Dad died."

"That was the only good thing during that time. That I got to meet her." I don't mention how I would have been able to meet Keith and the others if Mom and I hadn't been refused entry to the funeral. Despite the fire and brimstone that filled me when I got here, I think it's best to keep the more upsetting memories in the past for now. But I'm still curious enough to ask. "What are the others like?"

"Kevin and Kylie? Obviously, I'm the coolest of the three of us." Keith grins, which makes him look less like our father.

It's easier that way.

"Of course. Do they—did you tell them you were trying to meet me?"

Keith's face falls. "No. Not yet. I will, but the last family dinner had it's own special kind of drama, so I left you out of the conversation. Kevin...He'll come around. We've talked about you, watched the videos. Kylie... I wouldn't hold your breath. She's too much like my mother. She's a bitch," he says bluntly, then points his bottle at me. "I can say that, but not you."

"Wouldn't dream of it. Are they...married? Kids?"

"Kevin has three monkeys. Good kids, and his wife is pretty sweet, too. Kylie has two and a real dick of a husband, but I didn't say that. Her son—Gavin—there's potential, but her daughter is a lost cause. Lost, as in takes after her mother." Keith grimaces.

"That's too bad."

"I'm divorced," he says matter-of-factly. "My wife gave me the choice of the start-up company or her, and then walked out before I could decide. We've got two kids. Sasha and Jake."

"Maybe I could..." Meet them, I'm trying to say, but the words get stuck in my throat.

"Absolutely," Keith says with a beaming smile. "I think this can work out, even if you don't work here."

"About that...There's a lot to think about."

"How does your vlog work? Do you have sponsors that you're committed to?"

"Yeah, but it's more about the girls I'm committed to. Shae and Neely. It's kind of our thing."

"You've been doing it for a while."

"We've never really talked about not doing it." Part of me—the part that thinks this is really cool that I've met my brother, and he seems like a good guy—wants to unburden myself about Shae and Neely both. Tell him about Shae being sick and how it complicates what I feel about Neely, but if my confrontation with Natasha taught me anything, it's that I need to keep my mouth shut.

Plus, spilling Shae's secrets seems a betrayal, even worse than the dark thoughts that Natasha caused to swirl around my head.

The one where Natasha said we let Shae do whatever she wants, and we trot along behind her because—well, dying.

I'd really like to talk to someone about that, but the question is who. Neely would be my first choice; she's my first choice about anything, but since Grayson, a distance has opened up between us.

At least that's how it seems to me. And I miss her.

"I get that," Keith says slowly. "The three of you are pretty tight. But I have to ask—just how tight?" He has the same gleam in his eye that every guy has when they ask that question.

"Pretty tight," I say. "But not like that. They're my best friends."

"Must be nice to have friends like that."

"They're my family," I say truthfully. "Because, well, I never really had a family."

"I know," he says ruefully. "Well, maybe we can start to change that."

It's dark by the time I walk home. After we finished the pizza, Keith wanted to show me another one of his games in development, and we ended playing it for almost three hours.

I played video games with my brother. Did not see that happening in this lifetime.

Chapter Fourteen

Pepper

WE STAY LONG ENOUGH in Bollocks for Polly the waitress to look at us funny. I'm a common enough face in there so not to raise too many eyebrows, but usually I'm with Grayson. For me to be here with a *man*, and to sit laughing, both of us with suddenly so much to say, does raise some questioning glances.

For once, I don't care.

Even when Sally Struthers and Jemma Simmons sidle up to the table to ask about the rumours that Grayson is going to be the next Suitor, it doesn't bother me like it usually does.

"Your brother," Reuben ventures when they leave. "Adam told me a wee bit about him."

"Baseball god, reality show star, all around great guy? He tell you all that?" Like always, I can't keep the trace of bitterness out of my voice, even though I know it's not fair to Grayson. It's not his fault he's so good at everything. He doesn't try to make everyone love him more than me—it just happens that way.

And after talking with him about our father, I know he's as messed up as I am. Luck just hit him in the right places, like a perfect curve ball slicing the corner of the plate for the third strike in a big game.

I guess that takes a little more than luck to be able to do that.

"He did, aye," Reuben says. "I've no brothers, just cousins. I've always wanted a sister."

"For her friends? I used to say that the best part of having Grayson for a brother was his cute friends, but that kind of back-fired after years of unrequited love for Emmett. I don't know why I just told you that."

"Emmett...Shae's Emmett?"

"Is he? Kind of looked like that at the wedding, but I've not heard much." Nor have I asked, either Grayson or Dawson. It's like the first burst of friendship during that long night tapered off like blooms after a late frost. "Nothing ever happened with the two of us. Me and Emmett. There's never been a me and Emmett, except in my head."

"Can't say that's a bad thing." He glances at the empty glass before me. We each had a beer before switching to water; Reuben had the bacon cheeseburger and as soon as it arrived, had me regretting my order of chicken Caesar salad.

At least he let me steal some of his fries.

"I should be heading out. Work tomorrow, and all." I don't imagine the wistful note in his voice, because I'm feeling the same way.

"Me too."

He raises his hand in the universal signal for the bill and I sit quietly as he pays. That discussion happened when we first sat down and ended as quickly as it begun with Reuben telling me that since he owns half of Scotland, he can darn well buy me dinner.

It's hard to argue with that.

We walk back to the shop where Reuben parked the car. I'm surprised at the red, sub-compact car parked out front. "Do you fit in there?" I ask with a laugh.

"It's Adam's," he admits. "I don't have my own car."

"Me neither. I walk to work."

"Can I give you a ride home?"

"I don't mind the walk. It's kind of complicated getting back out of town. Here, you can just turn around and—"

"I may not have a car, but I know how to work one of those GPS things."

"Yeah. I have trouble with directions," I admit in a rush of words. "Dyslexia seemed to have affected my sense of directions."

Reuben stares at me for a long moment, and then gives a belly laugh.

"I didn't think it was that funny," I mutter.

"No, that's no—you live away out here, and we don't have cars, and it seems you might have trouble finding me, even if you can drive there."

I laugh weakly, even though I don't find the thought as funny as Reuben. "Maybe this is a bad idea. I mean, that *we're* a bad idea."

Reuben's laughter dies off and he takes my hand. "Or maybe it's the best idea."

I let myself into the house, the smile permanently etched onto my face. It's around the same time as I usually get home; thanks to Reuben's quick lesson in bread making, I missed the couple of hours I usually spend at the bakery at the end of the day.

The house is quiet. Mom already up in her room and Grayson out, with the usual lights left on for us.

"Pepper?" Mom calls.

"I'm home." It's the same exchange we have every night, but tonight feels different. I feel different.

"You better get up here and tell me what happened!"

My smile widens as I head upstairs, missing the creaking third step like I always try to. I let Reuben drive me home, explaining how we have moved to the tiny house after my father left. Even with me and Grayson helping, Mom didn't want to take on the responsibility of the big house we lived in with our father, with the lawn that spread back to the forest. It was easy telling Reuben things, letting loose the half-formed thoughts I never admit, even to myself.

We sat in the car for half an hour until I finally made him leave.

He didn't kiss me. It's the only thing that might have made the night even better.

Maybe not. Maybe it will make it better if we wait, just to see what happens. Because right now, I have no idea what's going to happen, only that I want it to happen *soon*.

Mom is curled up in her bed, television on to some police procedural drama, test papers marked with red pen strewn across the quilt. It's a much different room than the one she shared with my father—pretty and feminine with the quilt made of Grayson's baseball shirts and smelling of Mom's perfume. "So?" she demands, setting aside what she's working on. "Details. Maybe start with *who was that?*"

"Reuben." My voice sounds as silly as the smile on my face and suddenly I take a running leap onto the bed, sending papers flying and making Mom laugh. "He's nice."

"Must be more than just nice."

"He is." I flip onto my back, the scratch of papers under my bare shoulder. "I think I like him."

"That's a good thing to hear. Tell me more."

I give her a recap of things said tonight, by me and Reuben; how it felt to be stared at in Bollocks, how proud I was rather than self-conscious. How I can't stop smiling.

"And his family thinks that he might be descended from royalty, can you believe it? He said he owns half of Scotland, but he must have been joking because he's not like that, not pretentious or jerky arrogant, you know."

"Oh, Pepper." Mom sighs as she strokes my ponytail, the curls vanished with the long day. "I've waited a long time for you to sound like this."

I move up on the bed so my head rests on the pillow beside her. "What do you mean?"

"I mean, I've listened to Grayson gush about girls for years, but not you. Girls or boys. I never knew if you didn't want to tell me, or you weren't feeling it." She gives me a rueful smile. "Both made me a little sad."

"I'd tell you if there was anything to talk about. There just...wasn't."

"Are you sure? Because sometimes I think it's the very same reason that your brother tries so hard to find love. You, on the other hand, hide from it."

"Maybe."

"That makes me sad, too, and also very angry."

"I'm still angry that he left us," I whisper.

Mom sighs, and then silence as on the television, some square-jawed police detective tries to mansplain to an annoyed forensic person, only to be shot down by her.

"I was angry for a lot of years, sweetheart. You've got to let it go."

"I can't," I confess. "I try, really I do, but I still don't understand."

"It's simple. He loved her more than he loved us. That's not your fault, or my fault, or Grayson's—it's just how it was. She was his person."

"You deserve a person like that. It's not fair."

"Life is rarely fair, but you have to make the best of it. And then sometimes wonderful things happen, like your Scottish laddie." The way she rolls her r's in an attempt at the Scottish burr makes me laugh.

"I used to think Dad took her away because Peter was abusive," I admit.

"The last thing Peter Pike could ever be is abusive," Mom says firmly. "He's a nice man—a good man. Can I tell you a secret? I used to have a crush on him. And then they left, and it didn't seem right."

"It would have been perfect," I argue.

"It didn't feel right because I would have never loved him like I loved your father. He was my person. Sometimes when you find your soulmate, and think it's forever, they change their mind. Or maybe they were never your soulmate after all."

I think of Dawson's talk of soulmates and epic love stories and for the first time, wonder if maybe he had a point.

"Do you think he's dead?" I ask in a low voice. "Dad? It's been so long...years."

It's the first time in years that I've called him that.

"It would be easier if he was," Mom says in a harsh voice that suggests that she really hasn't gotten over her anger after all.

Dawson

I DON'T TELL MOM about meeting Keith.

I will, but I want to figure things out first. And to do that, I need to talk to Neely and Shae.

At least Neely.

I meet Neely at Fred's on Friday for lunch. Shae is late, as she always is, only this time a faint twinge of resentment begins to coil inside me, like tiny seedlings popping out of the earth.

They're easy to crush if you step on them.

I sit across from Neely, wondering if I'm imagining the tension between us. I haven't seen Neely since Wednesday afternoon when she ran out of Shae's after I voiced my thoughts of Grayson in front of her.

I should apologize, but I don't know how to bring it up. How do I say I don't have a problem with the guy as long as he leaves her alone? How with the Suitor show looming, Neely will only get hurt by Grayson.

There's a lot of other stuff on my mind as I sit across from Neely.

She looks tired.

I've always liked her in that T-shirt.

Is she really in love with me?

"How was your date with Pepper?" Neely asks out of the blue.

"Uh—" My glasses have started to slide down as I stare at the menu and I shove them back into place. "It wasn't exactly a date. I went to see her bakery in Ashbury, and we grabbed something to eat after. Cute little town."

"I haven't been there," she says, her voice cool. "Yet."

I'm definitely not imagining tension.

"How was *your* date?" I ask, not looking up from the menu, even though I already know what I want to eat.

"Great." She raises her chin slightly, a common tell when she's about to launch into an attack. "You seem to have a problem with that."

I don't think twice before I counter. "Maybe I have a problem that *you* don't have a problem with it. The reality show part of it."

"That's my business."

"It's not like you, Neely. This guy is obviously a player and you...He's not your type."

"And you seem to know exactly what my type is?"

Are we really doing this? And with no Shae to mediate? She's always been the referee between me and Neely; Neely may fix things, but Shae is the best at soothing hurt feelings and swings of temper.

Which Neely has both.

"You need a man who respects you," I say, trying to weigh my words with concern so maybe Neely will actually listen to me for once and—

"Grayson respects me! He's good and kind, and decent. He's funny and smart and—"

"Okay, okay, I don't need a grocery list of what's great about Grayson."

"I'm not giving you a list. I wouldn't give you a list. That's not me."

"I know." Neely would never give me such a list because she wouldn't see the need. She'd never fight for someone.

She'd never fight for me.

"Did you ever tell Shae?" My sudden question catches her off-stride.

"Tell her what?"

"About what—about us?" In an instant, I'm back lying on the lush grass of the vineyard, my shirt crumpled under us. Neely is in my arms, her bare leg slung over mine, her head resting on my chest.

It's so real that I flex my fingers, wanting to feel more of her skin against mine.

Neely's eyes are huge. I probably look the same because I feel like I'm walking a tightrope and it's a windy day. "No...details..." she stammers. "But, I think she knows."

Oh, she knows. For once I can read Neely like a book, and her expression says she's told Shae that the two of us slept together as clear as if it's written in red on her face.

"It's okay if you told her," I say. "I would have said something, but it felt...awkward. You know?"

"Very awkward." She's a little too quick to agree.

"You think it was awkward?"

"You just said it was!"

"I meant, telling Shae would have been awkward. What happened...that wasn't really awkward."

And that's as far as I get because Shae walks in and both Neely and I shift to her.

We order, chat to Mabel. Shae talks about Emmett and Denzel, and I do my best to keep the conversation away from Grayson.

I don't want to listen about Grayson when I have the touch of Neely's skin on my fingertips.

And then Shae brings up Antarctica.

"I thought we were waiting a few months before we took off again," Neely says, reluctance heavy in her voice. I know she has no interest in going to the bottom of the world, but is there more to it?

Did that little sliver of conversation affect her as much as it did me?

"I know, but we could cash in on the Denzel concert going viral and—"

Neely's voice turns sharp. "I told you, I'm back at school for the summer."

"I didn't know about that." Shae's eyes are wide with surprise. I remember Neely saying something months ago, how she really wants to finish her degree before she gets too old. We all laughed at the thought of us being too old, especially Shae.

No one expected Shae to make it to twenty-seven. It was always one more trip, one more birthday. No one planned for first jobs or university graduations—we never imagined we'd still be doing the vlog at this age.

"Yes, you did, because I clearly remember having the conversation," Neely says with the edge to her voice that she uses with me.

"Okay. I think that's great," Shae says. From the sound of her voice, it's not great at all.

"We could do something in the fall," Neely suggests reluctantly. "Or maybe we'll make it short and go before school starts."

It's now or never. I clear my throat. "I may have a job."

"A job." Both turn to me, eyes wide—one questioning, one almost accusingly.

I hunch my shoulders and soldier on. "Look, Shae, we've been doing a lot—Thailand, and right after Costa Rica." I glance at Neely, hoping for a shred of encouragement. "It's been nonstop, and I think it might be catching up with you. I know it has for me. It might be a good idea for all of us to get some downtime. You look really tired," I finish.

She does. The shadows under her eyes are beginning to look like she's gone a few rounds with Ronda Rousey.

"I'm beginning to get a complex, because that's all you say about me now. I'm still jet-lagged," Shae protests. "It takes a while."

"We're well aware of that. We're going through the same thing, but unlike you, we sleep. Take care of ourselves. I'm worried about you." Neely frowns at her. "You don't look good."

"I'm fine. I don't need the two of you ganging up on me."

"Have you been taking your vitamins?" Neely demands. "Because I know you're not sleeping. Your eyes give it away."

"I don't need your pity."

"Since when have I ever shown you pity? This is concern for my friend. You should be used to it by now."

"I know." The ding of the bell signaling our order pushes Shae to her feet. Running again. "I'll help Mabel with the plates."

How did we get here? What started out as a friendly lunch has turned dangerous. Suddenly, there are so many unsaid things between the three of us—the three of us who have always told each other everything.

"Are you okay?" I jerk my head up as Neely jumps to her feet, just in time to see Shae pitch forward, her head hitting the table with a sickening thump as she falls to the floor. "Shae!"

"Shae!" Neely shoves the table aside to get at Shae, lying limp, half under the table. "Oh my God—Dawson! Shae!"

She's so pale, her face winter white against the pink of her hair. I drop to my knees beside her, not knowing how I got there. "She's breathing."

"Of course she is!" Panic colours the edge of Neely's voice. "She can't—she's not—"

"Call 9-1-1."

"Don't move her!" she shrieks, fumbling with her phone.

"I know, Neely." My fingers press against the faint pulse in her neck. *Don't stop don't stop*, I chant silently, willing the blood to keep pumping, to make Shae okay…

And then Neely and I are in the ambulance with her, squeezed between the gurney carrying Shae's unconscious body and a monitor that beeps into my ear.

"She can't die," Neely whispers as the siren shrieks and the traffic along Queen Street miraculously moves out of the way. "She can't die. She can't die."

I grab Neely's hand. Yes, Shae can die.

Chapter Fifteen

Pepper

"**B**OTH OF MY BEAUTIFUL children at home on a Friday night," Mom sings as she sets the table. "What is wrong with the world?"

"I could be out if I wanted to," Grayson sounds exactly like he did as a kid when someone told him he couldn't do something. "I chose to stay home with you."

"Neely dump you already?" There's a childish sneer in my own voice. Grayson does bring out the best in me.

When I came home early for once, to find neither Mom nor Grayson home and nothing planned for dinner, I did what any good daughter would do—I got right back into the kitchen. And the small sigh of gratitude from Mom was the best reward.

She had looked tired when she stopped at the bakery this morning before school, her eyes shadowed and heavy. She must have been thinking of my father after I went to bed last night.

It's why neither Grayson nor I like to bring him up around her. We don't want her to relive the pain, start asking the questions—why? Why did he leave? What could I have done to keep him? Where has he been for all these years?

Mom might pretend she's all fine with the *Mrs. Pike was his person,* but I suspect that's not the whole truth.

So I make her pasta with green vegetables straight from Pike's farm and a homemade pesto sauce and vow to keep things light and happy tonight.

It's not difficult; my mood has been light and happy since I woke up with thoughts of Reuben on my mind this morning. And his text in the middle of the day made it even better.

"Neely and I are friends," Grayson insists. I wonder which one of us he's trying to convince. "Can you say the same about Dawson?"

I catch Mom's gaze. I don't know what makes me give a quick shake of my head. For whatever reason, Grayson doesn't know about Reuben's visit yesterday, and I don't feel like telling him. I want to hug it, like a favourite pillow, rather than have it pulled away and smashed in my face, like Grayson is prone to do.

"Yes. Dawson and I are friends," I say firmly.

"Too bad for you."

"Don't you mean too bad for you? Must be tough for Grayson Grant to be into a girl who can't stop thinking about her best friend." It's a shot in the dark, but I see from the twitch of Grayson's cheek that I hit my mark.

And then of course I feel bad about it. "It's better if you and Neely keep things strictly only friends with The Suitor coming up."

"I guess," he says sullenly.

"Are you still going ahead with that?"

"I guess."

I meet Mom's glance of concern. "Grayson, do you want to tell us something?" she asks gently.

"No," he says, his voice heavy with indecision. Then he gives himself a shake. "No, it's fine. I signed up for the show, I committed to the show. It's what I want. Neely...Nothing is really a sure thing, is it?"

"I think relationships must be hard for all of them because of the traveling." I add the pasta to the pot of boiling water and give the vegetables sauteing a quick stir. "Plus, the three of them are always together. This is almost ready."

"You're right."

"I know."

"You do, do you? You think you're the rightest little sister ever, don't you?" With a smooth move too quick to see coming, Grayson is up from the table and has me in a headlock while droplets of hot oil fly off my spatula.

"Grayson." Mom admonishes, sounding exactly like she did when Grayson would tease slash torment slash wrestle me in my teens. "Notice the pot of boiling water."

"And the veggies." The moment he releases me, I snatch a spear of asparagus from the pan and wave it at him.

"You think that's going to stop me?" He snaps his teeth and I whack him on the nose with it.

"How are the cupcake sales going?" Grayson asks, accepting the spear. "What did I say?" he wails as my face falls.

I turn back to the stove, all playfulness vanishing with the reminder that I haven't told Reuben that I make cupcakes for the bakery.

Or that I stole the recipes from him.

I've managed to push the thought away, the constant unease in the pit of my stomach of what he is going to say. I have to tell him; I have to be honest, come clean. But it's so much easier thinking happy thoughts; Reuben's smile, the way his hand brushed against mine, how much I wanted him to kiss me in the kitchen.

I still can't believe he didn't kiss me. Or that I didn't kiss him.

"Nothing," I mutter, giving the pot an angry stir with the spatula so now there's wayward piece of spinach caught in the bubbles. "It's good."

"I'd say it's good," Mom cuts in. "It was all I heard about today, how Abigail Freeman is getting cupcakes from Pepper's Pies and Pastries for her birthday party on Sunday."

"Her mother called in the order this morning." Mrs. April had done a dance of joy right there behind the counter when she took the call for two dozen cupcakes.

"Whatever flavours you want to make, she said," Mrs. April reported back. "Mix and match. Make it fun. Whatever you think a twelve-year-old girl would like."

"I don't even know what I'm making for it," I say now. "What flavour would kids eat? She didn't want just chocolate and vanilla."

"Ask Rufus," Grayson says, back at the table. "He'd know. He probably knows her."

"Oh, Rufus definitely knows Abigail." Mom smirks. "He knows *all* the girls."

Grayson puffs out his chest. "He learned from the best."

My comment about his influence on Emmett's nephew being anything but the best is interrupted by Grayson's ringtone.

"Neely?" He's out of the kitchen in a flash, and I hear the slam of the powder room door.

"What's that all about?" I wonder.

"I think he likes her," Mom says sadly.

"He shouldn't like her. Not if you want to get your fifteen minutes of fame during the family visit episode. And I know you want that."

The diet has already begun, the yoga classes increased because Mom is determined to look her best on television because my father will be undoubtedly watching the show.

She didn't tell me that, but I know.

Because I'll be doing the same thing.

Grayson returns as I'm dishing out the pasta. "You know Shae, Pep?"

"Shae from the wedding, Insta-star supreme?"

"Did you know she was sick?" I shake my head, biting my tongue so I won't add a comment about why would I care. "I mean, really sick. Dying sick."

"She's dying?" Of course I would care about that.

"Not anymore. Turns out all these trips they go on is because of some weird bucket list because they thought Shae was dying."

"But she's not?" Mom asks, even though she's never met her.

"Apparently not. Neely is crying and laughing at the same time."

"Is Dawson there?"

"Probably. Like you said, they're always together." He takes his seat and pulls the Parmesan across the table. "I wonder if this will change anything with them?" he muses.

The way he says it makes me wonder if this will change anything for my brother.

Dawson

"**S**HE'S NOT GOING TO die." Mike's voice is no longer the gruff rumble that it had been in the hospital when we got the news.

That Shae is not going to die.

He sounds as relieved as I feel, like Neely looks.

Mike drives us home, the crying and laughter of the hospital fading to an exhausted numbness that keeps conversation to a minimum.

Neely still looks stunned, her eyes red-rimmed from crying. Tears of joy, tears of relief, a release from what we thought was true.

No longer tears of sadness.

"'I can tell you with all certainty that you do not have Batten disease,'" I quote the *#hotdoctor* who gave us the good news. Shae made me post the picture with the hashtag, and unfortunately that's what I'll always think of him.

I'll do anything Shae wants right now, but for once, there's no hint of resentment about bowing to her wishes. She's not going to die.

"I love that," Neely says from the back seat. "I don't even care that they made such a mistake. She's not going to die."

"Oh, the threats of a lawsuit will come soon enough." I grin back at her as I throw the words over my shoulder.

"Probably. It really was a horrible mistake. To have us think that for so long..." She sniffs and I wish I could hop in the backseat with her to hold her hand.

I feel kind of naked without her fingers gripping mine.

From the terrifying ambulance ride where Shae lay unconscious, to the hours of waiting in the hallway outside Shae's room while they were running tests, Neely held my hand.

Is it bad that I'm as happy about that as I am about Shae?

It's different, of course. Shae is life and death, and Neely is just...love.

Neely has always been the light at the end of the tunnel that, deep down, you expect to reach one day. Hope to reach. But lately, Neely has seemed further and further away, and she kept moving in the wrong direction.

Even after my unreturned declaration years ago, she wasn't as far away as she's seemed this last week. I have Grayson to thank for that. Grayson has the opportunity to take Neely right out of my tunnel.

That thought makes me a little sick to my stomach.

So deep in my thoughts, I don't realize where Mike is headed until he pulls into the shared driveway between Shae's and Neely's houses. "Oh," I say, trying to hide my disappointment. "I guess I'll call an Uber from here." It's not that late, and it's not difficult to get home via transit, but being at the hospital all day has drained most of the energy out of me.

"No, I'll drive you home," Mike insists. "I wanted to get Neely here first. I'm sure Mama S. has a lot of questions for you."

"I told Adam," Neely says glumly, "and I'm sure he let Mama know. But she will want to know everything..." Her voice suggests it's not something she's looking forward to, and she's got every right to think that. As amazing as Mama S. is, she can be a little exhausting to deal with.

I roll my window down as Neely gets out of the car and look up at her as she pauses. "Thanks for the drive home," she says to Mike, hanging her arm inside the car.

Instinctively, I twine my fingers with hers.

"Dawson..." For once, Neely doesn't look angry or annoyed when she looks at me. She looks tired and almost wistful.

I tell myself that it's the exhaustion on her face that gets me out of the car. I get out of the car and, without a word, I pull her close into a hug.

It's one of the few times I've held her without Shae being with us.

Her arms wrap about my neck with a strength that's surprising, her head resting my shoulder. Even with the hospital smell surrounding us both, she still smells like Neely.

"She's going to be okay," I whisper into her hair.

"But what about us?"

"We'll all be okay," I assure her.

I'm willing to stand there all night with her and might have done that, had Mama S. not opened the front door.

"Neely?" she cries. "Is that you?"

Neely sags against me for one more moment, then pulls away. "I'm coming."

"Good luck." Her golden eyes are trying to tell me something but I don't understand what. Instead, I lean down and kiss her on the forehead.

I want to kiss her for real.

And then she's gone, swept into the house by an excited Mama S. so there's no one there to wave to as Mike pulls out of the drive.

"I didn't know if you'd mentioned things to Neely," Mike says as he turns onto Queen Street.

"Things...?" There are many things I want to mention to Neely right now, but still with the memory of her pressed against me, there's no way I can put them into words.

"Your mother?"

"Oh...that. No, I haven't had a chance. We haven't really spent much time together...other than today."

"Today was something."

"Yeah." That's all that's said. When we reach the apartment building, Mike parks out front and gets out to walk to the door with me. I figure out he doesn't do that to make sure I get in okay.

"Dawson?" Mom calls as I'm unlocking the door.

"And Mike," I say, gesturing for him to enter.

Mom stands in the hallway of the apartment, leaning on her cane, a tearful smile on her face. "She's going to be okay," she says.

Mike only goes to her and gathers my mother up into the biggest, tightest hug I've ever seen.

My own eyes are damp as I push past them.

Chapter Sixteen

Pepper

WE BREAK SALES RECORDS on Saturday.

"I couldn't believe that *everything* was gone." I laugh, kneading the bread dough in an automatic and relaxing motion. My iPad is propped on the counter before me so I can better see Reuben as we talk.

It's Sunday morning, and he's in the kitchen at Pain au Chocolate prepping for the day.

"All the loaves, even the day-old whole wheat ones, plus the cranberry focaccia that I burnt around the edges—gone! I thought we'd have to close the store because we ran out of everything, but they still came in for coffee. Poor Lexi was going crazy with the lattes." Still on a high from yesterday, my morning chat is much more chattery than the last few days.

I haven't seen Reuben in person since Thursday night, but we've talked a few times a day since then. It's quickly become a habit, one I look forward to. Reuben makes me laugh, commiserates with my stories about difficult customers, and already supports and encourages me more than anyone, other than my mother.

He told me more about Glinda and growing up owning half of Scotland. Last night I finally opened up about my father.

It's almost a relief to talk about him—the pressure I felt to be good at everything, to be the best at something, how his imagined disappointment still colours everything I do. But it's also nice to talk about good memories of him, things I don't want to share with Mom and Grayson because there are still so many hard feelings between them.

I admit that I honestly don't know if I want him to be dead or not.

I think, maybe, I can tell Reuben anything. He's that person; someone who will listen and give advice when needed, or just be quiet and understand. I've never had anyone like him before, and every time we talk, I get more and more excited about the possibilities. The what if.

What if Reuben is the one? What if he's my person?

And then when I'm in the midst of happiness, the ugly stuff will rear its head. The fact that I think I can tell him anything, except that I stole his recipes for cupcakes and I've been making them ever since.

"So why the change?" Reuben asks. I wish I could see the way his hands fold the pastry on the screen. I like his hands. I like watching them, wondering what it would be like if he touched my face again, or held my hand. "You were worried the first time we met. What's got them rushing in to buy Pepper's bread?"

I shrug, turning my face away from the screen. "No idea."

It's the cupcakes. Of course it's the cupcakes. Ashbury can't get enough of them, and yesterday, we had more than the regular townsfolks stopping by to buy. One customer yesterday told me she was from Cobourg, a little town almost an hour away. She had heard from a friend of a friend about this new place who baked the best cupcakes and had to come and try them.

She was eight months pregnant, and her husband looked resigned standing beside her, so maybe road trips for food was her thing.

Because of the run on sweet stuff, I spent a few extra hours in the kitchen after we closed yesterday, making enough to freeze in case we run out again.

Of course I don't tell Reuben that.

"Keep it up, whatever you're doing," Reuben says. It breaks my heart to keep the truth from him because he sounds genuinely happy for me. "Is Lexi coming in today? You'll be needing some help from the sounds of it."

I nod, glad to be off the *why* of the increased sales. "In the afternoon. Mom will be in this morning. I gave Mrs. April the day off."

"You need one of those yourself. You look tired, lass."

I close my eyes mid-smile. His accent sounds the best when he calls me lass, even better when he says lassie. "I'm closed tomorrow," I remind him. "But you have to work." My tone is rueful, and I try to smooth the expression so Reuben doesn't think I'm upset about that.

I'm not upset, but I would like to see him again.

Even though we've been talking nonstop, with the busy schedules of both shops, neither of us can see a way to get together.

"I wish I could come to help you," he frets.

His sweet offer only makes my stomach twist with guilt. "You have your own things to do."

"Aye, but that's what you do for your—" He stops with an almost frightened expression. "I'd like to help," he finishes.

"That's nice of you." What was he going to say? Was he going to say what he thought this was, or what it could become? "I'd like you to help," I add shyly.

"I'd like to see you again."

"Me too. But—"

"When," he finishes with a shrug.

"Maybe that's why I've never met many people outside Ashbury. It's too difficult."

"Aye, it's not too difficult. Don't be thinking that."

"I know—busy schedules. Maybe I'll figure out something for tomorrow." Each conversation we've had since Thursday ends like this. The more comfortable I become with Reuben, the more I want to see him again, and the less likely that will happen anytime soon.

"Let me know."

I leave a smudge of flour on the iPad as I end the call. Every time we talk, I'm left with a giddy smile, and a longing to keep smiling. I could talk to Reuben all day, even if it's only FaceTime. I've never felt like that with anyone.

And then the sick feeling in the pit of my stomach manages to wipe the smile off my face.

Sunday picks up from where Saturday left off—lineups and tables full of customers lingering over coffee, calling out compliments over the taste, the frosting, the flavour combinations.

Ashbury is definitely ready for gourmet cupcakes.

"You're doing so well," Mom sings as she waves goodbye to another happy customer, this one with a half-dozen lemon and lavender cupcakes and three loaves of bread. "This cupcake idea was brilliant."

"I think I'm going to stop making them," I say in a low voice. For once, I'm grateful for the lull in the lineup because of the quick burst of rain that soaked the sidewalk.

"Why would you stop?" Mom gapes, the same expression of surprise that Grayson wears. He's always looked more like Mom than I do. Maybe it's their personalities—happy, easy-going, always friendly.

I scowl, they smile. Except with Reuben; then I smile.

He hasn't left my thoughts all morning, and the regret seems to be swelling like dough on the first rising. Pretty soon it's going to explode out of the bowl.

"Because I stole the recipes." As I say the words, relief lifts off me like a heavy coat.

"Pepper?" Concern furrows Mom's forehead, but not disappointment. I don't ever remember her looking at me with disappointment, which only makes me wish I'd told her sooner. "Who did you steal them from?"

"Reuben. Or Pain au Chocolate, since that's where I got them, but I'm pretty sure they were Reuben's recipes." The relief of confession might help, but my shoulders still slump miserably. "He doesn't know I took them. He doesn't even know I make cupcakes, so I thought if I stopped, then he'd never have to find out. I really like him."

"Then tell him."

"I can't. I *like* him."

"That's why you need to be honest with him. Show him the respect of telling him the truth."

"But—no! What will he say?"

"You'll have to find out. But Pepper, don't start something with a lie. It will always be between you. Good morning," she says gaily as the bell tinkles over the door. "What can I get for you today?"

She's right. I know she's right.

But it doesn't mean it makes it any easier.

My customer services skills are lacking for the rest of the day as, in my head, I picture talking to Reuben.

I imagine it turning out both ways—Reuben, fine and forgiving, and him furious with me.

It's a toss-up which one is more likely. But late in the afternoon, long after Mom leaves and Lexi arrives to take over the coffee maker, I decide that I'll tell him the next time I see him. It has to be face to face, because over text would be the coward's way out. And FaceTime isn't the same as being there.

But I will tell him for the main reason that I'm tired of hiding.

I'm tired of hiding a lot of things.

Dawson

SHAE ISN'T GOING TO die.

It hits me Sunday morning, like remembering a favourite scene in a movie; when Westley and Buttercup roll down the hill, and she realizes who he is; the dance scene in Breakfast Club; when Samantha looks out the door of the church to find Jake Ryan waiting for her.

Shae will die someday, but hopefully it will be far, far away and we don't have to worry about it. Neely won't have to be so concerned about monitoring every sneeze and headache, carrying around vitamins and handing over cups of green tea.

Neely won't have to play babysitter to Shae.

Neither will I, but it's mainly Neely who takes care of her. Even more than her own mother.

With Shae's new diagnosis, I know things will change, but I'm not sure how. And something is stopping me from heading straight over to Shae's when I wake up Sunday. It's what I want to do—give Shae the biggest hug ever, and then demand *What do we do now?*

Neely will know.

But maybe that's the problem. For once, I don't know what Neely is thinking, and it might be something completely different from what I am. Now that Grayson is involved, I can't be sure of anything. She might want to keep travelling, or she might want to run off with the former baseball player.

She might even be planning on competing for Grayson's heart as one of the Suitor contestants.

I wouldn't put it past her, especially when I can't say a word about him without Neely getting upset with me.

Instead of going to see Neely and Shae and finding out what's what for my future, I head over to Grammy's.

I tell myself it's because I'm reporting on Shae's good news, but the truth is that I want someone to talk to.

Mike stayed over Friday night; I'm fine with it, but it's unsettling to wake up to find him so cheerful, like he just hadn't had the worst day of his life, and making waffles for breakfast. Mom tried to talk to me about it after he left, but there wasn't much to say.

I still don't know what to say about the two of them. Is it possible to be jealous of my mother's happiness? Because that's kind of how I feel right now.

When I get to Grammy's, I'm surprised to see neighbour Rachel at the front door arguing with a man. "Hey," I call out. "What's going on?"

"Oh, Dawson," Rachel says with relief. "I heard a thump inside, but Boen here doesn't think I should break through the window. I knocked, but Mrs. Gretchen isn't answering."

"What kind of thump?" I demand, reaching for the key Grammy gave me.

"A thump like...a body thump," she whispers, her eyes wide.

I push past her, key at the ready. "I'm Boen Carlisle," the man says awkwardly. "I live next door."

"Yeah, hi. Grammy!" I shout as I push open the door. "Are you okay?"

Silence through the house, then a faint, "Dawson?"

"Are you okay?"

"Don't come up here," Grammy orders as my feet hit the stairs. "Well, maybe you'd better."

Rachel and Boen are right behind me as I take the steps two at a time. Grammy's door at the end of the hall is open, and as I reach the top of the stairs, she appears. "I'm fine," she says, hands raised in surrender. "No need to panic."

"I heard a thump," Rachel says from behind me.

"That wasn't me," she says. If it's possible for a ninety-year-old woman to look disdainful wearing a bright yellow dressing gown that I brought her from France, than she does. "It seems Mr. Cullen slipped getting out of bed this morning, and I'm unable to lift him up. Maybe you boys can help me with that."

"Get out of bed—" I stammer, my feet halting. Rachel bumps into me from behind.

"Did she say what I think she said?" she whispers.

Grammy steps aside enough for me to see into her room. Sure enough, there is an older man lying on the floor.

Naked.

And if the tangle of sheets has anything to say about it, he did fall out of my grandmother's bed.

"Hello," I say politely, because what else is there to say to a naked man on the floor of your grandmother's bedroom?

Grammy tosses her second dressing gown to him, and he clamps the fabric over his crotch. "This is Mr. Cullen," Grammy says, without a trace of awkwardness. "My friend. My special friend."

Her special friend does not look happy to see us. He gives a bit of a growl, his face reddening.

Rachel covers her mouth with her hand to hide her giggles. "Oh, wow," she says. "Way to go, Mrs. Gretchen."

Boen pushes past me and kneels beside Mr. Cullen, who begins to struggle to put on the robe. "Are you hurt, sir?"

"It's this bloody knee," Mr. Cullen mutters. "I blew it out playing hockey years ago. Can never tell when it's going to give out, it just goes."

"And I can't lift him," Grammy adds helpfully.

"I think we should call an ambulance," Boen announces, pulling out his phone but Mr. Cullen reaches a liver-spotted hand and grabs it.

"If you think I'm being picked up and dropped in some emergency ward, buck naked and dressed in nothing but a silk robe, you've got another thing coming. I'll never hear the end of this in bridge club."

Grammy breaks the sudden silence by laughing. "Oh, Thomas, this is too good not to share."

"If you ever want me back in your bedroom, Caroline Gretchen, you'll keep your mouth shut about it."

My mouth drops open and I meet Rachel's wide-eyed stare. We both turn to Grammy, who has a discomfited expression on her face.

"I suppose I can keep it to myself," she murmurs.

Rachel giggles.

Boen and I help the elderly man onto the bed, then Grammy shoes us out so she can help him get dressed.

It takes a lot longer than I imagined, and I hear plenty of whispered murmurs through the door. Eventually, I move to the stairs so I don't have to listen.

"Mrs. Gretchen and him?" Rachel sits down on the stair below me. She looks like someone gave her a present, while I feel slightly nauseated. "That's so cool. I want to be her when I grow up."

"It's none of your business what she's doing in her own home," Boen snaps. "Mrs. Gretchen deserves her privacy and your respect."

"I respect the heck out of her, and it is my business when I hear the sound of a body falling out of bed and my neighbour is ninety-seven years old."

"That's how old she is?" I ask. It's better to think about her age than what Grammy is doing in that room. Or did in the room. With Mr. Cullen.

She's my grandmother, so I'm allowed to shiver a little.

"You didn't know how old she is? And obviously didn't know about her boyfriend." Rachel grins. "She's so cool."

"Cool," I echo. "And sexually active."

"Time for the talk!" This time Rachel's giggles turn into a belly laugh, which I reluctantly join in even though the thought of Grammy giving me details of her relationship isn't helping the queasiness of my stomach.

"We're old, not deaf," Grammy calls. "What's this saying about your own sex life that you can't stop giggling about mine?"

That wipes the smile off Rachel's face, and I don't miss the sideways glance she gives Boen.

Boen and I help Mr. Cullen down the stairs, and Rachel has his walker ready at the bottom.

"I'm fine," Mr. Cullen growls, waving off any further attempts to help as he slowly heads into the kitchen.

I can't help but think that he looks awfully comfortable here.

"I promised him a proper English breakfast," Grammy says, still wearing her dressing gown. "You're welcome to stay if you're hungry."

"As long as the gentleman is feeling better, I'll be off." Boen's words are clipped like I imagine they would be if he grew up in some pretentious, upper-class boarding school. But I can't fault him for the help.

"Thanks for your help." I hold out my hand. "Dawson Jacinto."

Boen gives me a nod and a firm shake. "I know. She speaks of you often. Mrs. Gretchen." He nods at my grandmother. "Don't hesitate to call if you have any further problem."

"Thank you, Boen."

"Rachel." The nod he gives her is sharp and curt, and without another word, he turns and lets himself out the door.

Rachel heaves a sigh as soon as the door closes behind Boen. "Why does he always seem like he has a stick somewhere it shouldn't be?"

"I wish the two of you would stop this silly war you've started," Grammy complains. "It would be lovely if the two of you could join Thomas and me for a hand of Euchre and a shot of schnapps one night. He does love his cards."

"And you like your schnapps." Rachel leans over and gives my grandmother a hug. "I'll come over with Dawson, unless he brings..." She looks expectantly over Grammy's white head. "Anyone? Bueller? Bueller?"

Not even the Ferris Bueller reference can get me to break a smile. "Nope."

Grammy gives a frustrated hiss. "Have you not noticed how someone older and obviously wiser, as well as *much* older, can easily sort out her love life, when the two of you are still running around, chasing your tails like one of your silly dogs? Not that I want the two of you together—you both have your person. Now do something about it. I'm a prime example that it's never too late. You're not dead until you stop breathing. There's been too many times to count that I was convinced I was a goner, but I kept taking one more breath after another and look at me now."

"Was that in the war?" I ask, mentally preparing myself to take notes.

"Oh, the Gestapo put the fear of death into me more than once, but the worst I think, was the accident. I left Duncan with a sitter, and I never thought I'd see him again, and that was the scariest moment ever."

"What happened?" Rachel asks, as caught up as I am.

"Oh, Clive had been drinking before we left. I never knew—I should have, but I didn't. By that time we lived together more like roommates than husband and wife. He hadn't slept in my bed in months and our—"

"Got the picture," I interrupt.

"Yes, well, it was snowing and the whiskey didn't help. I don't remember much but the bright yellow lights of the truck coming right for us. Closed Yonge Street for hours," she adds smugly. "I truly thought I was a goner that night but one breath after another, and look at me now."

"He—is that what happened to my grandfather?"

"Oh, no, not a scratch on him. They didn't even realize he'd been drinking. No, I had to wait another two years before I lost him. Died in his sleep, which is ironic, since if he'd stayed in my bed, I might have been able to save him. Goes to show that keeping your sex life alive will keep you alive. Remember that."

"Will do," I say grimly, wondering if every conversation with my grandmother is going to end up talking about sex now. "And now I'll be going."

It's time to figure out what's going on with my person.

Chapter Seventeen

Pepper

MY FEET START TO drag near the end of the afternoon, and I spend too much time watching the clock hands move from one chicken to the other.

Usually, a busy shop takes the edge off the long hours but today it's making it worse. Plus, a headache creeps around my temples, just waiting for a lull to attack.

Jena Markov at the counter is the opening it needs.

"What can I get for you today?" I don't try to sound cheerful with her because the first thing out of her mouth will undoubtedly be something negative.

"What's your brother up to these days?"

"You'll have to ask him." Jena has never admitted it to me, but I know she's a huge fan of The Suitor. There had been a lot of trips to my bakery during Grayson's season, a lot of inane questions as if I were going to confide in her.

Those days are long gone.

"I will. There are rumours that he's going to be the next Suitor." Jena leans a hip against the counter. "What do you think about that?"

"I think some people don't have anything better to do if that's what keeps them up at night."

She purses her lips. "You don't have to be rude about it."

"No, I don't, but it's so fun to be, don't you think?"

"I'm not being rude."

"No? You just swan in, fishing for information?"

"I actually came in for cupcakes. Eloise Freeman said the cupcakes for Abigail's party were quite nice."

"Quite nice. That's a compliment if I ever heard one." I'm not sure what's prompting me to finally speak back to Jena instead of running lines in my head, like an actor prepping for a scene. "What can I get you?" I wave an arm towards the display case just as an unholy screech comes from the direction of the coffee maker.

"I'm okay, I'm okay," Lexi cries as she runs cold water over her arm.

"Are you okay?" I parrot.

"She just said she was okay," Jena says sourly.

"Hot milk splash," Lexi reports over the sound of the water.

"Let me finish for you. There's burn cream in the back."

"I'm all good," Lexi insists, her gaze flicking to an annoyed Jena. "You finish with that. I can do this."

I exhale with a huff and turn back to Jena with a blank expression on my face. "Cupcakes," she reminds me.

"Which ones?"

"Do you have chocolate today? I can't believe you wouldn't have chocolate."

"I have chocolate today; chocolate with buttercream and dark chocolate frosting. Also, pink lemonade and vanilla with candied lemon rind, and marble with hazelnut icing." The hazelnut frosting is something I came up with, another non- Reuben recipe. "What can I get you?"

"Sounds...creative." The way Jena says it isn't complimentary in the least. "You're really veering off from the world of bread."

"What kind of cupcake, Jena?" I stand behind the display case, tongs in hand.

"You are in a mood."

"I'd like to see how badly Lexi is hurt, so—"

"I'll take four. Two chocolate, two of the other ones."

"Four. Sure." I snatch up one of the few remaining boxes under the counter. I'll have to see if Lexi can make more in the back before she goes.

"Eloise Freeman told me something else interesting." Jena's voice oozes, like burnt caramel.

"I'm sure she did."

"About your father."

I still, tongs held at the ready about to grasp the last cupcake. "What about him?" My voice sounds strange to my ears—high pitched and strained. It's not the first time the folks of Ashbury have dropped tidbits about my father, but it's been a while.

It's something I dread hearing about, yet I file away every morsel to go over and over it later.

"Eloise says Max's brother thought he saw him at a Blue Jays' game this weekend." Jena is smug, like she knows just how much that hurts.

I close my eyes for the briefest of moments. "Interesting."

"I thought so."

"Why is that?" With an amazingly steady hand, I manage to get the cupcake in the box and set it on the counter to close the lid.

I focus on the folds of the box, not what Jena is saying.

"I thought it might be fun if your dad showed up for a reunion of sorts. Especially if the rumours are true about Grayson being the Suitor. It'd be a great TV moment."

"No." The word swipes the smug smile off Jena's face. "It wouldn't be. Is that it? Sixteen ten."

Jena shows me her debit card, and I push the machine over to her. "When's the last time you spoke to him?" she asks, trying for casual.

"That's none of your business. None of my life, or my family's, is any of your business so I'd appreciate if you stopped trying."

"I'm only trying to be a good friend."

My chest swells with all the anger I've felt for my father. "Is that what you call it? Because I can recall more than a few times when you made me feel the very opposite of a friend."

I open my mouth to begin the list when a movement out of the corner of my eye catches my attention. Lexi, slipping the cardboard sleeve over a to-go cup, stares at me with an expression of amazement.

"Never mind," I mutter.

"Pepper..." Jena begins in a weak voice.

"It doesn't matter. Have a good day. Next?"

Jena stands there with the box of cupcakes in her hand for a long moment before she finally steps aside.

I really wish she stayed, because Reuben is the next customer in line.

My whole body deflates at the sight of him. After wanting to see him more than anything, and for him to be *here*...at the worst possible moment to show up...

"Cupcakes?" Reuben asks, the accent and his expression making it sound like an accusation.

"Reuben..."

"I dinnae ken you make cupcakes."

I close my eyes, rubbing at the ache behind my temple. "I didn't before I met you."

How can I say that so calmly?

He nods, and keeps nodding, his face shuttering so I have no idea what he's thinking. "I dinnae need to ask where the ideas come from."

"From you." The words burst forth with a huge exhale.

"Where did you get the recipes?"

"Also you," I admit in a small voice. "I took pictures of your recipes when I was at Pain. The night we met. I didn't know you then."

"But you ken me now."

My eyes prick like I've rubbed them with sand, and I swallow the rising lump in my throat. "I should have told you," I say in a rush. "Things have been bad here, and I needed something to make money...I didn't know you."

Reuben steps back, his expression stricken and somehow stoic. Why does it feel like I've slapped him? "I'm sorry I took them...I'm sorry I didn't tell you—"

He turns and heads for the door without a word.

"I'm sorry," I call after him.

He stops, his hand on the door, and I want to run to him, beg him to stay, to let me explain.

But I don't move.

"I would have given them to you, had you asked," he says over his shoulder.

Then he's gone.

Dawson

SUNDAY AFTERNOON TRANSIT IS a frustrating way to move around the city, even when you're not in a hurry. And for some reason, there's a clock ticking down the minutes until I can see Neely.

To tell her...what? What am I supposed to say?

I want to tell her about Mom and Mike, Grammy and the mysterious Mr. Cullen.

I want to tell her I met my half-brother, and about the job offer.

I need to tell her about Natasha knowing about Grayson being The Suitor, so he can get a warning before it breaks.

I want to know if Shae not dying has changed anything for her, because I really think it's changed things for me.

But even without talking to Grammy, I really want to find out how Neely feels about Grayson. That's the ticking time bomb. Because if I'm too late, and he's wiggled his way into her heart—

It's been a week. Neely's heart has been closed like a store in the middle of a pandemic, so how could Grayson have gotten in there so quickly?

Maybe...

All I want, all I've ever wanted, is for Neely to be happy. If Grayson can make her happy, so be it. I will keep any non-friendship thoughts to myself and get used to Neely never being my person.

But can he make her happy? If he goes on The Suitor, that will mean the end of anything with Neely. Unless he gives it up for her.

Part of me wishes he would, if only to make Natasha's big reveal totally worthless.

I want to talk to Neely. I miss her.

I hop off the streetcar right at the end of Neely's street, like I've done hundreds of times before. But this time my feet are impatient, my hands jammed into the pockets of my joggers as I hurry down the street.

I'm halfway there when I see them.

Two people step out on the sidewalk and start walking towards the beach. Neely's golden hair is pulled into a messy knot at the back of her head, Grayson striding along, towering a full head and shoulders over her.

As my feet slow, I see Grayson take her hand.

I stop walking.

Chapter Eighteen

♥

Pepper

REUBEN WALKS AWAY.

I didn't know you. Even replaying the lame excuse in my head makes me wince. How can I say that to him, like he means nothing to me?

It would be so easy if he meant nothing.

"He didn't say anything?" Mom asks as I sit at the kitchen table with lowered head, dunking the last of my Cheerios into the milk. I'm so late this morning, and the worst thing is that I don't even care. I need to be at the bakery in a half hour to open and here I sit, trying to see which of the O's can survive my merciless drowning attempts.

"Coopcakes," I say, mangling the word with my attempt at a Scottish accent, just like I've mangled my life. "He said coopcakes."

Mom puts her hand over mine, halting the dunking. "I meant, he hasn't called since Sunday?"

I spent Monday at the bakery, cut off from human contact and playing the most depressing music I could find in the crate of CDs.

But I did get enough bread baked so that I could sleep in this morning, and everything else ready for another day of record sales.

The cupcakes I forced myself to make were probably my best batch yet. I don't even want to put them in the display case.

I shake my head, unable to answer Mom because I can't find any words that won't show how miserable I am.

"You're going to be late opening the shop," she murmurs.

"I don't care."

"Pepper."

"I really don't, Mom. And don't think this is all about Reuben. I would never let myself get this miserable over a man. Or a woman."

"Then what is it?"

"I put everything I've got into the bakery, and what do I have to show for it? Nothing. I barely break even—"

"What? You didn't tell me that." Her surprise only makes me feel worse. I've always had Mom's full support, and now, seeing her disappointed in me, is like kicking me when I'm down.

"It's not something I'm proud of. And to get ahead of things, I end up stealing from the guy I really like." I stir the dregs of milk in my bowl fast enough to create a little whirlpool. I wish it could suck me down.

"In your defense, sweetheart, you didn't know that you were going to like him all that well when you took them, right?" Mom raises her eyebrows with an encouraging smile.

I exhale with a frustrated huff. "I don't deserve you defending me about this."

"I'm a little tired of hearing of what you don't deserve. You're bright and beautiful and so talented. You deserve the world, Pepper."

I stare into my bowl. For some reason, the first time I made bread pops into my mind. I remember showing it to my father, so proud of the lumpy loaf, my mouth watering from the smell.

"That's great, Pep, but you're not going to spend your life feeding people." My father dismissed the bread with a quick wave of his hand. "Now, I thought we'd get you out on the ski hill next weekend, see how you take to that. There's got to be something you can do, and do well."

He never accepted me for what I was, always trying to better me.

"Do you think my father knows about my bakery?" I ask suddenly.

Mom leans back, surprised by the question. "I don't know. This doesn't have to be about him, Pepper."

"I think it might," I say slowly.

"Start small, start with Reuben first," she urges. "Talk to *him*. Don't worry about your father."

"Kind of tough when he clearly doesn't want to have anything to do with me." I can say the same about my father.

"You don't know that. He was upset."

"I don't think that's going to change."

"Pepper, you need to try."

"It won't do any good."

"How do you know that? Don't you think he's worth fighting for?"

I go back to staring into the bowl. Of course Reuben's worth fighting for. He's worth everything. He's worth so much more than me, and that's why it will never work. "There's nothing I can say to make this better," I say.

"You can try with an apology," Mom says in a firm voice. "And you can fight for him. Show him that he's worth it. That you're both worth it."

Something in her voice has me looking up. "I never fought for your father," she adds in a hollow voice.

"He left *us*."

"I knew there were problems," she admits. "I never thought he was so unhappy. I was focused on you and Grayson and I thought—I thought we'd be okay."

"There's something else about yesterday," I say, hesitant to bring up what Jena had said. With everything about Reuben, I'd almost forgotten. But now, I wonder if it's more important to tell her than keep musing about what I did wrong with Reuben.

Mom insisted that Grayson and I talked to a therapist after our father left. Ever the dutiful daughter, I sat on the couch and expressed my anger, and even cried—the last time I did so in front of someone. Three sessions, and I considered myself purged of my father's sins and never spoke his name again.

I had no idea if my mother ever spoke to anyone about him. Did she hide it inside like I did, pretending the hollowness was normal?

Does she even miss him?

Mom watches me with an expectant expression. "Something Jena Markov said," I say reluctantly.

She grimaces. "That girl never has a nice thing to say about anyone."

"I know, but, this is different. She said, my father—Dad—was seen at a Blue Jays game on the weekend."

I watch closely and catch the flicker of pain move across her face. "He did like baseball," she says slowly.

"Do you think he's in Toronto? That close to us?"

"I don't know. But it wouldn't surprise me."

"But..." The thought of my father being so close, having always been so close, creates a mixture of emotion that I don't understand. Anger and frustration, sadness and regret, and a swirl of anticipation.

It's the anticipation that I don't understand.

"Why didn't you fight for him?" I ask in a quiet voice. "After he left. Why didn't you go after him? Ask him to come back?"

"He hurt me so much I didn't want him back. He humiliated me. Even if he'd asked, I doubt I would have taken him back."

"But what about us?"

Mom smiles sadly. "I know I deprived you of your father, and I've had to live with that. It's the one time in all my years of being a mother that I've been selfish. I let my pride win out."

"You had no idea if he would have listened. Or come back."

"I know. I've told myself that same thing for years. But it all comes down to the fact that I wasn't willing to fight for him. Which is why—" She squeezes my hand. "That I can say with the utmost certainty, you need to fight for another chance with Reuben. Now, you take my car—"

"I don't know where to find him," I protest.

"You can find his patisserie. That's where he'll be, because that's where you were all day yesterday, even though it was your day off. You're upset and that's where you wanted to be. Reuben will be the same."

I nod because she's right. I know Reuben will be there.

"I'll drive you if you want."

I glance at the clock, my stomach tight at the thought of not only seeing Reuben but finding my way into the city. It would be so easy if I let Mom drive me, but I can't. "You have school."

"This is more important."

I think about the classroom of children waiting for her. "No, it's not."

"Everything you do is important to me, Pepper."

"This is important to me, but not important enough for you to miss work. Maybe if I knew how it would turn out." I push away from the table and take my bowl to the sink. "I'll drive you to school and then I'll...see."

Dawson

"Keith? It's Dawson. Mind if I stop by sometime this week?"

I leave a message for my half-brother on Sunday night, long after seeing Neely and Grayson, happily hand in hand, like the happy montage in some happy romantic comedy.

After another day of video games to distract myself, I fall asleep watching Die Hard Monday night. It really is a good Christmas movie, and the only romantic moments happen at the end. Sure, John McClane was saving the building because of his wife, but he would have done it anyway, even if she wasn't being held hostage.

I don't want to watch a romance. I can't think of two people in love because it hurts that it's not me feeling that way.

Or am I? Am I really, still after all this time, in love with Neely?

I think so. I think that's why the sight of her with Grayson hurts so much.

Back at the beginning of puberty, when I was worse than Farmer Ted when it came to being obsessed with girls, my mother sat me down to give me the 'talk.' It was filled with analogies and what ifs, giving me no real information that I could take back to my buddies, who were even more obsessed than I was. But there was something Mom told me that stuck, even fifteen years later.

"After you have sex with someone," she had said, "you can never go back to just holding hands."

After all the years since that night I spent in Neely's arms, I've been trying to prove my mother wrong—that Neely and I could stay friends even after sleeping together.

But seeing Neely and Grayson together like that has made me realize that I've been fooling myself. I love Neely because she's my best friend, but I'm also *in love* with her.

And I'm tired of pretending that I'm not.

"So what's going on in that big brain of yours?" Keith asks Tuesday morning as I sit across from him in the glass box of an office. I brought him coffee from the Starbucks at the corner. It's not Adam-quality from Pain au Chocolate, but it's caffeinated, and Keith seems to appreciate the effort.

"Big brain?"

"Our father let it slip a few times how smart you were," Keith admits. "You can understand how it didn't really endear you to us. At least until we were more mature. Obviously, I'm still jealous." Keith grins as he leans back in his chair, and something unclenches in my chest.

I like him. I like my new half-brother.

"Did you know Grammy—Grandmother—has a boyfriend?" I ask.

The front legs of Keith's chair crash to the floor. "What? How'd you figure that out?"

"I saw them."

"Please tell me you didn't actually see them."

"I walked in to a naked man on her bedroom floor." I give him the recap, happy that he has the same reaction I do when it comes to our grandmother's love life. "I should call to make sure he's okay," I finish, not looking forward to the thought.

"You are totally the favourite grandchild," Keith says with a teasing smile. "And you should be if you had to go through that."

"I'm happy for her…"

"But no child needs to see that." He grins sympathetically. "Better you than me, bro."

"Thanks." It surprises me how easily Keith and I slid into this relationship. There's bantering and teasing and everything I would have expected had I spent my childhood with a sibling, but it happened so quickly that it seems surreal.

Plus, part of me keeps waiting for it to go away.

"Speaking of child, how's your mother?" Keith asks over the lid of the to-go cup. It's a polite question but he doesn't meet my eye.

"You don't have to ask," I tell him. "I get that it's weird."

"I feel like I should," he admits reluctantly. "I liked your mother. She was always nice to me."

"She has a boyfriend too," I confess. "I just found out. He's the grandfather of my best friend."

"That's…odd."

"You're telling me." Keith is the only person other than Pepper that I've talked to about this and it's a bittersweet feeling. I want to tell Neely but nothing about Neely has worked out since she met Grayson. "Again—happy for her but…"

"It's not cool thinking about parents and grandparents having sex," Keith says with a shiver. "Mom remarried, but I don't think it's any happier than her first marriage. I'm just glad I wasn't faced with any R-rated images of them."

"Consider yourself very lucky."

"It's nice to think that you can still find love when you're that age," Keith muses. "Although I'm having such a hard time dating these days, there's no way I'll be picking up the ladies when I'm old and gray. Grayer," he adds, touching the salt-and-pepper patch on his temple.

"Yeah. It's not easy."

"Girl problems?" he asks sympathetically.

"Only the unrequited kind." Saying that out loud is easier than I expected. "I think I'm in love with Neely, only Neely isn't in love with me."

"That sucks," he commiserates.

"It does."

"Are you sure? I've seen the videos, and she's always looking at you."

"Because I'm usually the one filming." I finish my coffee with a long swallow.

"No, not then. When she stands beside you, or when you laugh. You always seem...nice. Like you have fun together."

"I do have fun with her," I say, staring at the empty cup in my hand.

"Maybe she's having fun with you, too. More than friendly fun."

I look over Keith's head, to the big window overlooking Queen Street, hope filling me like a balloon. Then, "No," I decide with a shake of my head. "I'd know."

"Like guys can ever tell what a woman is thinking," he scoffs.

"Point." Do I listen to a brother's advice? I'm not ready yet, since things are complicated enough even thinking of Neely right now. "But that's beside the point. I'm not here to talk about Neely."

"You're here to tell me you want to work for me," Keith says with the utmost confidence. He grins as my expression of surprise. "You're not the only one with a big brain in this family." He raises his coffee cup. "Welcome aboard."

Chapter Nineteen

Pepper

My HANDS GRIP THE steering wheel tight enough for my knuckles to turn white. I really don't like driving; really, really don't like it when I don't know where I'm going.

Mom had programmed the address of Pain au Chocolate into her GPS before I dropped her off at school. She even put the red dot on my left hand, like she used to when I was a little girl.

If Reuben is at Pain au Chocolate, I will be able to find him.

At least that's what I keep telling myself as I follow the directions the nice English lady on the speaker gives me.

When I'm not thinking about my father.

Driving does give you time to think and reflect about things. Ashbury to Toronto is long enough for me to sort out more than a few things, things I haven't given enough time to think about.

I don't blame my mother for not fighting for him. When someone walks away from you, it's really hard to take a step after them.

I've never been able to do it. Walking away is it for me. Leaving means the end.

Or does it?

"Five hundred metres on your left is your destination," the voice from the GPS says.

I recognize the strip of stores with the wide window of Pain au Chocolate. It's open, like I knew it would be.

I know Reuben is scheduled to work.

Now I just have to make myself walk in there.

It takes longer than I expect.

When I finally pull open the door, the smell of coffee and sugar hits me like a blow and I stand for a moment, eyes closed, breathing it in.

It's also a good way to drum up any last bits of courage.

"Pepper?" My eyes fly open to see a smiling Adam behind the counter. "You're Pepper, Pepper from the wedding. With the Suit-or brother." Adam looks delighted to recognize me.

"Yes," I say weakly. "You're Neely's brother."

"Not that you're all about your brother, although he's quite good-looking. Don't tell Neely that." Adam gives a theatrical grimace. "She may not appreciate it if we both think he's hot. In fact, we've never—"

"Is Reuben here?" I interrupt, unable to handle another moment of hearing about Grayson's hotness.

"Well...yes. Just a sec and I'll pull him from the kitchen."

The three tables are full, but there's no one in line. I move closer to the counter, admiring the glaze on the pastries. A plate of cupcakes sits by the cash, a mix of chocolate and vanilla. Simple and each one is perfect.

My head jerks up at the sound of the kitchen door, at Reuben standing there, clearly unwilling to come any closer to me. I can't read the expression on his face, and the lights glint off his glasses, masking his eyes.

"Reuben." There's a pleading note in my voice that I catch and correct. No. There will be no begging, no crying. In and out, and say what I need to say. "I'm here to apologize."

Adam squeezes past him. "Apologize for what?" He looks at me and then back at Reuben. "Oh. Oh!"

"You did your apologizing," Reuben says stiffly.

"Not enough. And not to M.K."

"She's not here." Adam's dramatic whisper is loud in the quiet shop. "Why don't the two of you go in the kitchen to talk?"

"I don't deserve privacy. Let me just say what I need to say." I take a deep breath like I'm about to jump in a pool. "I've been trying for my whole life to make my father proud of me so he might come home. The bakery was my best chance, and I couldn't even make it work. I took your recipes as a last-ditch effort to turn things around. I've been desperate because I know my father will be watching, because of Grayson. I wanted him to be proud of me, too." I take a deep breath and notice the flicker of Reuben's jaw. "That was wrong. Not only wrong of me to take your recipes and lie to you, but it was wrong of me to be so concerned about what my father might think of me. He gave away any right when he walked out on us, and it's about time that I realize that. I finally understand that I'm enough for *me*, and I don't care what he thinks. But I care what *you* think, and I hope someday you can find it in yourself to forgive me."

I take a last, long look at Reuben. He still hasn't said anything. "That's it," I say, my voice cracking. "Please give M.K. my apologies. I'm so sorry."

And then I turn and walk out.

Dawson

A FTER KEITH AND I sort out the logistics of me working for him, I head to Shae's. I need to tell her and Neely everything.

I have a job. A nine-to-five—or eleven-to-seven—job that will pay me to play video games, to design and advise and tell people what I like and don't like. I never imagined my posting on Quora and Reddit about Fortnite and Call of Duty would be anything but a time-waster, but Keith said reading some of my old posts was better than a job interview.

"You really know your stuff," he said.

It will be hard not planning the next trip with Shae and Neely, harder still to tell them I'm not going be able to go for a while, but having a job that lets me do what I'm interested in will help.

I'm not looking forward to telling them, which is why I've spent the last half hour listening to Shae talk about Emmett; about what to do about him, how to make up for a lie, which really wasn't a lie, but a withholding of truth.

"I need to make a grand gesture," Shae says, lying on the living room floor.

That's what they do in the movies. If this was a movie, I would have snuck out to see Bender in his cell. I would have the ghetto blaster up in the air and played it outside Neely's bedroom window.

We don't have a song, though.

The ghetto blaster never really worked in Say Anything, because Diane had to work out a few things first. Like me.

There's a break in Shae's monologue, and I open my mouth to start.

"I'm scared," Shae says before anything can come out of my mouth. "I don't know how people do this relationship stuff."

Neely, sitting on the floor beside her, gives a snort. "You're looking at me like I should know what you're talking about. Ask Dawson, since he's got the string of broken hearts to remind us what a lady-killer he is."

Any shred of hope I might have dwindles away like smoke. There's no point then, if that's what Neely thinks of me. That's what I've been doing—trying to find a replacement for her, trying to find someone to share the big love with, and in doing so, made her look at me all wrong.

I've done everything wrong. "I'm not a lady-killer," I say quietly.

"Really?" Neely sneers. "Who are you with this week?"

But before I can respond, Shae clears her throat. "Uh...Neely... .?" Shae waves her phone before my face. "Is Grayson a sure thing for The Suitor?"

"He hasn't signed the contract yet, so it's not official."

"That's not what Instagram says."

Insta...Natasha. My heart sinks. I never told Natasha—but I didn't deny it either. I hold my breath, ready to hear the worst about Shae.

Neely grabs Shae's wrist to stop her waving the phone and squints at the picture of Grayson. "What does it say?"

"That he's the next Suitor." Shae pulls her hand back to read the rest of the post. "Oh, no."

"What?"

"This isn't from the show." She looks straight at me. "Natasha posted this. Natasha just told the world that Grayson is the next Suitor."

"How could you?" Neely demands.

"I didn't do anything," I say, fighting to make my voice straight and convincing. "I'm sure it was just a good guess. She's a huge fan of The Suitor, so of course that's where her mind would go." My shoulders slump miserably. I can't tell them what really happened with Natasha.

"How could she know?" Neely persists, shaking the phone at me.

"Like I said, a good guess. C'mon, Neely, really?" I glance at Shae, who shakes her head, so I know she's stepping out of this fight. "Pepper asks us not to say anything, so of course I wouldn't. Why do you even have to ask?"

"So you'd keep your mouth shut for Pepper but not for the rest of us?"

"What does that even mean? You know I'd do anything for the two of you and your friends. Where's this coming from? Are things that bad with you and Grayson?" I can't stop that from sneaking out and hide my grimace.

"There is no me and Grayson, thanks to this." Neely's voice is shrill and rips through me like a knife.

"What's that supposed to mean? I thought—I don't know what I thought," Shae says quickly, her gaze shifting to Neely, to me, and back to Neely, as if she doesn't know where to look.

Or what to say.

"What's going on?" I demand. "Neely? Talk to me. There's more to this, isn't there?"

"I can't." Neely suddenly collapses into the chair, hands covering her face. Beside her, Shae looks ready to burst.

I want to drop beside her. I want to take her in my arms and tell her everything will be okay.

I want to tell her Grayson isn't worth it.

"You can tell me anything." I feel like a hypocrite, because I can't do the same. "C'mon," I say, the image of her accusation, the anger in her golden eyes, too much for me. "You're my best friend."

"I don't want to be your friend!" Neely bursts out.

I take a step back like she hit me, like she's crumpled my heart in her hand.

"I can't watch you and Pepper. I can't do it anymore. There's always someone new, and it takes a bit for me to get my head around it, but Natasha was gone and there was Pepper and I can't do it anymore. I won't."

The kitchen is silent, save for the drip of the coffee maker and Shae's soft sigh. "Why won't—?"

"I'm in love with you."

Neely says it. Not me. I don't say it but Neely...

Neely *loves* me? How...why...how? I can't find the right word. I can't find any words because it's like fireworks have gone off in the middle of a thunderstorm, because Neely's expression is like being in love with me is the worst thing ever.

"Just go," Neely groans when I can't answer. I can't even ask.

"Neely..." I manage. When? How? But again, the words don't come. I've been struck mute right there in Shae's kitchen with so much to say.

"I'm going if you won't." Neely jumps to her feet and I take a step to stop her because if she leaves, this is over, I'll never be able to fix it and—

"Neely." My phone chimes and instinctively, I glance down at it.

Then everything gets much more confusing.

"I've got to go," I tell them, and rush out the door.

Chapter Twenty

Pepper

I CAN'T BEAR TO sit in the car for longer than it takes to punch in a new address in the GPS because it would be horrible to wait for Reuben to come rushing out of the patisserie to find me and have him not appear.

It would be the perfect movie moment if he would run out the door just as I'm driving off.

But my life is not a movie, and there's no Reuben rushing out the door.

I take a deep breath—and one last look at the window as I drive away. I can't see if he's watching. If he is, he'll see me leave.

The voice tells me to turn right onto Davisville, and then I'm off to find my father.

When Jena told me he'd been seen in Toronto, it was easy enough to look him up. I found addresses for three Howard Grants, but two had apartment numbers, and I knew my father would never live in a high-rise building.

He told me once that he loved wide-open spaces. That's why we had stayed in Ashbury, for the fresh air.

It surprises me that he settled in a big city.

An hour and a half later, I find out that he's not exactly in the city.

The GPS sends me northeast; out of the clogged streets and houses tight together to where the trees tower and fields spread wide between the roads.

Turn left. Turn left. Your destination is on the right.

I slow to a crawl as I approach and have to keep reminding myself to breathe. The house is smaller than the one we used to live in, but just as well kept. There are two cars in the drive.

"He's home," I say aloud as I park down the street.

This time there's no waiting to drum up my courage, because if I don't get out of the car right now, I'm not going to do this.

I'm not sure what I'm going to do, but I'm doing something. With shaky steps, I head across the lawn dotted with grass seed to the door.

My father lives here.

Behind this very nice door, in this very nice house. With another woman, who is not my mother.

It takes a long moment before I can lift my hand to press the button. The doorbell rings inside, signaling I'm here.

I'm here to see my father.

I stare fixedly at the container with pansies spilling over the edge as I wait until footsteps come towards the door.

Breathe. Keep breathing. And don't run away.

The door opens in slow motion and I brace myself on the side of the house.

A gasp. "Pepper?"

Lily Pike stands before me, looking a little grayer, a little more lined, but the same woman who used to hug me goodnight when I slept over at Ellie's.

"Is my father here?" My voice is creaky, like I haven't used it in a while.

Lily nods, eyes wide and staring. "Howard," she calls. "Howard, come here."

The footsteps are upstairs, heavy and slow. "Lil, I—"

"Howard."

He stops halfway down the stairs, as soon as he can see me standing outside his door. "Pepper? Pepper!" he cries, his steps now quick on the stairs. "What are you doing here? It's so good—"

And then he takes a good look at my face. "What's the matter?"

"You live here. You live *here*? Two hours away from us."

My father turns to Lily with an expression of resignation; the same expression as Grayson when he's caught in a lie. "There's a lot we need to say."

"You don't get to say anything. Except for why—not why you left. Why you didn't tell us where you were. I thought you were *dead*," I spit out. "Is that what you wanted?"

"We didn't want to make you choose." Lily's face is ashen with tears in her eyes. "We knew you'd all be okay with Peter. With your mother."

I have absolutely no sympathy for her.

"That's cowardly of you." I look from Lily to my father. "You're both cowards, and selfish...and mean, and horrible. You left without a word and expected us to be okay with it? No one was okay. We didn't know if you were alive or dead...or why you didn't love us enough." My voice cracks at the end.

"Pepper." My father reaches out a hand, tanned with gray-blond hair sprinkled on his forearm. "Of course I loved you. Love you. I love both you and your brother, and Lily loves Emmett and—"

"I don't care." I breathe through my nose, once, twice, until I settle enough to continue. "That's what I'm here to say. I don't care anymore about where you live or why you left, or what you think of me. I don't care if you're proud of me. You threw away the right to all of that. I. Don't. Care." I nod, and keep nodding as I step back. "That's all I wanted to say. I don't care. And there wouldn't have been a choice. I would have always picked Mom."

I don't remember how I got back to the car. I only know that I get in, turn it on, and head home as quickly as I can.

Dawson

THIS TIME I'M TOO impatient for transit and call an Uber as I head up Neely's street towards Queen Street, cursing myself for never getting a car. I could have borrowed Mike's, but I didn't have the sense to ask for it before I ran out, and I definitely can't go back for the keys.

Uber it is.

When I reach Pain au Chocolate, a long fifteen minutes later, Grayson is inside, leaning against the counter and talking to M.K. I don't even notice the smiles on their faces as I push open the door.

"Dawson!" Adam calls, eyes widened dramatically with surprise. "What are you doing here?"

Wordlessly, I point to Grayson.

"Okay..." Adam's surprise turns to confusion. "What's going on? Where's Neely?"

"She's not here because we're about to have a conversation about her," Grayson says. "An important conversation that you shouldn't tell her about."

Adam's hand stops on the reach for his phone. "Not tell my sister something? I'm not sure about this."

"I think you should let Dawson talk to her first."

I throw up my hands. "What am I telling her? Why am I even here?"

It was his text that sent me running out of the house.

Grayson:

Emergency. 9-1-1. Need to talk to you pronto about NEELY. ASAP. Come to Pain au Chocolate.

He sent two others while I was on the way there.

It was a good idea at the time, but the farther I got away from Neely, the more I realize I shouldn't have run out. Grayson's text had been a life line out of situation I didn't know how to deal with.

I should have dealt with it. *I love you, too.* That would have fixed everything.

Now I'm forced to explain things to Grayson, apologize for telling Natasha, and find out if he's in love with Neely.

The light at the end of the tunnel is the headlight of an oncoming truck, and it's about to flatten me.

"Let's sit down." Grayson escorts me to the farthest table like I'm sleepwalking. Maybe I am, because why would Grayson want to meet me to talk about Neely.

Unless there's something wrong with Neely that she hasn't told me. My heart falls at the thought. After years with Shae, after the good news that puts a skip in my step, there can't be anything wrong with Neely.

But there can be. I know that all too well.

"What's going on?" I demand even before Grayson sits down.

"Pepper tells me there's nothing going on with the two of you," he begins, all casual and comfortable, almost like he's enjoying himself.

"Pepper? Why would you think? She made me a sandwich. That's it. Did she think...?" I trail off, remembering how Pepper had leaned over and kissed me. It had been a total surprise—not a bad one, but definitely a surprise since I didn't get the sense there had been anything like *that* brewing between us.

There's been so much else going on that I'd forgotten all about meeting with Pepper. When was that? Last Monday? Tuesday? It seems like a lifetime ago.

Pepper—friend.

Neely—right now I have no I idea.

"*She* didn't think that," Grayson clarifies.

"But Neely did." His nod confirms it. No wonder Neely has been annoyed with me. It also explains the stupid lady-killer comment, the cry that she can't deal with me and Pepper. "But why...?" I trail off, still confused as to why I'm here.

"Do you have any idea how long Neely has been in love with you?"

If it wasn't for Neely's little outburst, I would have laughed off Grayson's question. But during that small amount of time racing from Shae's to Pain au Chocolate, things started clicking into place. A thousand and one things; all the frowns and sharp words about girlfriends, her comfortableness when we're alone and how she tenses up even when joined by Shae. How when I look at her, she looks pained and frustrated, like she's being denied her favourite toy. Could that really mean...? "I think I don't know what's going on," I say weakly.

This is like the worst math class I've ever been in, when I need the teacher to slowly walk me through each step.

Grayson doesn't look anything like a math teacher.

"How could you not know she felt that way?" Grayson demands, his tone accusing and more than a little scornful.

"Why would I be here with you if I knew she was in love with me?" I shoot back. "Did she tell you she loves me?"

"She did, the night she asked if I could distract her enough to get over you."

"She said that?" I ask in a voice full of awe. But then, "She wants to get over me?"

"Which hasn't happened, as much as I've tried," he says with a rueful smile. "Apparently I'm not as irresistible as I thought I was."

I stare at the wall, feeling for once like Jake Ryan, but when he called Samantha's grandparents. "So she does love me."

"You said you didn't know."

"She just told me."

"Dude!" Grayson cries loud enough for heads to turn. "Why are you here?"

I shake my head, trying to dislodge the non-Neely thoughts. There aren't many right now. Her tear-streaked face as I hurried out the door, her *I'm in love with you* gasp that cracked everything wide open. "You told me you had to talk to me about Neely. You used shouty letters. I had to come and see what was going on."

"Not if she'd already told you!" He points to the door. "Go! Get back to her."

"Tell me what's going on first," I plead. "I had no idea she loves me."

"For a smart guy, you're pretty stupid."

"I'm not," I protest. "I told her I loved her years ago, but she never said it back, and then shot me down with this prepared speech that felt like...like she really shot me. What was I supposed to do?"

"Fight for her?"

"There wasn't anything to fight for."

"There's always something to fight for. The easiest way to get a woman to fall for you is show her you're interested."

"Maybe for you. I poured my heart out to her, and got nothing. Nothing. There was nothing to fight for because there was nothing there on her side."

Grayson cocks his head to look at me. "Does she know this? Because from what I got from her is that there's a lot on her side."

Why didn't Neely ever say anything about this to me? Or why didn't Shae, because she had to have known. How could I have wasted so much time?

When I look up, Grayson is staring at me like he knows exactly what I'm thinking. Maybe he does—I wouldn't have put it past me to say it out loud. "C'mon, dude," he says, pushing the chair back with a loud scrape. "Let's get you back to her, and then you can figure out the rest of your life."

"Wait," I say as we reach the door. "I have to get her a cupcake."

Chapter Twenty-One

♥

Pepper

I T'S ALWAYS BEEN A dream to have my own business; something that I'm responsible for, that I can grow and take care of the way I want to. But right now, as I stand outside everything I've ever worked for, Pepper's Pies and Pastries feels like an anchor weighing me down.

It feels like a mistake.

The big window, with the red vinyl letters stuck to it, seems to stare accusingly at me. I spend hours making it shine and sparkle, only to have those drunken idiots barrel through it, looking for fun and a good snack.

I've given up so much for this place, driven by some inane plot to make my father proud of me, some way to compete with Grayson.

Grayson has never wanted anything other than the best for me. And my father didn't care enough to stay.

It wasn't anything I did or didn't do; nothing Grayson did, or even my mother. It wasn't even some defect in my father. In fact, you can say he followed his heart because he picked Lily Pike over our family. He picked love over us.

Nothing I could have done to stop that.

Still hurts.

But along with the hurt comes an odd sense of freedom, the knowledge that it wasn't my fault, wasn't anyone's fault. And as much as I want to go home and tell Mom and Grayson this, instead, I unlock the front door of my shop. This is where I need to be right now.

I might have started it for the wrong reason, but I still love Pepper's Pies and Pastries.

I need a new name. Pepper's Bread. Pepper's Baked Goods. Pepper's Cakes and Cupcakes.

Not that.

The key sticks in the old lock and I glance over my shoulder in the hope that no one sees me. I've stayed closed on a Tuesday, which I've never done before. Although part of me—the insecure little girl part—wonders if anyone noticed, the mature, grown-up part knows that if I'm seen opening now, I'm going to have a lineup within minutes.

I like that grown-up part of me. She's knows what she's doing.

The lock clicks just as there's a shuffling step from behind me. Pulling out the key, I brace myself, trying to get in the baker-with-the-awesome-coffee mode when all I want to do is hide away for a little while longer until I can sort out my life.

"Lassie?"

The voice is questioning, but not angry or shy. He sounds like he's... concerned.

I drop my keys and turn to see Reuben. Right there on the street, standing beside a sleek, shining black car. His apron is gone, hands shoved in the pockets of his jeans as he steps towards me. I can smell the scents of butter and chocolate and sweet things.

He smells like a sweet thing.

"Whose car is that?" I have to say something. I can't just jump into his arms, even though that's really what I want to do. My heart is doing a drum solo in my chest and it's hard to breathe.

"Is it the same one you borrowed before?" I ask, my words rushing to fill the unknown between us. "When you were here on Sunday, when I tried to explain and did such a bad job of it that I had to try again but now I don't know if—"

Without a word, Reuben stoops and picks up the keys. "You'll have a lineup round the corner if you don't get inside," he says. "There's been three knocks on the door since I've been waiting." Reaching around me, he opens the door and gives me a little push.

"Why are you here?" I ask blankly as I shuffle inside.

"To the *cidsen*," Reuben instructs. "So you'll not be seen. Unless you mean to open?"

"No, not now. I don't know why I came here. I don't know what's going on." Reuben shuts the door, locks it with a decisive click.

He's here. I don't know why or how or...*why*...but he's here.

"I'm glad you came here," he says. He won't meet my gaze, but something about his expression tells me he's not mad.

I think.

Whatever his emotions might be, Reuben follows me around the counter, the shop lit only by the sun coming through the big window. The chairs sit upside down on the tables, the floor pristine enough to eat off. Yesterday, I spent as much time here as I did baking in the kitchen, my muddled thoughts a perfect soundtrack for cleaning.

The display case is empty, the bread baskets on the wall, bare. The coffee machine is silent for once, but the aroma of the beans still hangs in the room.

My bakery feels like it's waiting.

But Reuben is right; if I stay out here by the counter, someone will knock on the door, wanting coffee, a loaf of bread, a cupcake. I lead the way into the kitchen, left perfectly clean when I finished yesterday.

But looking at it from Reuben's eyes, all the evidence of me making cupcakes is right there—the box of cocoa powder left out, the piping bag drying by the sink, a plate with the scraps of candied orange. "Why are you here?" I repeat.

"To see you," Reuben says like I asked about the colour of the sky.

"Oh. Why?"

Reuben chuckles. He *chuckles*. My life has never been more confusing, and he laughs.

My lips curve up into a hint of a smile, some of the tension lifting from my shoulders like the steam released from the frother.

"You had your say, but you never gave me mine," Reuben points out. "I drove right here, right after I bought a car."

I blink, because I don't think I heard that right. "You bought a car?"

"Aye. Seems necessary, now I've a reason to drive out of the city."

Everything about me collapses and I grab the edge of the counter before I end up on the floor. "For me?"

"Aye, lassie."

I close my eyes and feel warm hands on my arms. But not yet. First, I have to say it. "I went to see my father," I blurt out.

"Aye, and how was that? I'd wondered if that's where you were off to. Work it all out?"

"No. *No!*" The word escapes in a shout. "I didn't want that, to work it out. I told him I don't care what he thinks. I told him—or I should have—that I'm tired of living my life trying to make him proud of me." I halt, studying Reuben's expression.

I feel like I'm nine again and my father told me to jump off the diving board into the pool at the aquatic centre. I had stood there, legs shaking, staring at the water three metres below, his shouts to *jump* echoing in my head.

I jumped because my father told me to.

"And that's because of you," I finish.

Reuben nods, with a smile that might be pride. "Is that so?"

"It's because of you," I say. I catch my bottom lip between my teeth and prepare to jump because I want to. "I have to thank you for showing me there's more to me than this place." I pinwheel my arm. "Because of you, I know now that I want more than this. I want you, but I understand if you can't—"

"I dinnae say anything about can't," Reuben cuts in. "I dinnae say anything a'tall."

"If I let you say something, what would you say?"

But he doesn't say anything, just stares at me with green eyes, studying my face like a map.

And then he kisses me.

One moment I'm standing there, and the next I'm caught in his arms, my mouth pressed roughly against his. I have a second to respond, a half-second to realize what's happening before he lets go.

"No," he says, stepping away from me. "Not that."

"Oh," I say in a very small voice.

"I want to kiss you," he says, his words almost indecipherable in his rush. "I've wanted it since you were first in my kitchen, but not like that, me throwing myself on you."

"Trust me," I whisper. "I wouldn't mind."

Reuben looks at me and laughs. "Pepper." His hand cups my cheek. "I've always made a muck out of moments like this. The lass laughed at me for my first kiss. With Glinda, you know how that turned out. I've never had this before, and...I don't even know what this is."

"Me neither," I whisper. I clutch at his hand cupping my cheek, my own laughter bubbling up.

It's not a laugh, it's a giggle.

"I don't want to muck it up," he says.

"I always muck things up," I admit. "But it always kind of works out."

"I'll give you the recipes," Reuben vows. "I'll give you anything you wish, anything you need."

"I know," I say, leaning into his hand on my face. "I'm sorry I didn't tell you. I'm more sorry about that than taking the recipes, although I feel really bad about that."

"I know. Don't. I've got me own bags to carry lassie. But mebbe we'll try to carry them together?"

"Aye."

Reuben's hands are on my waist and he lifts me onto the counter, like I'm as light and fluffy as his best cupcake. The stainless steel is cool under my pants, and thankfully clear of flour. We're eye to eye now, and as I fight to catch my breath from the nearness of him, he rests his forehead against mine.

"The accent," he says in a low voice. "Not so much."

"Really? I thought I was getting b—?"

This time, his kiss is soft and gentle, and so much better. I wrap my arms around him and fall into it.

From far away, the banging on the front door invades into this very nice moment. I might even say it's as good as a movie moment.

Reluctantly, I pull away but the banging doesn't stop. "Someone saw me," I whisper, dropping kisses onto his mouth, his cheeks, his nose. Kissing a beard is a revelation. It's softer than I expected, but I imagine it will give a bit of a burn if we keep this up.

Which I plan to.

"You're a wanted lassie." Reuben snakes a hand around my back and I arch into his chest, already so close, but wanting more.

"They'll go away," I promise, my kisses finding his lips again.

"But I won't." His mouth curves under my lips and a giggle bursts out.

"That's a good laugh," I tell him quickly. "A very happy laugh. A laugh that means I don't want to move or deal with anyone... just want to stay here. With you." I fall into his kiss once more, and all the goodness and rightness of this moment is threatening to spill out, spill over, like an overflowing cupcake tin.

"Give me another minute here and then we'll open up," Reuben murmurs against my lips.

I like the sound of that.

Dawson

GRAYSON GIVES ME A ride back to Shae's. "She still might be there," I say as he looks for parking along the street. "Just park in the driveway." The ticking clock has changed to a constant chant in my head. *Hurryuphurryuphurryup.*

"Look, bro, it's your fault that you left," Grayson reminds me.

"Because you sent me the text and told me to meet you."

"You could have called."

I point to the drive between the houses with a shake of my head. "I'm not doing this now."

"Just tell her—"

"I don't need advice, I need to get out of the car! I'm good," I add, taking a deep breath. That's when Natasha pops into my mind. "Actually, I need to tell you something."

"That you told that girl I was going to be the next Suitor?" Grayson's voice is calm as he pulls into the drive.

"I didn't tell her, but I didn't *not* tell her either," I admit. "She knew and wanted me to confirm it or she'd tell everyone about Shae's illness. Which isn't a thing anymore..." I trail off. "For a minute, I was ready to throw you under the bus. It would have

protected Shae and it would have solved the you-and-Neely problem."

"Which really isn't a thing either," Grayson points out.

"No, but I didn't know that."

"Seems there's a lot you don't know, dude."

"Yeah." I take another deep breath. I'm taking a stand. This time, I'm not willing to blindly follow the path I'm on, like Cameron in Ferris Bueller. "I didn't tell Natasha about you being the Suitor because Neely would have never forgiven me. That's the only reason."

"Probably wouldn't have forgiven you," he agrees.

"No. Neely is—" I search for the right words. "A little intense when she's angry."

"I got that." Grayson laughs. "She's downright scary. But all good women are like that. You should see my sister when she's riled up." He gives me a rueful smile. "It's too bad things didn't work out with you and Pepper."

"There was never anything," I say. "She's great but I'm not for her. I don't even eat that much bread."

"Plus, you've been secretly in love with Neely for years."

"Plus that." Staring out the car window at Neely's house, I give my head a shake. "I can't believe she didn't know."

"I'm going to suggest you're doing something wrong, then. Now, get in there and do something right."

"You're a good guy, Grayson. I wish—"

"That it could have worked out for me and Neely? No, you don't."

I grin. "No, I don't."

He jerks his head to the door. "Get in there and fix this."

There's more I need to say to him, but now isn't the time. Instead, I'm out of the car and up the steps to Shae's front door just as it opens.

"Where did you go?" Shae demands, a bundle of offended, defensive girl anger in one tiny little package complete with pointing finger that pokes me in the chest. "How could you run out right after she says she loves you? Do you know how hard that was for her? Even if you don't feel the same, there's no excuse for being such an unfeeling, insensitive jerk of a—"

I grab her hand before she pokes me again. "Where is she?"

"Went home, heartbroken, because you are a—"

"How long has she felt like that?" I ask urgently. "Because I told her years ago how I felt."

"No, you didn't!"

"I'm pretty sure I did. The night in Italy." My heart beats like it's about to self-destruct. If it's this bad telling Shae, I'm going to explode when I tell Neely. "That night after we...you know."

"I do know, and I know Neely didn't say anything about a declaration of love from you," Shae says, eyes wide and unconvinced.

"I said it," I insist. "I said...I said I loved her. *I loved her.* I love her," I finish.

Shae gives a gasp audible from the inside of the house and claps a hand over her mouth. I want to shove her aside and find Neely to tell *her* all this, but Shae has always come first.

This is the last time I put her before Neely. I love Shae, but as a friend, and Neely—

"That night, I told Neely that I loved her," I say, sounding as calm as I ever have. "I said that I knew then I felt more than friendship, and I wanted more than a friendship with her. She said nothing."

Shae shakes her head slowly. "Neely never told me this."

"I waited for her to say something back, but she never did. I must have fallen asleep. Because when I woke up, she was getting dressed with that annoyed look on her face. She told me it had been a mistake, that it would never happen again. And then she left."

"She told me that. But you agreed with her."

I throw up my hands, the frustration of that long-ago night still there, so close to the surface. "What was I supposed to say? I didn't want to hurt our friendship. I didn't want to hurt you, if we couldn't agree on this and you had to get in the middle."

"It's my fault?"

"Of course not, but you're part of the why I didn't argue. I couldn't."

Shae's mouth still hangs open. "All this time? But you had girl-friends. So many girlfriends!"

"I didn't love any of them." Whirling, swirling thoughts click into place faster than I can comprehend them. "It's only ever been Neely."

"The whole time?"

"I think so. Maybe."

"You could have been together the whole time." Shae clutches my arm. "Maybe she didn't hear you?"

"How could she not hear me?"

"Asleep, passed out...high on sex hormones. What are those things called...pheromones?"

"I don't think they make you deaf."

"Well, something must have crawled into her ear because I *know* she didn't hear you, Dawson. She would have told me."

"What would she have told me?" I whisper, afraid to hope because the regret of so many wasted years is going to be overwhelming.

"She would have said she loved you too."

I close my eyes. Regret, yes, but still relief floods me like warm syrup. Neely might have said it, and Grayson may have confirmed it, but having Shae say it like that makes everything real. But then I picture Neely's face. "And now? She didn't seem happy about it."

"Well, no, because—" For the first time she looks over at Grayson standing by his car and listening to our conversation. "Things change."

Grayson holds up his hands. "I am respectfully stepping aside."

"That's why I went to talk to him," I say to Shae. "I only want Neely to be happy."

Shae nods, still looking at Grayson. "How's Emmett?" she calls.

"No, this isn't about Emmett!" I cry. "This is my life now. Me and Neely."

"Well, stop wasting time and go talk to her," she orders. "Are you leaving?" she asks Grayson, who hasn't moved.

"I kind of want to find out how it turns out," he admits.

"Well, come in and talk to me," she says. "And you—" She points to Neely's house. "Go."

I go.

It takes all I have not to push past Mama S. and hotfoot it up to Neely's room, but I can't. I've waited long enough so I can force myself to take a minute and answer her questions, to taste test the sauce she has simmering on the stove. Nothing will work out if Mama S. is mad at me too.

Finally, I make it through the gauntlet of Neely's house and wait as Mama S. knocks on the bedroom door, bouncing impatiently on my toes.

"Neely, Dawson is here," Mama says. "He says—"

"What? No!"

My heart sinks but I'm not about to let Neely's anger ruin the best chance I have with her. I push open the door and my heart squeezes to see Neely sitting on the bed, one of her old stuffed animals in her lap. "I have to talk to you."

"I'm fine." Neely keeps her head down, sheets of hair covering her cheeks. "Everything is fine."

"It's not but it can be." I don't remember the last time I was in her room and my gaze darts around, noticing the lack of clutter, the pictures fixed to the mirror, the giant Pikachu that I won for her at the CNE leaning in the corner. "I brought you a cupcake."

Neely's head jerks up, her eyes as cold as her voice. "You left to buy a *cupcake*?"

"I went to talk to Grayson."

Through all this, Mama S. is still at the door, her head swiveling like she's watching a Grand Slam match. I smile apologetically as I make to close the door. "Thanks, Mama S., but do you mind?"

"Keep both feet on the floor," she cries as she's cut off from the drama.

The door shuts and I'm alone with Neely. I've never been alone with her in her room. Suddenly I'm fifteen and Shae is pulling me over to meet her best friend and I'm faced with an absolutely gorgeous Neely, like some kind of golden goddess, a perfectly beautiful girl.

I was Duckie, faced with the first sight of Andie in her dress.

Even back then she had the same expression of annoyance on her face.

"Twenty-seven years old and she still thinks I need a chaperone," Neely grumbles, staring at the tattered zebra in her lap. "Where's my cupcake?"

"Downstairs. Mama S. wouldn't let me bring food up here." The bed creaks under my weight as I sit down. How do I do this? What do I say?

"Of course she wouldn't." She tosses the stuffed toy on the floor.

I take a deep breath. "Grayson says you've only been pretending to date him."

She rolls her eyes but won't look at me. "So?"

"I'm glad."

"That you're humiliating me right now?"

"I'm not trying to. I'm trying to tell you that I love you too."

Slowly, ever so slowly, she meets my gaze. "Why?"

That isn't the reaction I expect. I have no idea what to expect. Even when this sort of thing goes awry in the movies, it's never this awkward. "Have you seen yourself?"

"You mean as a friend...right?" Everything about Neely is closed off and tight, like she's piling on the armour so she doesn't get hurt in the fight.

I can't sympathize with her. I want to be kissing her right now, not fighting with her. "Do you know how frustrating you are?" I demand.

"I'm frustrating? You run out with your tail between your legs just after I tell you something utterly, horribly embarrassing, leaving me—"

That's when I decide that the only way to make her stop talking, and get on with things, is to kiss her.

So I do.

Her lips are pillow soft and as sweet as they were years ago. All I want to do is dive in and enjoy, relish the fact that I'm here and she's here and this might be the big moment I've been waiting for since I was fifteen, but I don't. I need things on the straight and narrow before I dive in, because I don't want any more years of uncertainty.

So I pull back, leaving Neely with her eyes closed, hand still reaching for me.

Her eyes flutter open. "What...? Why?"

"Ready to listen now?"

She fixes her gaze on me and nods. We're close enough that I can see the shades of golden-green and flecks of brown in her eyes, the three little freckles on her nose, the scar on her forehead peeking out from under her hair.

This is really happening.

I think.

"Just to be clear—you really love me?"

"You're not getting me to say anything unless you explain why you kissed me," she snaps.

Does she really not get it? Does she really not know that I've loved her forever? I guess I haven't exactly been waiting around for her, but she *didn't say it back.*

"Grayson texted me about three times today," I say without preamble.

"Why?" Neely's eyes narrow with a glinty steeliness, like she has something to hide. Which she does, if Grayson was only an act.

"The one that came in just after you said what you said was literally a 9-1-1 call," I say as if she hasn't spoken. "It even said 9-1-1, in shouty caps, so I read it. Grayson wanted to see me—needed to see me. So I ran over to Pain au Chocolate to talk to him." I pause and Neely impatiently motions for me to continue. "He said he knew there isn't anything between me and Pepper."

"He texted you about Pepper?"

"Because everyone thought we were getting together. Or he thought it, and therefore, you, too. Did you?"

"I've stopped thinking of you with anyone," Neely whispers. "At least I try not to."

I tip a finger under her chin, lift it so Neely is forced to look at me. "I didn't know how you felt. I hoped...but I never knew."

"You...hoped?"

"Of course I hoped. It's everything I've ever wanted." I smile sheepishly. "At least for the past week it has been."

"Dawson..."

"Grayson needed to know how I felt about you."

"Me?"

"Yes, you." I mouth the words, in the most perfect Jake Ryan impression. Neely has watched Sixteen Candles with me more times than I can count. She'll get it.

She gets it.

"It's always been you," I say in a halting voice, "only I never realized it. I mean, deep down I knew it, but I didn't know you knew it."

"You're not making sense." She pokes at my knee and I know what she's doing. It's the same thing she does when she scared or so excited and can't believe something is happening. She grabs my hand or touches my arm, or once in France, in a hot air balloon, she grabbed my finger so tightly that I lost the circulation. There's been so much like that during the trips and the travels and all the years we've spent together, and I know Neely has had trouble believing some of the experiences were real and not something from a dream, because I've wondered too.

"I'm real," I whisper.

"Why?"

"Jeez," I say with a shake of my head. "For a smart girl, you are absolutely clueless."

"I'm not, I'm just confused."

"I know. I love knowing something you don't. But now—can I kiss you now, and explain everything later?" I reach out and cup her face. "We should have been doing this for years."

"Oh."

"That's all you have to say?"

"Take your feet off the floor," Neely whispers, and I don't need any other invitation.

This time, I need to touch her to make sure she's real, because once my lips find hers, and her arm is around me, it all becomes a dream.

A dream. A moment as good as any in a movie. It's real and it's epic and—

"Don't stop now!" Neely cries.

"There's more," I say. I might have stopped kissing her, but I'm not letting Neely go, not for a long time. "That night in Italy, the night we—that was the best night of my life."

"Me too." She bites her lip, not able to look me in the eye. "In the morning—"

"I told you I loved you that night."

Neely jerks back so fast she almost rolls me off the bed. "What?"

"I told you I loved you that night. And now I'm telling you again, only I want to make sure you hear me."

"You did not!"

"I'm pretty sure I did. Shae figures you were asleep."

"How could you not notice I was asleep when you said something like that?"

"I just told the girl I was in love with that I loved her. I was barely breathing myself, so forgive me for not checking on you."

"I—you—really?" Now she looks at me with wonder. "You told me you loved me?"

"I did."

"What did you say?"

I shake my head. I remember every word, but the words of twenty-two-year-old me isn't what I want to say now. "I said I want a serious girlfriend," I say, reciting the line from Sixteen Candles instead. "Someone that I can love, that's gonna love me back."

"No, you didn't." Neely smiles and brushes the hair from my forehead. "You like your movie quotes, but if you really said that..." She pauses, like she's waiting for me.

"That I love you," I finish, the words so much easier to say now that she's awake.

"That you love me," she echoes, with such a smile of happiness that my heart is about to burst. "You'd use your own words."

"You'll never know," I tease, leaning in to claim another kiss.

"Wait." She pushes against my chest so I stop, a breath away from her mouth.

"Kind of tired of waiting," I growl.

"I love you."

This, I can wait for.

"I'm sorry I was asleep."

I laugh with disbelief and Neely's happy expression morphs into the annoyed one I know so well. "I think that might be the first time you've ever apologized to me."

"It is not."

"It might be."

"I say sorry when I do something wrong. I just don't do much wrong. But being asleep the first time you tell me you love me, is kind of bad."

"No." I kiss her again, and again, tiny drops on her lips to stop the words of regret. "This is when we need to be together. This is how it is supposed to work out. This is when we finally get to be together. Not then, or a year later. Now. And don't worry." I lower her back onto her pillow. "I'll say it again. And you can say it again. And we can say it together...over and over and..."

And then I kiss her again. Anything else I need to say can wait.

I'm not waiting any longer for her.

Epilogue

♥

Three Months Later...

SHAE BOUNCES ON THE couch, her shoulder knocking Emmett's arm when she gets too high. "Who's he going to pick? Who's he going to pick?" she chants.

Beside her, Rufus echoes her chants.

"We'll never know if you don't keep quiet and watch," Neely says.

Tonight is the finale of The Suitor and Neely and I were invited to Emmett's house to watch it with his family.

Shae has been practically living there for the past month.

I never thought she'd be the type to live in the country, but as Neely puts it, it's been good for her. Getting into a routine after years of travelling has been tough for all three of us, but Shae has adjusted to the early hours with surprising ease.

I'm lucky that Keith lets me make my own hours, especially when Neely doesn't start classes for another few weeks and has a tendency to tempt me into staying in bed with her.

I moved into my own apartment three weeks ago. We're not officially living together, but it's only a matter of time.

After that afternoon, when Mama S. started banging on the bedroom door, asking what we were doing in there, I pulled Neely over to Shae's. Grayson was still there, and so he had a front row seat as I told them everything—about my brother and my job, and my conversation with Natasha.

And then Mike came out of the kitchen, and we both told them about Mike and my mom.

By the end of it, I thought Grayson was a pretty good guy, which is why it's not that strange that Neely and I are here with his family watching the last episode of The Suitor. Grayson has two women left, and by the end of the two hours, he's supposed to be engaged to one of them.

Tough decision. Neither of them are Neely, but they both seem pretty nice.

"Have you heard from Pepper?" I ask Mrs. Grant.

"It's too bad she couldn't make it back," Neely adds.

A month ago, Pepper closed Pepper's Pies and Pastries for the last time, and left with Reuben. They started in Scotland, made their way to Paris and have been haunting the patisseries of France, from what I got from Pepper's Instagram page. The plan is for them to return in a few weeks, do a complete renovation of the bakery, and reopen it.

Together.

Reuben gave his notice at Pain au Chocolate and will be moving to Ashbury.

I'm happy for her.

I'm happy for everyone.

Shae has now moved onto Emmett's lap, and his arms are wrapped around her to stop the bouncing. Ellie and

James—whose wedding started this all—are curled up on the other end of the couch. Peter Pike seems to be giving quite a bit of attention to Shae's mother, who is smiling more than I have ever seen her.

Back home, Mike is no doubt watching the show with Mom.

And Neely and I are together.

"How can Grayson pick one of them?" Shae wants to know. "How does he know?"

"If I have it solid for a girl, I'll ride by her house on my bike. I'll do it like a hundred times a day," I recite.

Heads spin in my direction. Neely rolls her eyes. "Pretty in Pink," she says. "But you've never ridden by my house on your bike."

"I will do that first thing tomorrow," I promise. I lift the hand that's held tight to mine all night and bring it to my lips.

"It's so sweet to see you all so happy," Mrs. Grant says wistfully. "Love is really in the air. I wish Pepper and Reuben could be here. I might have hoped one of you couples would take this as a sign to make it official."

I glance over and meet Emmett's gaze. "Well," I say, my other hand reaching into the pocket of my pants to catch hold of the little box.

Remember that Emmett has a brother? Meet Ethan and Davis, and get more Rufus in Don't They Know it's Christmas!

And find out what happens with Grayson on The Suitor in Falling for The Suitor!

If you enjoyed the cast of characters from my Don't books, I'd love it if you joined my mailing list and find out more!

When you sign up for my mailing list, you'll get a copy of the short story, **Cupcake Connections**!

In Pain au Chocolate patisserie, the cupcakes are becoming more popular than the pastries. Reuben, the big, burly Scotsman, is an expert on sugar and sweets, but his love life has fallen flat.

And when one of the customers catches Reuben's eye, Adam decides to help him win her over. While planning a makeover for Reuben, Adam digs into Reuben's past and discovers that Reuben is doing just fine on his own.

Packed full of character cameos from Beautifully Baked, Unexpectingly Happily Ever After and The Hidden Past of Pippa McGovern, Cupcake Connections is a sweet story about finding your own way.

Sign up now!

Acknowledgments

As I get ready to publish, the pandemic is still ongoing in the world. Who would have thought?

For Don't Stop Me Now, I made a slight change from the other books in the Don't trilogy—I make mention of the pandemic! See if you can find it! But seriously, like Don't Tell Me You Love Me, and Don't Want to Be Friends, I have pretended the pandemic doesn't exist. It's the only place I can.

The Don't trilogy has been a bit more serious than comedic, but hopefully you found some laughs as well as some love within the pages. It sort of reflects where my head space has been for the last year or so. But with all the chaos and challenges of the world, you still have to find time for the little things that make you happy. Eat those cupcakes!

Time for thanks—to Nita for sorting out my head with Pepper, and Regina for loving Reuben and Dawson. Thanks to Kaitie, Sam, and Sarah for giving me the bare minimum of quiet to write this, to my Fri-yay ladies for inspiring me, and to E for listening.

And thank you to YOU for reading, and coming back for more me.

About Author

Holly Kerr is the author of twenty-five chick-lit, romantic comedy, and women's fiction novels. She grew up a farm girl but now calls Toronto home, where she lives with her three very tall children, following their sports exploits like any dutiful mother.

She's a lover of Marvel movies, Star Wars movies...really, any movies, and has a surprising amount of worthless pop culture info stored in her head. She likes oceans over mountains, tea over coffee, and can mix a darn fine dirty martini, with extra olives, of course.

Visit her at www.facebook.com/HollyKerrAuthor and www.hollykerr.ca to sign up for her newsletter.

LOTS OF LAUGHS.
LOTS OF LOVE.

Suitor Science

Hating the Chemistry Teacher
Falling for The Suitor
Fraternizing with the Ex
Marrying the Billionaire Best Friend
Loving the Wrong Guy
Finding the One

Love & Alliteration

Perfectly Played
Beautifully Baked
Pleasantly Popped

Don't

Don't Tell Me You Love Me
Don't Want to Be Friends
Don't Stop Me Now
Don't They Know It's Christmas

Sisters in a Small Town

Coming Home
Hanging On
Stepping Up

Charlotte Dodd

The Secret Life of Charlotte Dodd
The Missing Files of Charlotte Dodd
The Best Worst First Date Ever
The Hidden Past of Pippa McGovern
The Last Stand of Charlotte Dodd

Unexpecting
Unexpectingly Happily Ever After

Absinthe Doesn't Make the Heart Grow Fonder

Oceanic Dreams – I Saw Him Standing There

Kid Lit

The Dragon Under the Mountain
The Dragon Under the Dome